the Haunted Yarn Shop Mysteries

Last Wool and Testament

"A great start to a new series! By weaving together quirky characters, an interesting small-town setting, and a ghost with a mind of her own, Molly MacRae has created a clever yarn you don't want to end."

—Betty Hechtman, national bestselling author of *Yarn to Go*

"A delightful paranormal regional whodunit that . . . accelerates into an enjoyable investigation. Kath is a fascinating lead character." —Genre Go Round Reviews

"A delightful and warm mystery . . . with a strong, twisting finish." —Gumshoe

"Suspense and much page flipping! . . . I loved the characters, the mystery; everything about it was pitch-perfect!" —Cozy Mystery Book Reviews

"The paranormal elements are light, and the haunted yarn shop premise is fresh and amusing."

—*RT Book Reviews*

Praise for Other Mysteries by Molly MacRae

"MacRae writes with familiarity, wit, and charm."

—*Alfred Hitchcock Mystery Magazine*

"Witty . . . keeps the reader guessing."

—*Publishers Weekly*

"Murder with a dose of drollery . . . entertaining and suspenseful." —*The Boston Globe*

Also by Molly MacRae

Last Wool and Testament

DYEING WISHES

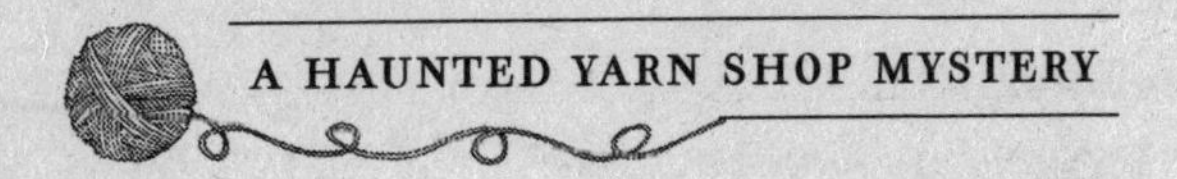

Molly MacRae

OBSIDIAN
Published by the Penguin Group
Penguin Group (USA) Inc., 375 Hudson Street,
New York, New York 10014, USA

USA | Canada | UK | Ireland | Australia | New Zealand | India | South Africa | China

Penguin Books Ltd., Registered Offices: 80 Strand, London WC2R 0RL, England
For more information about the Penguin Group visit penguin.com.

First published by Obsidian, an imprint of New American Library,
a division of Penguin Group (USA) Inc.

First Printing, July 2013

ISBN 978-0-451-23956-3

Printed in the United States of America
10 9 8 7 6 5 4 3 2 1

For the Little Wool Shop,
opened in 1935 in the Market Square in Lake Forest,
Illinois, by my grandmother
Katharine Vincent Canby

ACKNOWLEDGMENTS

It takes an agent, an editor, friends, and a family to raise a writer. To raise a mystery writer it also takes putting up with questions about blunt instruments, red herrings, poisons, and plot twists. For every ounce of support they give me, I'm grateful to my agent, Cynthia Manson, my editor at Penguin, Sandy Harding, my colleagues at the Champaign Public Library, my writing friends, and members of the Champaign Urbana Spinners and Weavers Guild. Special thanks to Kate Winkler, whose knitting needles produce not only catnip mice but magic. And above all, thank you to the guys at home who do the laundry and the shopping and who cook, wash dishes, and cheer me on with love and dark chocolate.

Chapter 1

"Where are the lambs?" Ernestine asked when she and I caught up to the rest of our group at the pasture fence. "Did Kath and I dawdle too long? Have they already run off to play?"

"Oh, sorry, Ernestine," I said. She was spry for being nearly round and almost eighty, but I'd been sure I was doing her a favor by walking slowly down the farm lane with her. As it turned out, she'd been the one waiting for me because I couldn't help stopping to take pictures of our beautiful Upper East Tennessee springtime along the way. She kindly hadn't complained, but now I felt bad because we'd expected to see Debbie's new lambs frisking in the field. "Did we miss them, Debbie?"

"No. They're with their mamas," Debbie said, "at the far end, over there under that beech tree." She pointed across the hillocky field.

Not knowing much about lambs or their mamas, I wasn't surprised they weren't hanging around at the fence waiting for us. Debbie seemed puzzled, though, and it was her farm and they were her sheep, so I mimicked her scrunched nose and stared across the field where she pointed. I could just make them out standing in a white huddle under a huge tree.

Ernestine put her cheek to Debbie's extended arm, using it and Debbie's index finger as a sight. Her head barely reached Debbie's shoulder, and as she squinted toward the sheep, her thick glasses flashed in the sun. Concentrating and leaning into her squint the way she did, and dressed in a gray sweater and slacks, she looked like a grandmother mole trying to bring the world into better focus. She wasn't as blind as a mole but she probably didn't see the tree, much less the sheep, at that distance.

Thea and Bonny, the other two women with us, had already gotten tired of straining to see the sheep. Thea, in jeans and a Windbreaker, climbed up and sat on the fence. Bonny was checking her phone for messages.

"I don't get it," Debbie said. "Usually they'll come see if I've brought treats. And the lambs are always curious. But I don't think they've even noticed us."

The five of us, members of the needle arts group Thank Goodness It's Fiber (TGIF), had met up that morning at Debbie Keith's farm, Cloud Hollow. Thea and Ernestine had been smart and had carpooled with Bonny, letting her navigate the half dozen winding miles up the Little Buck River valley from our small town of Blue Plum. I'd driven out alone, arriving last and feeling as though I'd made it despite, rather than because of, Debbie's directions, which included the near-fatal phrase "and you can't miss it."

We'd all looked forward to spending the morning in Debbie's studio. She was going to teach us her techniques for dyeing yarn and wool roving by "painting" them. Unfortunately, in her flurry of preparations, Debbie had locked the key to the studio inside it. She'd phoned her neighbor across the river, who kept an extra set of keys for her. The neighbor said she'd drop the keys off on her way to town and we'd decided to make the most of our wait by walking down the farm lane to visit the new lambs. But, as we saw, the lambs and their mamas were otherwise occupied.

"Can't you call them?" Thea asked. "Whistle for them or something?"

"Not at this distance," Debbie said. "I'm not loud enough. And that's not really how sheep work, anyway."

"See, Bonny?" Thea said. "I told you that's what Bill is for."

"I know what a sheepdog is for," Bonny said. She brushed at something on her black pants legs, maybe imaginary dog hair. "But dogs in general don't like me, except to bite, so I don't like them back. And I make it a point to never give them the chance to bite in the first place. No offense intended—I hope you know that, Debbie—but I am much obliged to you for putting what's his name in the house."

Debbie, still looking at the distant flock, waved off Bonny's tepid thanks.

I was pretty sure I heard a muttered "wuss" from Thea, but Bonny, farther down the fence and engrossed by her phone, didn't catch it. When Bill, Debbie's border collie, had bounced out of the house with her after she'd phoned for the spare keys, Bonny had taken one look, jumped back in her car, and slammed the door. She'd refused to come out, even though Bill appeared to be a perfect gentleman, until Debbie graciously put him back in the house.

Bonny pocketed her phone as she made a disgusted noise. "The morning's turning out to be a complete bust, though," she said. Ernestine tried to shush her, but Bonny continued grousing. "Driving the whole blessed way out here and trying to find this place was bad enough, but now we're standing around in wet grass and accomplishing absolutely nothing."

"But isn't it a beautiful morning for getting nothing done?" Ernestine asked.

No one could argue with that. It was the kind of gorgeous spring day in the foothills of the Blue Ridge Mountains that looked like the inspiration for an Easter card. The world smelled of fresh breezes. Also of the wild onions I was standing on. I stepped back from the fence and took a picture of the grassy lane we were in and another where the lane disappeared around the next hill. Then I snapped a few candids of the other women.

Thea, sitting on the top fence rail, was a tempting target. Her orange Windbreaker was stretched across her broad back, making her look like a giant pumpkin perched on the fence, her brown head making the stem. I skipped that picture, though. Thea was our town librarian and defied all stereotypes associated with that position except two—she was single and she had more than two cats. But she was far from being hushed and, in fact, called herself the Loud Librarian. I knew she'd be loudly unappreciative of a picture taken of the particular view I had in my lens.

Ernestine and Bonny stood farther along the fence, Ernestine distracting Bonny from her grumbles by asking about her winter in Florida. Ernestine's white hair became a dandelion nimbus as she turned her wrinkles to the sun, eyes closed behind her glasses. She was retired from a number of jobs, most recently as receptionist for my late grandmother's lawyer. She had a dry sense of humor and although her eyesight was failing, she easily saw the good in people and frequently apologized for their shortcomings.

I'd met Bonny for the first time that morning. The only things I knew about her were what I'd just heard—she'd returned from Florida the week before, she was a gung ho spring, summer, and fall member of TGIF, and she didn't like dogs. She also seemed to be expecting a phone call or expecting someone to answer a call she was trying to put through. And she wasn't patient.

At a passing glance, she looked to be on the good side of fifty. But after studying her face and hair in my viewfinder, I suspected she was closer to the upper end of sixty and had a hairdresser and possibly a plastic surgeon under orders to fight for every year they could gain. She was solid without being overweight and there didn't appear to be anything soft about her, except the pretty sage green hand-knit sweater she'd pulled on before we set out to see the lambs. Even her hair was under control, no wisps flying astray. My own dark red curls danced with every wandering breeze.

Debbie stood at the fence, a hand shading her eyes, staring across the field toward her sheep. With her blond braid down her back she could have been a Norse maiden scanning the horizon for sails. My grandmother had liked to say Debbie looked as though she'd stepped out of one of Carl Larsson's watercolors. She had that bright, decorative look of the young women in his nineteenth-century domestic scenes. Debbie worked part-time at the Weaver's Cat, the yarn shop in Blue Plum that had been Granny's pride and passion up until her death a little more than two months earlier. The shop was mine now, which made Debbie my employee, but truthfully, she and the shop's longtime manager were still teaching me the stitches of owning and running the business.

At the shop Debbie tended toward long skirts and embroidered tops, hence Granny's Carl Larsson comment, but that morning she was wearing farm-sensible jeans, a navy blue hoodie that brought out the blue of her eyes, and a great pair of red tartan rubber boots that I coveted. She had four or five inches on me, though, and I'd heard she was strong enough to toss a bale of hay or hold a sheep between her knees for shearing, so I didn't plan to try wrestling the boots off her feet. Part of her strength, mental as well as physical, came from successfully running her farm alone since the death of her husband three or four years earlier.

Framing each face in my camera, I realized we were a nice range of ages. Debbie was in her early thirties, I'd turned thirty-nine two months before, Thea was an honest mid-forties, Bonny could cover both fifties and sixties for us, and Ernestine capped us out with her nearly eighty. I snapped another picture of Ernestine smiling at Bonny, who was showing her the size of something by holding her hands out and looking from one hand to the other, maybe telling Ernestine a Florida fish story. Thea turned and I was able to get a picture of her face in profile.

"I know what the sheep are doing," Thea said. "It's Monday-morning book group. They're reading *Three Bags Full* and making plans."

Debbie gave a quick smile but didn't look as though she'd really heard Thea. "Hey, Kath, have you got a zoom on that camera?"

"Good idea." The camera was new to me, one of several I'd inherited from Granny, and I hadn't played around with all the features yet. I fiddled with the adjustments, held the camera up, and fiddled some more before finding the beech tree and the sheep in the lens. "Okay, got them."

"What do you see?" Debbie asked.

"Sheep. And . . . something? Nope, they shifted for a second but now they're not budging. They're standing with their backs to us."

"Well, I think I want to go out there and see what's going on with those girls," Debbie said, still staring across the field. "That's so unlike them. Anyone want to come with me?"

"Sure." I looked at the others. They might have come

prepared for playing with pots of dye, but Debbie, Thea, and I were the only ones wearing anything on our feet suitable for crossing a wet pasture.

"Come on, Thea, we'll go with her," I said.

"Sorry, no." Thea shook her head. "Mud, maybe, but these shoes don't do ewe poo."

"You two go on and round them up," Bonny said. "We'll stay here holding up the fence and cheering you on."

The others laughed and Debbie and I climbed over and started across the meadow. The sun felt as yellow as the patches of buttercups and warmed every delicate shade of green in the fields and woods around us. A flock of clouds meandered high above in the soft blue sky. The mud and the ewe poo were mostly avoidable. But through the camera's zoom I'd caught a glimpse of something under the beech tree that wasn't right. From the behavior of the sheep, Debbie knew something was up, too, but from her own behavior I didn't think she had any idea what. She was a fast walker and I skipped to catch her.

"Debbie, I need to tell you—"

"Look at them, would you?" she said. "It's like they're standing in a prayer circle. They don't look scared, though. I hope one of them isn't hurt." She walked faster.

"It isn't a sheep."

"Sorry, what?" She didn't slow down.

I grabbed at her arm. "It looked like a person."

Debbie turned her head, nose wrinkled. "What?"

"Well, I'm probably wrong. I only got a quick look when a couple of the sheep moved, and it was hard to tell. Wow." We'd gone about three-quarters of the distance from the fence to where the sheep stood under the tree, and not only was the size of the tree more amazing the closer we got, but the sheep—my goodness. I'd pictured a flock of Mary's little lambs—petite things prancing and nibbling grass—or at least not what I was seeing, which was more along the lines of a herd of Saint Bernards. "Wow. You know, I thought sheep were shorter than that."

"They're Cotswolds."

"That makes them big?"

"Yup, Cotswolds are big," Debbie said. "The older ewes weigh a hundred seventy, a hundred eighty pounds. If your boots don't have steel toes, try not to get stepped on."

I wondered how I'd avoid that if the whole flock turned and suddenly came at me. Did sheep do that?

A couple of the lambs heard us and finally decided we were more interesting than whatever the herd mentality was still engrossed in. They frisked toward us, very cute with their spindly legs and wagging tails even if they were taller than I'd expected. Debbie stopped and greeted them by name.

I was brave and went closer to see what was capturing their mamas' attention. And immediately wished I hadn't.

"Debbie?"

She was down on one knee making goo-goo noises to her babies.

"Debbie? Hey, Deb. Debbie! These sheep over here need you." That brought her head up. "And we need the sheriff." It was probably too late for an ambulance.

Chapter 2

I hadn't known how sad sheep's eyes could look. Debbie's flock stood like woolly mourners around two bodies at the base of the beech tree. Debbie, good shepherdess that she was, checked first to see if any of the animals were hurt. Then, when she was sure they were uninjured, she reacted.

"Oh my God oh my God oh my God oh my God." She stared at the dead man who'd been cradling the dead woman in his arms. "Oh my God, what's he *doing* here?"

"You know him?"

She nodded, couldn't speak, started to shoo the sheep out of the way.

I stopped her. "Leave them if they'll stay. They make a good screen so the others back at the fence can't see."

She looked back toward the road, wide-eyed. "Oh my God."

"Do you have your phone? Can you call 911? Debbie!"

She whimpered but pulled her phone out. Then stopped and stared again. "Are you sure they're dead?"

How could they not be? The woman, young and pretty and fallen sideways from the man's arms, had two wet red blossoms in the middle of her chest. The man, not much older, his head fallen forward, had drying strands of blood from the corner of his mouth and his nose and a terrible hole in his right temple. A gun lay on the ground near his right hand.

"Make the call, Debbie, and stay here. I'll see if there's anything, any—"

I pushed between two of the sheep and knelt beside the bodies in the hope of finding a pulse. I reached toward the woman, stopped, then made myself touch her wrist and push aside the blond hair to feel the side of her neck. Cold. Cold. She was gone. He was gone, too.

But when my hand fell away from him, it brushed against his sweater and an immediate twist of love and unbearable sorrow jolted me. I looked at my hand as though it should somehow be glowing. Of course it wasn't. Tentatively, I laid the tips of my fingers on his sleeve again. How could they feel what they were feeling? I moved my fingertips to the woman's pullover and a rush of terror knocked me back on my heels.

I worked hard to swallow a scream, control my breathing. Worked to explain away the transferred emotions. It was delayed shock. It was my overactive imagination. It was the incongruence of finding violent death in this field of buttercups and new lambs. It was not, could not, be what my beloved and possibly delusional grandmother wrote in the letter she left for me to read after her death. It wasn't any kind of special talent or ability or anything to do with hidden secrets. It wasn't.

"They're coming."

I looked up. Debbie pointed at her phone. I stood up, rubbed both hands on my jeans, scrubbing all sensation from my fingertips. Pushing the memories of love, sorrow, and fear into what I hoped was an unreachable corner of my mind. "What did they say we should do?"

Debbie stood staring, arms hanging at her sides. She'd

let her phone slip from her hand. I picked it up. "Are we supposed to stay here? Debbie?" I looked at the phone. She'd shut it off. I looked at her. She was shutting off, too. "Okay, come on. Let's go back to the road." I started to take her by the elbow but pulled my hand back before I touched her. "Come on."

She started walking with me but turned to look back at the tree and stumbled.

That time I did grab her elbow and was relieved when I didn't feel anything more than her trembling arm. We stood for a moment and I continued holding on to her, but I was afraid I was losing her.

"Debbie, did you warn the dispatcher about the sheep?"

"What?"

"About how big they are and about how the sheriff's people need to be careful and not let them step on their toes?"

Debbie shook her head as though she didn't quite believe how foolish the words coming out of a city girl's mouth could be. She didn't answer me, though, and looked back toward the tree again.

"Or what if the sheep are startled by the uniforms or the shiny badges and charge at the cops? Because, you know, those sheep really are big." I didn't need to see Debbie's face that time to know I did sound idiotic, but at least I'd prodded her mind in another direction.

"They'll be fine."

"The sheep, too?"

She made an impatient noise.

"Well, good, so come on, we can go back to the road and the sheep will be okay and the police will be okay. But are *you* going to be okay? The guy—was he a friend? Who is he?"

She turned and started across the field toward the

road again. The sheep, their vigil disturbed, followed us in single file.

"I know both of them," she said. "His name is Will. Will Embree." Tears ran down her cheeks, but her voice was steady. "And, Kath . . . that's Shannon Goforth."

I shook my head. "I'm sorry. I don't think I know who either of them is."

"You must have heard of Will Embree. Or, I don't know, maybe you haven't. There was some stuff happening at Victory Paper a couple of years ago that he got mixed up in and blamed for. There were protests and he was one of the protesters and it got real ugly."

I remembered reading about it. Ugly was right. And deadly. Granny had sent me the articles from the *Blue Plum Bugle*, but it made the national news, too. Victory Paper International ran a pulp and wood product mill on the Little Buck, farther up in the mountains above Blue Plum, near the North Carolina border. The company had been accused numerous times over the years of causing massive fish kills in the river. The company always denied responsibility, pointing to reports from its own and from state and national inspectors. It had also denied responsibility for the odiferous brown foam that floated down the river from time to time. There wasn't anything unusual, as far as I could remember, about the back-and-forth of accusations and denials. The concerns for the river were reasonable and the corporate responses typical.

What I'd enjoyed reading about in the *Bugle* articles were the odd misfortunes that befell Victory Paper. One involved graffiti depicting dead fish—hundreds of bloated, belly-up fish painted on the outside walls and windows of the mill and on just about anything else within range of a can of spray paint, including dozens of fish on each of the company vehicles. The artwork had taken a lot of time and a whole lot of paint. In a festive touch, the empty spray paint cans were hung like ornaments from a tree inside the security fence surrounding the plant. The pictures in the *Bugle* were great.

Another misfortune involved a quantity of brown organic matter of unspecified but hinted-at origins. It was left on company doorsteps. Once or twice a week. For months.

But then there'd been another fish kill and local environmental groups staged a raucous protest, surrounding the mill on all sides, with people up in trees and on the river in canoes and kayaks, and in the river, too, in wet suits and fishing waders. It was the kind of thing I'd like to have witnessed and maybe taken part in. Had Granny been younger, I think she would have been one of the first up a tree or in the water.

"Some guy died, right?"

Debbie nodded. "Terry Widener."

"He drowned?" But it wasn't an accident and the guy the authorities were sure did it had taken off into the mountains and no one had seen him in the two years since. It was a sad story for everyone involved. "I'd forgotten all about that."

"Will didn't kill Terry," Debbie said, her face tight.

"Wait, you mean that's him? That's *the* Will Embree back there? Good Lord. What's he doing here?" I realized I'd echoed Debbie's words from when she first saw him. Except her words sounded different somehow. "That guy didn't look like someone who's been hiding out in the national forest for two years." He didn't. He was clean shaven with trimmed hair. His jeans were worn and his sweater pilled and faded, but he had on new-looking running shoes. He looked more like a poor graduate student than a mountain man on the run. And when had I noticed all those details? "How did you recognize him?"

She didn't answer, slowed our already slow pace, then stopped. "We're going to have to tell the others and I don't think I can. No, I know I can't. I can't. No. Oh my God oh my God." Her voice had started low and urgent but ended in that string of rising babble. Before it reached hysteria, I squeezed her elbow. Maybe too hard, but squeezing it was less obvious than a slap on her cheek and just as effective. She closed her mouth and yanked her arm away.

"Sorry, Debbie. But it's going to be okay. You don't have to say anything. I'll tell the others there was an accident and we're waiting for the police. That's all they need to know and they'll be okay. And then the workshop will be good for everyone, don't you think? It'll be color therapy. Is everything set up? What colors have you got for us? Aw, and look at that"—I pointed at the sheep—"the lambs are following us to school. So come on." I took her elbow again and urged her toward the fence and the other women.

I was practically babbling by then. Of course we weren't going to continue with the workshop. And if Debbie had set out pots of red dye for us, she'd probably throw up when she looked at them. But I hoped my yammer would act as a dampener to drown out her own thoughts. It didn't, though.

"You don't understand." She pulled away from me. "That's Shannon Goforth back there." Again she said the name as though it should mean something to me. "Bonny Goforth's daughter."

"Bonny Goforth's daughter," I repeated, shaking my head, still clueless.

A couple of the older lambs pranced past us and up closer to the fence. Thea hung over the top rail with a handful of grass. Ernestine reached between the rails with her own handful. Bonny had climbed right over and into the pasture. And then the name clanged into place.

"*Bonny's* daughter? Oh my God."

Chapter 3

If by rooting ourselves out in that field Debbie and I could have kept the terrible news from the others—from Bonny—we would have. But as our ears picked up a siren and its wailing grew louder, what we'd seen under the tree became too painful for Debbie to keep inside, and she had to tell Bonny.

Bonny stood, uncomprehending, until the siren whooped to a stop and we saw the deputy climb out of the car. Then she looked across the field at the tree. She started toward it. I reached for her, caught her sleeve, and she turned and crumpled in my arms. As soon as I touched Bonny, I wanted to let go. The surge of emotion from her rocked me, made me gasp. It wasn't raw grief or anguish I felt, though. It was pure, violent hate.

We stayed with Bonny, intending to surround her and cocoon her, while more police arrived and took over the far end of the field. She sat with her head on Ernestine's shoulder, breathing hard and shuddering. Ernestine stroked and patted her back. Thea and Debbie sat facing them. No one seemed to care about the damp grass anymore. I sat apart from the group, slightly behind Thea.

When Bonny became coherent, she wanted to follow the police, to be with Shannon, but she listened when

Ernestine told her to wait there with us. She didn't agree to wait quietly, though.

"You knew him," she said, lifting her head from Ernestine's shoulder and jabbing her chin at Debbie. "You were in school together." Debbie nodded and blew her nose. "Then you know he wasn't worth the sheep shit in your field."

"Don't," Debbie said. "Please don't start that now, Bonny. Not now. You're right. I knew Will. I knew Shannon, too, and I am so sorry. You had a lot to be proud of in her. But I know Will could never kill anyone, and Shannon knew that, too."

Bonny bowed her head, biting at her lip. She became fascinated with a cocklebur seed twisted in her sock. "And how well did you know Will?" she asked. "There's no way he eluded the authorities all this time without help. That's another well-known fact. So who helped him? Got any answers to that?" She looked at Debbie again, but Ernestine answered.

"I thought there was a whole network of environmental folks helping him," Ernestine said, "stashing camping gear in caves and tucking canned goods into hollow trees and what have you. That was in the paper, wasn't it?"

"And I think people and the Internet have Will Embree confused with those Appalachian yetis you sometimes read about or maybe the Keebler elves, or any number of other silly theories floating around out there," Thea said. "We need to keep this real. Not blow it up into some kind of conspiracy. Will Embree was a human being and now he's gone. Whatever he did or didn't do, let's show the man some respect."

"Thank you," Debbie said.

"My daughter deserves respect," Bonny said.

"Yes, she does," said Thea. "She surely does. She was as smart and pretty as they come."

"And more," Bonny said.

"Yes, she was."

"And Will Embree deserved a prison cell. Will Embree was out to kill Victory Paper. He was responsible for Terry Widener's death two years ago and my daughter wouldn't be shot to death out there now, in some sheep pasture, if it wasn't for something else Will Embree must have been up to."

"Bonny, you can't blame him for this," Debbie said. "You don't know what happened and you didn't see them out there."

"Oh, and you do know? What do you know? Exactly what do *you* know about what happened?"

"That's not what I meant," Debbie said quietly.

"When was the last time you saw him?"

Debbie shook her head.

"Kath, you were out there," Bonny said. "You saw. You're the impartial witness. You tell me what happened."

I'd hoped to stay out of it by staying mostly out of view behind Thea, but Thea hitched over so I could be part of the group. As I reluctantly scooted forward, it occurred to me we were now arranged very nearly the way the sheep had been standing around the bodies, but without their silent, sad-eyed contemplation.

"I don't know what happened," I said.

Bonny pounced on my careful phrasing. "But you've got eyes and you saw something, so tell me what you guess."

I saw the need burning in *her* eyes and heard the grief in her voice. But the hate I'd felt when I held her was still there, too, and the irrationality that can follow a terrible shock. None of that seemed to be anything she could help, and certainly no one could blame her for an entire maelstrom of emotions. But my guesses based on the wounds, the location, the gun lying by his hand, and Shannon in Will's arms—none of that needed to be the catalyst for the storm taking over Bonny's life.

"No." I shook my head. "I can't. Guesses aren't—" I hesitated. "Guesses wouldn't be respectful of your daughter. They wouldn't be respectful of either of them."

"She's right, Ms. Goforth," a familiar voice said behind me. "It's best not to speculate at this point. Ma'am, may I say how sorry I am for your terrible loss? And if you don't mind, you should come with me now."

The owner of the voice, Deputy Cole Dunbar, was not my favorite law enforcement officer, and it was unlikely he ever would be. Not because of his meticulous behavior in a situation such as this—he was at his grave best speaking to Bonny. And not because of his looks. There was no flab on his large frame and he was always neatly turned out in his perpetually starched and stiff uniform. It was more his whole personality and approach to life. He was prissy, pissy, and perpetually superior and had a contradictory dash of boorishness that vacillated between being an undertone and being a really annoying overtone. He irked me and he seemed to take pleasure in knowing he did.

My private name for the irritating Deputy Cole Dunbar was Clod. I tried to be careful, though, and never referred to him by that name to anyone else and never called him Clod to his face. After all, he did carry a gun.

But at that particular moment I was happy to hear Clod Dunbar agree with me about guesses and respect, and it didn't even make me jump out of my skin to find him standing behind me. Maybe Bonny shared some of my ambivalence toward him, though. Her only acknowledgment of his presence or his request was a flicking glance. Then she leaned forward toward me.

"Okay, no guessing," she said, low and urgent, "but

you can find out for me. You know what it's like when people start making up stories. And I heard how you beat these clowns to the answer a few months ago."

Deputy Dunbar coughed behind me, and that time I did jump. I moved aside, too, but he chose to walk around our small circle to reach Bonny rather than step into the middle of it.

"Come on with me now, Ms. Goforth. I'll take you to see your daughter."

He took Bonny gently by the arm and helped her up. He told the rest of us we could go on home after answering a few questions from one of his colleagues and that he'd have a deputy take Bonny and her car home later. I might have imagined the hard look he gave me when Bonny grabbed my arm and said she was counting on me.

We took turns answering questions for one of Dunbar's colleagues. I went last. The questions were simple: Name, contact information. How close had I gotten to the scene? Had I touched or moved anything? When I rejoined the others, Debbie was looking and sounding as though she shouldn't be left alone, either. She was stuck in a loop, alternately apologizing for the dye workshop that never got started and staring at the ground.

"Why don't we see if your neighbor brought the spare key and then we'll help you put everything away?" I said. "And we can reschedule the workshop. That's no problem."

"You could do it, Kath," Debbie said, still staring at the ground.

"Well, sure, we'll all be happy to," Thea said.

"I mean she could find out what happened. Like Bonny said. You could do it, Kath, and we could help. Like last time."

I took a chance and put my arm around her. She was

taut, brittle. She didn't flinch, though, and neither did I, thank goodness. No errant emotions buzzed between us. I held her that way until she relaxed a fraction; then I spoke quietly in her ear. "We saw the same things out there, didn't we? Don't you think maybe we already know what happened?"

She didn't just flinch then; she yanked herself away.

"We do *not* know what happened. We know what we saw, but we do *not* know what happened. And depending on who looks for answers and then quits when they find the easy and obvious ones, we might never know what happened."

"Debbie—"

"You know that can happen. You've seen it happen. So please. For their sake if not for Bonny's or mine."

This really was irrational, and I didn't know how to handle it. Snap her out of it by telling her how ridiculous it was? Agree with her to calm her down? Messy situations like this were exactly why I'd preferred dealing with the predictability of concrete chemical analysis and textile preservation in my professional life. Of course I was also the one who now sometimes felt emotions when I touched fibers. And then there were the one or two other less-than-normal matters waiting for me back in town—speaking of totally irrational . . .

"Please," Debbie said.

I was also the one who, with the help of a "posse" that included Debbie, Thea, Ernestine, and a few others, had unraveled several mysteries and murders before the professionals. Mainly before Deputy Cole Dunbar. Breaking his nose in the process. Except that the posse wasn't responsible for breaking Clod's nose. That was down to me alone. Me and my fist. It hadn't been one of my best moments.

I glanced at Ernestine and Thea. Ernestine always

looked innocent no matter what went on behind her thick lenses. Thea was again uncharacteristically quiet. They'd both enjoyed being part of the posse. They both looked very slightly hopeful now.

"Please," Debbie said.

"Let me think about it. Maybe give it a couple of days. Okay?"

"Okay. But I want you to say yes." She clasped the top of her skull; then she put her hands to her cheeks and shook her head. "I don't think I even know what I'm doing. This was such a beautiful day. Now it's a nightmare. And I made lunch for all of you and what am I going to do with all of that? And isn't that a *stupid* thing to worry about?"

"You can feed it to the deputies," Ernestine said. "I believe they'll be here with you for a while. Now, come along." She took Debbie's arm. "You can get me back through the fence so we don't need to call for more help."

After Debbie convinced us she'd be all right on her own, I was glad to give Ernestine and Thea a ride back to Blue Plum. I hoped their navigational skills would make for a shorter return trip. Ernestine insisted she'd be more comfortable in the backseat. Thea looked at my two-door Honda, didn't argue, and held the door for her.

"Well, this has been a morning for the books," Thea said, settling in beside me. "Of course I say that every morning. But what a terrible, horrible shame. Saying 'poor Bonny' doesn't begin to cover it."

"Does she have other family in the area?" I asked.

"They're not close," Ernestine said. "When I get home I'll start the TGIF phone tree and we'll get some casseroles going over there."

"That's a good idea," I said. Visions of a hand-to-hand

tuna noodle brigade went through my head. "I'm sorry about missing Debbie's dye workshop, too. I was looking forward to it."

"Were you?" Ernestine asked. "If you don't mind me saying so, I was surprised to see you. After all, you're Ivy's granddaughter. Surely you learned at her knee, and I would have thought she'd left all her special secrets with you."

Special secrets? My eyes flew to Ernestine in the rear-view mirror. How could she know anything about the secrets Granny mentioned in her letter?

"Ivy was an artist, though," Ernestine went on, unaware of my alarm. "That's the simple truth. She was an artist in everything she did. Debbie is good, and her use of color is exciting, but in the end no one dyes the way Ivy dyed." She paused. "Oh dear. There was no way for that last part to come out right, was there. I am so sorry."

"It's okay, Ernestine. You know Granny would've laughed. In fact—"

"Whoa, whoa, whoa," Thea said.

"Whoa, what? I haven't even started the car."

"I know. I'm calling for a subject change because you ignored the opening I gave you when we got in. *A terrible, horrible shame? Poor Bonny?* You know, the whole reason we aren't playing with painted wool. Tell us what happened out in that field."

Ernestine tsked.

"You're as anxious to know as I am, Ernestine. Don't pretend you're not."

"But we could at least let her buckle her seat belt first," Ernestine said.

"I wish I could forget what happened out there." As if that were possible. I believed what I'd told Debbie, that we probably did know what happened. But why it happened and how it came to happen—there in her field and on this bright morning—those questions swam around in my head threatening to make me dizzy. "I'd really rather not talk about it," I said, finally rolling down the drive.

"Right," Thea said. Then, when I turned left onto the main road, "Where are you going? I said right."

"I thought you were agreeing not to talk about what happened."

"It's a wonder you ever did get here. Which way did you come? Cherry Grove Road or Buncombe?"

"Hard to say. Maybe both."

"Would you like me to drive, dear?" Ernestine asked.

"No, thank you, Ernestine."

Thea got us going in the right direction, and by the time we crossed the Little Buck I had my bearings. We traveled beside the river for two or three miles in a broad, level valley and I remembered coming out this way with Granny, when I was a child, to pick strawberries at one of the farms. Later in the year there would be acres of tomatoes and more acres of pumpkins. The river was wide and smooth here, stretching and relaxing after its rough tumble through the mountains. It chuckled softly, inviting folks to fish from its gravel banks and bars, or step in for a swim, or go for a lazy paddle downstream, slipping past willows and alders.

But don't you turn your back on that river for a minute, Granny used to tell me.

"That isn't a river that mixes well with alcohol," Ernestine said from the backseat.

"Are you reading my mind back there, Ernestine? Granny used to say something like that."

"I'm practicing because two of my grandsons are getting old enough to think they know better. I don't suppose many rivers do mix with alcohol, but there's something about this one that seems to attract more than its share of fools."

"That's because fools are easily fooled," Thea said.

Talk of the river brought some of my questions bubbling to the surface. "How far upstream is Victory Paper from here?"

"Maybe ten miles as the fish swims," Ernestine said.

"You'd never know all that mess was up there, though, to look at the Buck down here," Thea said. "And depending on who you talk to, that goes right along with fools being fooled. There might be fish in that river, but you won't catch me eating them."

"So who all was mixed up with the protests when the guy drowned two years ago? Will Embree, but was Shannon, too? Is that why Bonny is so set against him? She thinks he led Shannon astray?"

"Oh, my land, no," Ernestine said. "Those two couldn't have been at more opposite ends of that argument. Shannon was the spokesperson for Victory Paper."

"What? Holy cow. No wonder Bonny reacted that way."

"Bless her heart," Ernestine said. "And bless theirs, too. They had their whole lives ahead of them. Here's your turn coming up, and this will take you right on into Main Street. Goodness. It will feel good to be home." She said that as though we'd been in another country and gone for days, but that was the way going back to Blue Plum affected the people who loved it.

When I'd driven into Blue Plum to bury my sweet grandmother, I'd looked at the town fondly but with the eyes of someone only stopping through. I'd spent many joyful summers there with Granny, playing storekeeper in the Weaver's Cat, learning to weave on her massive floor loom, taking walks with her and listening to her stories of the town she'd lived in her whole life. But I'd come to say good-bye to Blue Plum's quaint streets and antique buildings, good-bye to the Weaver's Cat, to

Granny's house, to her friends, and to dear Granny. She'd left the shop, the building it was in, and her house to me, but I had my own career and I was following a different pattern. I planned to pack whatever memories would fit in a rented truck and take them back to Illinois, and I wasn't sure when I'd ever be back.

Almost as soon as I'd arrived, though, my neatly organized life was upended. In so many ways. So many sad but not terribly unusual ways. And in a few decidedly abnormal ways, too. The list of abnormal ways included, though it wasn't restricted to: losing my textile preservation job at the state museum in Illinois, discovering Granny was Clod Dunbar's personal prime suspect in a very nasty case of murder by poison, and receiving the letter Granny wrote telling me she had certain "talents," making her "a bit of a witch." She'd ended that fey letter with the news that I might have inherited her "talents" and she'd hidden her secret dye journals somewhere in her attic study at the Weaver's Cat for me to find and use. Or not. The decision to witch or not to witch being mine.

I mean, really. And on top of all that I'd somehow ended up with a depressed . . .

"Are you going to the Cat?" Ernestine asked.

"I can swing by your house," I said, happy she'd interrupted my manic reminiscence.

"No, dear, the Cat is fine. I'll enjoy the walk home. What about you, Thea?"

"Sure, the Cat's fine. This was supposed to be my day off, but I might as well head over to the library. Maybe if I slip in the back door, I can put in some stealth time in the office and no one will ever know."

"So Shannon and Will and Debbie all knew each other?" I asked, slipping into my own metaphorical back door.

"The way I heard it, Shannon and Will dated in high school," Thea said.

The image of her in his arms came back to my mind along with the confusion of feelings, the love and the terror. "That explains a lot and nothing at all."

"Well, we can't help you sort through it," Thea said, with exaggerated patience, "because you still haven't told us what happened."

"Let me park."

We waited behind a tour bus as several dozen seniors creaked down its steps onto the sidewalk and steadied themselves for an assault on the shops. Then I turned the corner and pulled into the lot across the side street from the Weaver's Cat. Thea turned toward me when I shut off the engine. Ernestine moved to the center of the backseat so she could see between the headrests.

"First," Thea said, "have you thought about it, like you told Debbie you would? Are you going to investigate? Are you redeputizing the posse?"

"There hasn't been time to think about that. I was busy driving without getting lost or crashing, remember? But really, I meant it when I told Debbie I don't think there's anything to investigate."

"She thinks there is," Ernestine said.

"She's distraught. That's wishful thinking. And poor Bonny's in shock and wants the whole thing to not be true. No one and no amount of investigating can help her with that."

"Then convince us Debbie's wrong," Thea said. "Tell us what you saw."

"Okay. Basic description only, though." I was surprised by how choked up I suddenly felt. I hadn't known Shannon Goforth or Will Embree. But their broken lives had just shattered two women in front of my eyes. I held my breath for a moment, then breathed out slowly, using a trick I'd learned to calm myself before speaking in front of large groups.

"It looked like a murder-suicide, like he shot her and then himself. There was a gun on the ground near his hand. I've never seen anything like that before, though, and I've never seen gunshot wounds, and I don't really know what a murder-suicide looks like. I just know I don't want to see anything like it again. But here's what I don't understand. It looked like he was cradling her in his arms. Why would he do that if he shot her? Unless maybe he was sorry he'd killed her? I don't know. And I'm not sure, and I don't know why I think this, but maybe I shouldn't have told you that much. And if investigating means digging around in their private lives, into things that aren't anyone else's business, then I'm not sure that's something I want to do."

"Bless their hearts." Ernestine put her hand on my shoulder and nodded. "Thank you for telling us. Don't worry about spreading stories, though. All of that and more will be around town before you sit down for supper tonight, with details you never saw and more that never existed. Well. I believe I'll go on home now and start the phone tree. Bonny's going to need strength and kindness."

Thea helped Ernestine out, then came around to my window with a different look in her eyes. "You can't fool me," she said. "You're already on the case."

"No, I'm not, because it isn't a case. There aren't any suspects. It's a murder-suicide, Thea. There's nobody to suspect of anything—even if I do wonder about why he was cradling her and even if Debbie insists he'd never kill her. Neither of those sentimental interpretations changes the facts. If that's what they are." I wished I'd quit throwing in qualifiers.

"See? I told you. You *are* on the case. You're looking

at this from your ivory tower scientific perspective. That's good. And don't worry about suspects. You'll come up with some or you'll come up with something else."

"The Illinois State Museum is not an ivory tower."

"But you *are* on the case."

"I don't think so." I meant that to come out with more certainty and shook my head at that failure. "I haven't made up my mind yet." Rats, I hadn't meant that to come out at all.

Thea patted my shoulder, too, before turning around and heading for the library. I sat in the car awhile longer, drinking in the sanity of the symmetrical lines of the Weaver's Cat across the street. Since the upheavals in my life, the Cat had become my refuge of choice. Granny's lovingly tended pet occupied the three floors of a nineteenth-century row house on Main Street. The square, high-ceilinged rooms contained enough colors and textures to lure and possibly drown any fiber artist or needle crafter brave enough to look in the front windows or dip a toe inside.

"Wool, cotton, herbs, dyes, bricks, wood, women, gossip, coffee, and, if we're lucky, a hint of cinnamon or chocolate," Granny had rattled off when I told her I wanted to chemically analyze the Cat's particular scent so I could reproduce it and let it loose in my museum lab back in Illinois. "I've spun them together for years. The proportions are a secret recipe, though. I'll leave it to you in my will." Instead of that secret, she'd left me a few others not quite so straightforward as a recipe for aromatherapy. And she'd left me the Cat.

I locked my car then, and ran rather than walked across the street to my refuge. Where it turned out parts of the morning's story had arrived ahead of me.

Chapter 4

Ardis Buchanan, longtime manager of the Weaver's Cat, gave me a subdued wave from behind the sales counter when she saw me. Ardis was at least a foot taller than either Granny or I had ever hoped to be. Every so often she made token complaints about thinning hair and a spreading waistline, but for the most part she couldn't be bothered to worry. If the Cat was my refuge, Ardis was my rock. A rock that always smelled of honeysuckle, but steady and reliable.

"No need to be here, honey, if you don't want," she said when I reached the counter. "I've just hung up from Debbie."

"How's she doing?"

"Says she'll be here in the morning as usual. But between you and me, she didn't sound so 'as usual.'"

"Coming in to work might be what she needs."

"That and finding out what happened."

"I don't think there's much question about what happened," I said.

"Much." She nodded.

"There's no reason to think the police will miss or misinterpret anything."

"Miss and misinterpret," she said, shaking her head sadly.

"I said 'or.'"

She dismissed that quibble with a flick of her wrist. “Ernestine said you’re considering reconvening and re-deputizing.”

“You’ve talked to Ernestine already?”

“And Mel,” Ardis said.

“What did Mel know? She wasn’t there.”

Melody Gresham was another member of the original posse. She was also the owner and operator of the best café in town and would have been up to her talented elbows in pastry dough for hours by the time Debbie and I made our discovery in the sheep pasture.

“Quick is how word spreads in most towns,” Ardis said. “Like blue lightning is how it spreads in Blue Plum. And think about this—if information walks in here, and it sprints into Mel’s, can you imagine how much of it will be sitting around sipping iced tea and ripe for the picking at the always wonderful and often hysterical Historical Trust Annual Meeting and Potluck come Saturday night?”

“Huh. You’re right.”

“Of course I am. So what do you think? About re-deputizing the posse?”

“Right now I’d like to stop thinking about all of it, so if you really don’t need me, I’ll be in the attic. Land of the never-ending opportunity to sort and organize. That’s what my brain needs.”

“Mine needs lunch,” Ardis said. “If I see Joe I’ll send him over to Mel’s.” Joe was Joe Dunbar, Deputy Clod’s brother and a complete yin to Clod’s yang. “Would you like something?”

“Sure. Popeye salad, dressing on the side. If you don’t see him, let me know and I’ll go. Has the cat behaved himself?”

“Good as gold. He came down for his bite of breakfast, asked after you, then took himself back upstairs to the land of the rarely ending naps. He needs a name, you know."

"Still working on that."

I loved Granny's private study in the attic, loved its snug proportions and angled ceilings, its built-in cupboards and bookcases. It had been the place where Granny worked the bugs out of one project and designed the next; read the latest on rigid-heddle looms, hand spinning, and natural dyes; or simply put her feet up and stared out the dormer window and dreamed undisturbed.

For me, the study wasn't quite so private. Two others also loved it and spent time there—the cat and a ghost named Geneva. I hadn't believed in ghosts until I met Geneva. And there were times I wished I *hadn't* met her so I could stop believing in the other odd things that had entered my life recently. Nothing against her personally.

I still didn't know much about her. I had reason to believe she'd lived sometime during the nineteenth century, but pegging her age and era more specifically wasn't easy. She didn't like being pressed for details about her life or death and it didn't help that she wasn't ever any clearer to my eyes than someone seen through a ripple of water.

Cat and ghost were both in the window seat when I reached the study. The cat raised his chin in greeting, but before I could say hello, Geneva put her nose in the air and vanished. I shook my head. Ghosts. Go figure. Maybe I would find out what that snub was about and maybe I wouldn't. I was definitely on a learning curve, but I was coming to realize ghosts were a lot like cats. They were finicky and they needed a certain amount of downtime. And just as a woman shouldn't have too many cats, if she could help it she probably shouldn't have too many ghosts, or she might end up being called a crazy ghost lady. Or just plain crazy. The crazy part was something I worried about because, crazy as it seemed, the cat and I were the only ones who saw or heard Geneva. And that sometimes made my life difficult, or at least tricky.

Before we met, Geneva had lived, for lack of a better word, in the caretaker's cottage at the local living history site. She didn't haunt the cottage in the traditional sense, because the caretaker hadn't known she existed. But she did haunt—as in spent every second of every day in—the room where the caretaker left his television permanently on, and she'd developed an insatiable appetite for cop shows, talk shows, old movies, Westerns, and reruns of fifties and sixties sitcoms. All that accumulated pop culture gave an interesting twist to her personality.

I scritched the cat between his ears and he obligingly started his motor. I never had found out where he came from, but he'd arrived looking as though he'd stuck his paw in an electrical outlet. The vet said she thought he might have been tossed out of a moving car, poor old guy. He bore the world no grudges, though, and after a few months of hard napping and gentle cosseting, he was becoming quite the dapper fellow. He was a lovely ginger tom with a white bib and a white fur mustache that turned upward as though it curled at the ends. The only problem was what to call him. Geneva tried a new name every few days, but our agreement was that we both had to like a name, and so far that hadn't happened.

The three of us actually got along fairly well. We clicked, the cat, the ghost, and I. Maybe because of what we had in common—loss, disorientation, the need for a place to anchor. Maybe the reasons weren't important.

I gave Mr. No Name's chin a rub for good measure, then did a slow three-sixty of the room, pivoting on my heel and wondering where I should start. Where did one begin to search for secret journals? And really search, not just bemusedly, skeptically check around? Because I had kept an eye out for the journals when I put Granny's papers and desk in order, but at that point it didn't surprise me when I didn't find them.

I didn't bother asking myself when I'd started believing the journals existed. Anyone who previously hadn't believed in ghosts, who now shared a cat with one, shouldn't spend too much time examining beliefs.

The journals, according to Granny's letter, contained her recipes for special dyes that allowed her to help her neighbors *out of certain pickles from time to time*. She didn't specify what she meant by "help," "pickles," or "from time to time," but she thought the whole thing was marvelous and was sure I would, too. Maybe if everything else in my life hadn't fallen apart at the same time Granny died, my reaction would have been more enthusiastic.

But even if I obviously hadn't known Granny as well as I thought, I did think she would understand my need to sort, straighten, and organize my life back into some semblance of order before looking for her journals. So that's how I'd filled my hours and days since I'd packed my belongings in Illinois and moved to Blue Plum, telling myself I was busy and productive and was not avoiding the journals. But now their time had come.

I continued my slow three-sixty of the room. It wasn't a large space. It was the finished part of the attic, walled off from the rest and made cozy by my grandfather, who had enjoyed woodworking as much as Granny had enjoyed her fibers and weaving. He had built the bookcases, too. I'd looked through the books on the shelves, in case the journals were disguised and in plain sight. That would have been too obvious, though, and not safe enough if she was concerned about prying eyes, and I didn't find them there.

Granddaddy had found Granny's desk as a derelict at the flea market and refinished it for her. It was one of those old, heavy oak teacher's desks, and Granny said she never wanted to know how he got it up the three flights of stairs and around the last tight corner into the study. I'd looked the desk over carefully for false-bottom drawers and secret panels. No luck there, either. Granny was clever, though, and she was confident that I was clever, too. She wouldn't hide the journals where it was too hard to get at them. Maybe under a hinged floor-board?

Geneva floated back in while I was crawling around examining, tapping, and attempting to pry.

"You can grovel all you like," she said. "It won't make me feel any better."

"Sorry?" I sat back on my heels and pushed my hair behind my ears. "What are you talking about?"

"Me. You left me behind this morning."

"Is that what you were in a grump about a few minutes ago? You said you didn't want to come with me."

"And then I changed my mind, but you'd already left without me." She looked at me and waited. I waited, too. "Well, I can see you aren't going to apologize, so I'll be kind and forgive you for that. But *then* . . ." She stopped and heaved a throbbing sigh.

"'Then' what?"

"You didn't *tell* me. I had to hear about it from a customer just now, and she was buying the most horrible shade of orange rug wool while she was talking about it. The whole experience was too much." She had a tendency to billow when she was upset, and she tended to upset herself with her own melodrama. I scooted back to give her more room.

"Are you talking about what happened at Debbie's farm? Geneva, I was going to tell you."

"But you didn't."

"Because you left, but I was going to."

"Really?"

"Of course. I knew you'd be interested."

She blew her nose. "Okay. I feel better."

"Good. So now tell me what you heard, but first, do you know who the woman was that you heard it from?"

"Besides being someone with painful taste? No, I have no idea."

"What did she look like?"

"That is such an uninteresting detail compared to what she said. Why does it matter?"

"I just wondered if it was one of the women at Debbie's this morning, except I don't see how it could've been. You know Debbie and you've seen Ernestine and Thea often enough. I'm sure it wasn't Bonny. What did the woman look like?"

"Her hair was straight and stringy, much like her figure."

"Well, no, that doesn't describe any of us."

"I don't know Bonny, but I imagine her grief will work on her so that she begins to fade away," Geneva said with some relish. "That is a sad fact of bereavement, except perhaps in your case. You were not stringy when we first met, and even though you've suffered through the death of your dear grandmother and the loss of your job and your home and all your friends and—"

"Is there a point you're trying to make?"

"Yes. I've noticed that you have become less stringy since we met. I thought I should mention that to show how accurate I am at describing people."

Said she who need never worry about gaining another ounce for all eternity. I was glad I'd asked only for the salad for lunch. "Thank you, Ms. Eagle Eye. The point is, who was this woman, where did she hear about what happened, and when, and how far has the story already spread?"

"Maybe she was the murderer." Geneva billowed in and out, excited by that thought.

"Calm down. She wasn't. It was pretty clear, even to me, what happened. I don't think anyone's going to be looking for a murderer."

"That's not what I heard."

"Really. Well, maybe you'd better tell me what you did hear."

"Oh good, because it is a good story and I think I can tell it with true inspiration. Marshal Dillon would like to hear it, too, though, so you sit next to him."

Now was not the time to argue over the cat's name or his interest in crime. I sat cross-legged beside him in the window seat. He woke long enough to climb into my lap and purr before falling back asleep. Geneva floated into the middle of the room, wispy arms artfully poised.

"You give me my cue," she stage-whispered.

"Oh, for . . . Okay. Begin."

And she did, launching into a short but dramatic retelling of what she'd heard. Or maybe it was her own, more colorful interpretation of what she'd heard. The basics were accurate—a young couple dead under a tree—but in this version they were found with their arms twined around each other, both were murdered, there was more blood than I ever wanted to hear about again, and no weapon was found.

"Um—wow—thanks, Geneva. That was—gee—that was vivid. You know, though, I think maybe the woman you heard the story from might have confused a few of the details."

"Well, she probably didn't see it in person. That could be why," Geneva said, sounding even-keeled and ready to forgive the woman's excess rather than explode at my questioning of her rendition.

"If that's the story she's telling, then, no, I'm pretty sure she didn't see it in person." I stopped and thought about that. Unless she'd been with the deputies and EMTs who responded, but then she wouldn't have gotten the details so wrong and in fact might still be on duty out there, not here buying rug wool. That meant either an exaggerated story was already running around town, something Ardis and Ernestine warned me would happen, or Geneva was the source of the embroidery. The former would be hurtful to Bonny when it reached her ears, as it was sure to. As for the latter, it seemed disrespectful to Bonny and to the dead to let Geneva continue spinning that yarn, even if the cat and I were the only ones hearing it. Calling her out on the embellishments would be treading dangerous ground, though. Maybe if I approached it from a detective's point of view.

"You know, Geneva, if we were investigating what happened—"

"Are we?" She billowed toward me, empty eyes wider than I'd ever seen them.

"Investigating? No. You might hear Debbie and Ardis saying something about me looking into it—"

"But you told them you couldn't do it—"

"Exactly."

"—on your own."

"What? No, that's not what I said."

She didn't hear me. She was over the moon. She was also all over the room, whirling and squealing with delight, like a crazed balloon someone blew up and suddenly let go. The squeal wasn't a pleasant noise, and the whirling was going to make me sick. I closed my eyes and covered my ears, and that's how Joe Dunbar found me when he trotted up the back stairs to say he'd brought lunch.

Chapter 5

"Kath? Hey, are you okay?"

When I finally realized there was someone else in the room besides the berserk ghost, I opened my eyes. Joe, younger brother of the antagonistic Deputy Cole Dunbar, was crouched in front of me, peering into my face. The cat had left my lap and was sitting next to me, following Geneva's acrobatics.

"I heard what happened," Joe said. "Ardis said you and Debbie found them. That was a hell of a thing to happen. It must've been a hell of a thing to see. *Are* you okay?"

"Yeah, I am, thanks. Thanks for asking. I was . . ." I couldn't think of a good ending for that sentence.

"You looked as though you were trying to blot out the whole world," he said.

"Sometimes it helps."

"Fishing's good for that, too. It's good to have a place where you can get away. Be alone."

If he'd been aware of Geneva swooping past his head doing bad Clint Eastwood imitations, he wouldn't have been so philosophical. She was calming down, though, and being the nosy thing she was, circled him a few times, then settled in the window seat on the other side of the cat. Ghost and cat sat watching Joe as though he were the most exotic creature to set foot in the attic. Joe held his hand out and the cat sniffed his fingertips, then rubbed the side of his face against them. Geneva reached a wispy hand forward.

"So, Joe," I said, hopping up and startling him so he dropped his hand and sat back on his heels out of Geneva's reach. "How's Maggie?"

"Same as ever," he said, getting to his feet. "She's a sweetheart."

Those two statements didn't go together, in my experience of pretty Maggie. She was Granny's cat, whom I'd also inherited. But Maggie's "as ever" when it came to her opinion of me was the same as that of every other cat Granny had ever had—intense dislike with occasional swatting. It was an interesting phenomenon that baffled Granny and saddened me. But Maggie liked Joe, and after thumbing her nose at me, she went to live with him.

"Have you got a name for your guy yet?" he asked.

"No, still working on it."

"We are not," Geneva said. "Marshal Dillon likes his name and it's as fine as they come. Oh, but wait. I've had a thought. It's rather brilliant. Harry Callahan. Dirty Harry." She bounced and billowed at her own brilliance. "It suits him, don't you think?"

I squeezed my eyes shut to blot her out for a moment. Forgetting Joe. He grabbed my elbow.

"Are you sure you're all right? Maybe you stood up too fast."

"Could be."

"Your salad's down in the kitchen. You should go eat."

"And while you're doing that, Dirty Harry and I will be on stakeout in the shop," Geneva said. "We'll gather intelligence and report back after your luncheon date."

Brilliant.

My luncheon date was wishful thinking on Geneva's part. Joe Dunbar was nice enough, and he was nominally a member of the posse, but it seemed to be a general principle that Dunbars and I had trouble mixing. Anyone glancing at me and noting the lack of a ring on my finger and the absence of PTA meetings in my thirty-nine-year-old life might extend the mixing principle to me and men in general. To them, I would say, be patient. Miracles happen. Witness the cat who actually liked me and sat in my lap. And at least I hadn't socked this Dunbar in the nose.

But Joe had some baggage I wasn't too sure about. One of those bags had to do with burglary that might or might not be a habit. The one incident I knew about could have been a first-and-last-time deal, and no one else I knew and trusted seemed to worry about there being a sketchy side to him. His brother, the starched deputy, *did* seem to worry, but I didn't particularly trust his brother. Besides, Clod's worries might be nothing more than brotherly baggage.

Joe had some saving graces, too, though, so I tried to keep an open mind. One of those graces was his tendency to *avoid* his brother. Another was what Geneva noticed—not only was he nice enough; he was also nice to look at. Whereas his brother was tall, solid, and mulishly stubborn, Joe was tall, spare, and scruffy in an artistic, outdoorsy sort of way, and he had an easy, accepting manner. Geneva referred to Joe as my gentleman caller, convinced we were an item. Reminding her we weren't was a waste of breath.

Joe's most telling grace was his affection for my grandmother and her apparent affection for him. I still wondered why, if they were such pals, I hadn't known of his existence until recently, but I had an idea the baggage thing might be a factor there, too. For now it was enough to know he'd liked her and she'd trusted him. Ardis trusted him, too, and that said a lot.

But Joe didn't join me for lunch downstairs in the kitchen. I didn't ask where he was off to and he didn't volunteer the information. He was a man with many trickles, if not streams, of income. He was a sought-after fly-fishing guide and he taught the occasional fly-tying class for us at the Weaver's Cat. He was also a more than decent watercolorist and did a fairly decent business selling his paintings at another shop in town. A regular Renaissance man, with baggage, was Joe Dunbar. But solo fishing up one or another secluded mountain creek was his go-to way of passing a lovely afternoon. Or so he said.

Geneva did join me over lunch to give her first intelligence report. The cat followed her into the kitchen. He purred and twined his furry self around my ankles, and I was still enough in the early sappy stage of cat cohabitation that I found it utterly charming. If he'd asked to share my salad I would have simpered and given him a leaf or two of spinach and a bite of carrot. But he wanted dry, crunchy, fish-smelling things, so I tipped some of those into his bowl. The way he dug in and smacked his little cat lips made his lunch look and sound better than mine. I'd left the dressing off, remembering Geneva's observation of my increasing lack of stringiness. Her opinionated remarks were taking some getting used to. I was definitely still in the early, perplexed, "why me?" stage of being haunted.

"I hope you appreciate what I'm doing for you," she said, hovering across from me, elbows not quite on the table. "Although I don't want you to think I begrudge spending my precious time listening for a clue that will crack the case wide open while you sit out here eating. Alone. Do you know, though, for every customer with something interesting to say about the murders, I have to keep awake through a dozen boring conversations? It's exhausting." She yawned to prove it.

There almost certainly hadn't been a dozen customers in the shop, all carrying on conversations, boring or otherwise, during the ten or fifteen minutes she was on her self-assigned stakeout. And, far from sounding bored, she sounded keyed up. If her eyes could be, they would be glinting.

"But you did hear something interesting?" I whispered so I wouldn't embarrass myself by being overheard in case Ardis or a customer was near the kitchen.

"I heard quite a lot about self-striping sock yarn. It's on sale today and is always fascinating, if you enjoy listening to Ardis run on about such things. If I weren't such a good detective, I think I might try my hand at being a shopkeeper."

"You're a good tease, anyway. What did you hear?"

"I have you wondering, don't I?" She wriggled with satisfaction. "I'll give you a hint, but the full information is too long and important to rush the details. All the details are extremely interesting, of course, but I can't stop to tell you the whole fascinating story now, because some of us are doing important and extremely interesting jobs and must get back to them." She sat back, clapping her soundless fingertips together beneath her chin, and said nothing more.

Self-important and extremely irritating ghost. She'd probably been an irritating woman, too. I waited and counted to ten. Then counted ten more for good measure and forced a smile. Bit my tongue. Raised my eyebrows in a "what gives?" sort of way.

She dropped her hands to the table. "You aren't being very cooperative. I am expecting you to explode with curiosity."

"And I'm waiting for you to give me your crumb of information," I whispered, "so you can return to your very important job and leave me to finish my very bland salad."

"You're hissing at me."

I leaned farther across the table and hissed harder. "We're in a semipublic place. I'm being careful so I'm not pegged as the next crazy person, and you're making it seriously difficult."

"If you were to pretend you're talking on your telephone, you could speak in a normal tone of voice and not upset me."

"Oh." I sat up, snapped my mouth shut, and pulled my phone from my pocket. "My gosh. Why didn't we think of this before?"

"It will look more realistic if you put the phone to your ear," she said.

"Good thinking."

"I'm brilliant, aren't I?"

"And smug. But brilliant, yes. So what did you hear?"

"Well, and now I fear we've run out of time. I did warn you." She sat back and sighed grandly. "Unfortunately you wasted what time we had with your usual nitpicking, and now I see Dirty Harry has finished his lunch and we must return to our stakeout." She rose, nose in the air, and floated toward the door.

"After all that, you're not going to tell me? You've got to be kidding."

"Come along, Dirty Harry." The cat actually looked up from contemplating his empty dish and started after her.

"I am not calling him Dirty Harry," I snarled into the phone.

"Him, who?" Ardis asked, zipping in the door.

She zipped straight through Geneva. I'd never seen

that happen before and couldn't help staring. It didn't affect Geneva, didn't part her wispy form or displace it. She saw me staring, though, and turned her back with a *hmph*.

"Do you feel that odd draft?" Ardis looked back over her shoulder, then at me. "Oh, sorry, I didn't see you were on the phone."

I held up a "one moment, please" finger, finished the charade by saying good-bye, and flipped the phone shut. "Him, the cat."

"Oh, well, I should hope not." The cat rubbed against her ankles and she leaned over to pet him. "You've cleaned up into a fine-looking fellow, haven't you? You're not a dirty anybody."

"Tell her the name has nothing to do with hygiene," Geneva demanded.

"Don't worry, Ardis," I said. "Dirty Harry is just another of those ridiculous suggestions people offer for his name. You should hear some of them. Absolutely nutty. But I'll come up with the right one, one of these days." I felt bad as soon as the words were out of my mouth. That was carrying tit for tat further than I should have, even if Geneva had started it. She was gone, though, and I couldn't apologize to her in front of Ardis, anyway. And if I thought hard enough, I could probably come up with several more ways to rationalize not going after her to tell her I was sorry.

I asked Ardis if she and the shop were set for the afternoon. Of course they were. I was the only one who needed help when I was alone in the shop. I was the one who didn't know what she was doing professionally or personally. Or, as it turned out, paranormally. I told Ardis I'd see her in the morning, abandoned the search for secret journals again, and went home.

And found the Spivey twins waiting in the shadows of my front porch.

Chapter 6

If I had seen Shirley and Mercy on the porch before I pulled into the drive, I would have goosed the gas and gone around the next corner on two wheels. It was possible I overreacted to the Spiveys, but it was a genuine gut reaction, and going with my gut often worked.

But I didn't see them. I was out of the car and walking up the steps, foolishly looking at my keys and not peering warily around for invasive cousins—even if they were only cousins several times removed—before they emerged like chameleons from the background. Heaven only knows where they found sweat suits the same yellow as the house. Although I had no trouble picturing them sneaking over to compare the outfits to the paint and returning them for a refund if the color didn't match.

"We came over as soon as we heard," the twin on the left said.

There was a way to tell one sixtysomething twin from the other, thanks to Mercy's wearing only one particular cologne. The kindest thing anyone could say about her scent was that she wore it sparingly. Unfortunately when the twins stood shoulder to shoulder a comfortable distance away, that clue was useless.

"We know how much you value our advice," the right-hand twin said.

"And after the shock of finding the bodies, even

though you seem to attract an unnatural number of them, Mercy thought you might need consoling." It was Shirley on the left, then.

"Gosh." That was the best response I could come up with on short notice.

"We know, we know," Mercy said, coming toward me and looking as though she planned to pat me on the back.

I dropped my keys in my purse so that I didn't forget myself and unlock the door and invite them in. In the short time I'd been back in Blue Plum, I'd managed to avoid either Spivey setting foot inside, scented or unscented.

"Let's back up, though," Shirley said.

"Good idea," I said, retreating before Mercy's advance.

"Not literally," Shirley said with a tsk.

"Oh, I don't know," I said, continuing to back.

"She meant back up to what I said about advice," Mercy said.

"And how much you've valued ours before, in similar situations," Shirley added.

It didn't surprise me that the conversation was heading in a suspicious direction. That was a hallmark of Spivey interactions. What surprised me was how quickly we'd veered down that suspicious path.

I stopped with my back against the front door.

"We have information," Mercy said.

I looked from one to the other. I felt like a trapped animal, but they misinterpreted my eyebrows rising in alarm as an invitation to continue.

"Information guaranteed to help you solve the Enigma of the Intimate Enemies," Shirley said. She leaned closer, scrutinized my face, and then straightened. "There you go, Mercy," she said with satisfaction. "Didn't I tell you we would kill two birds by calling it that?"

"I still like the Case of the Sinister Stalker," Mercy said. "'Enigma' sounds too highfalutin. You're right about the birds, though, except I make it three." She held three fingers in her sister's face. "We've piqued her interest." She folded down one finger. "We've proved we have valuable information to contribute to the investigation." She folded down a second finger. The third finger, her index finger, she turned and pointed at my face. "And look at her eyes, Shirley. If you ignore that stunned and unattractive squint, you can see that she's not just interested in our information; she's already a believer."

The odd thing was that I did believe her, despite my betraying eyebrows, which I knew had lowered and pulled together. I would rather have thought my eyebrows looked perceptive and comprehending more than stunned, but I decided I could go with stunned, too. Shannon and Will involved as intimate enemies? Will as a sinister stalker? Either image could make sense of that horrible scene under the tree and whatever it was I'd felt when I touched their bodies.

And maybe I was stunned, because I found myself inviting the Spiveys in. That must have stunned *them*, because they sat in the living room, as un-annoying as I've ever experienced them, and they didn't attempt to roam or snoop. I wasn't so staggered that I offered them iced tea. They were kind enough not to draw attention to that lapse.

"First," Mercy said.

"Yes," Shirley interrupted, "first, if you use either of the titles we just told you for this case, then you should give us credit."

"That isn't what I was going to say, but it's a good point." Mercy looked at me.

I cleared my throat.

Mercy hurried on. "And there will be plenty of time

to discuss it later. I was going to say that we have two pieces of information. The first is that Will Embree and Shannon Goforth had a history."

"They dated in high school?"

"That part is common knowledge," Shirley said. "Their history after high school isn't."

"We're talking about two years ago," said Mercy, "during the protests at Victory Paper. Will and Shannon—the violent protester and the company's loyal mouthpiece—were secretly engaged."

The twins sat back, looking pleased, each crossing her right leg over her left and letting her right foot swing.

"If it was a secret, how do you know about it?"

"Ah. Thinking like an investigator. That's good," Shirley said. "Unfortunately, we can't tell you."

"Yet," Mercy quickly added. "Our source told us in confidence, and we should check with her, um, with our source, before saying more."

"Hmm. Okay. What's the second piece of information?"

"Shannon Goforth told our source she was being stalked," Shirley said.

"By Will Embree?"

"No."

"Then by who?"

"By whom," Mercy said.

"That's where you come in," said Shirley, "because we don't know."

After they left, I sat down in one of Granny's old blue overstuffed chairs. Almost immediately, I got up and switched to the other overstuffed chair because Mercy's cologne lingered in the first. Breathing more easily, I knitted my fingers behind my head and chased a flock of fluttering questions around for a while. They were about as easy to catch as an explosion of grasshoppers.

I did finally latch onto a couple of conclusions, though.

The first was that everyone else was right and I'd been deluded. I *was* on the case. The second was only something I needed to remind myself of. That anything the Spiveys said should be doubted until verified.

The ghost and the cat were both in the kitchen when I let myself into the shop the next morning. He was hungry and she was sulky. And so we started another day.

I fed the cat and checked to see that the three of us were alone. It was my turn to open the shop, though, so I didn't expect to find anyone else in for another half hour, and indeed didn't. Geneva was moping in a small heap in a corner of the kitchen near the trash can. I couldn't help thinking she'd watched for me to arrive and then thrown herself into the corner when I unlocked the door.

"Geneva, may I apologize for being so childish yesterday?"

"Will it make you feel better?"

"Yes."

"Then please don't."

"I think I will anyway."

"Why bother?"

"Because that's what friends do. I'm sorry I was spiteful about the cat's name."

She didn't respond to that, but she followed me out front, like my own personal Great Dismal Fog, and watched as I flipped on lights and put the till in the cash register. She also didn't bring up the "very important and fascinating" information she'd claimed to overhear. If *she* hadn't been so irritating and childish about that, maybe we wouldn't have erupted into our latest argument. I didn't remind her of her behavior, though, and the information could wait until she was in a better mood and I had time to pay close attention.

The cat helped himself to a pool of morning sun collecting under one of the front windows. He stretched himself out to soak in it and started cleaning his paws. Geneva drifted over to a display of new, undyed Icelandic wool yarns and nestled in among the creams, browns, grays, and blacks.

"Why are you wearing a skirt today?" she asked.

"No special reason. I felt like it. It was hanging in my closet. The weather's nice. I haven't done my laundry." I shrugged. "Any one of those reasons. Take your pick." It was just a pencil skirt. Herringbone. It was my favorite skirt, though. In fact, it would look good with a sweater knit from some of the wool she was cuddling.

"I choose none of the above," she said.

"It wasn't really a multiple-choice question, Geneva. That's what I meant when I said no special reason."

"I also don't choose that answer." Her voice, so often light and insubstantial, except when she was moaning or howling, had dropped in timbre. "And I think you will have to admit that I know what I'm talking about. I have insights that are beyond your understanding." Her hollow eyes watched me and she swayed sinuously back and forth.

I stopped fluffing the scarf display. I tugged at my skirt and adjusted my tights, suddenly self-conscious.

"Your skirt, blouse, and black stockings tell me you are feeling sober, structured, and professional," she droned. "They tell me you have made a decision. What you put on your body is a direct reflection of how you feel and how you approach your life."

"Oh now, come on." I tried to laugh. "What is that? Fashion advice from beyond the grave?"

"No, it is reality at its best. That was practically a direct quotation from *What Not to Wear*." Her voice lost the sideshow-medium quality and rose toward bubbly.

"Have you ever watched that show? It's chock-full of insight and drama. I'm always on the edge of my seat waiting to see if their contestants are able to spend the entire five thousand dollars they're given appropriately and in time. And I've just thought of how you can make up for being snide and spiteful about Dirty Harry's name. Why don't you take me on a shopping spree and I'll be your fashion coach? I've had so much experience watching the show that I'll be able to steer you away from the blunders you make so frequently. Or here's another good idea: Why don't you install a television in my room upstairs? It can be your choice. Shopping or a television, either one is fine with me. Isn't this fun?"

She was into choices that morning. Maybe as a result of being in television game show withdrawal. The choice I made was to leave unsaid quite a few things, several of which went beyond snide and spiteful. But before I could congratulate myself for having that strength of character, I told a lie.

"Geneva, do you remember why I'm living here in Blue Plum now? That I lost my job? I can't afford to buy you a television. And even if I could, if you wanted to watch shows like *What Not to Wear*, if the show is even still on, you'd need cable or satellite and I can't swing monthly payments like that. The same goes for a five-thousand-dollar shopping spree. Even a hundred-dollar shopping spree. Money is tight. I'm sorry."

A retort to her comment about my frequent fashion blunders almost slipped out, but at least I was able to wrestle that back in. And what I told her was more a half-truth than a total lie. Buying a television and subscribing to cable or satellite were out of the question. And shopping with her as a fashion coach was definitely out. But if I thought that soothing her ghostly feelings by leaving a television on day and night in the attic was a good idea, I could give her mine or the one I'd inherited with Granny's house. I didn't think it was a good idea, though. It was a *terrible* idea. Even if Geneva didn't have a brain left to rot with ceaseless television viewing, I didn't want the constant background noise up there in the study. I also didn't want anyone else to hear it and think it was background noise *I* enjoyed or needed. And I didn't want Geneva thinking the study was *her* room.

She sighed and drooped. "I'm sorry you are so poor."

"I'm better off than many people, but thank you. So are you interested in fashion?"

She didn't answer.

"I know you like all the colors and textures in the shop. What's your favorite color?"

She shrugged.

"Do you know that I can't see you clearly? For instance, I can't really tell what you're wearing."

At that she looked at me and cocked her head. Then she rose from her nest of Icelandic wool and spread the skirt of whatever she wore. It rippled but didn't catch or reflect any of the sunlight streaming in through the window behind her. There was no shimmer of color or glimmer of life to it. It didn't cast a shadow.

She floated several feet closer and the shelves I could half see through her seemed to undulate as though I saw them through rising heat waves. The clothing hung on her without much shape of its own and obscured what shape she had, though she didn't appear to have been a big woman, either overall or in any strategic places. The garment was long, down past her ankles, and I realized I didn't know what she wore on her feet, if anything.

"Will you come closer?" I asked.

"Oh, pshaw, what do you want to see this old thing for?"

"It interests me. It's what I do. Or what I did. I guess

it's what I still could do if I found another job. Didn't I ever tell you what my job was? I'm a textile conservationist. I study and take care of materials made of fibers. Everything from tapestries to rags. Coverlets, crinolines, long johns, ball gowns, you name it. Very old stuff, usually."

"Well, la-di-da," she said. She gave me a mock curtsy, but then she sashayed another few feet closer and held still for a few moments.

It made no difference, though. Looking at her made me want to blink my eyes or squint to focus them better, and proximity didn't help. The details of the fabric weren't clear enough to see a pattern or weave. It could have been a knit, for all I could tell, although it didn't seem to drape or move like one. Then again, she didn't move like any person I knew in this world, so maybe the way the fabric moved didn't mean anything. But whether it was a nightgown or a dress or a shroud, I still couldn't say. I only knew there were no hoopskirts or voluminous petticoats involved.

"I wish you would describe what you're wearing for me," I said. My fingers itched to get hold of whatever it was so I could examine the construction, the seams, the actual material.

"Why? What good would it do either of us?"

"I could write an article for *Preservation* magazine about it," I said answering what I considered to be a silly question with a silly answer. "I'd call it 'My Ghost Predates Polyester: A Paradigm for Unraveling the Preservation of Paranormal Textiles.'"

"Would I be famous?"

"Oh, I'm quite sure the preservation world would be talking about both of us for a long time. What do you think? Should we go for it?"

While she appeared to be seriously considering that,

another thought struck me. What would happen if I *could* get hold of her dress? Would I find the patterns of wear I looked for when studying textiles? The sort of day-to-day stains I found on some pieces of clothing? And when I touched it, would I "feel" her emotions? Which emotions would they be? Would I get a clearer sense of her current state of mind or would I suddenly be plugged into the emotions she felt when she died? That notion sent a shiver down my spine.

"No," she said, twitching her skirt and turning her back on me. "I've decided we should not go for it and I won't describe anything for you. You should not write that article. Think how unpleasant my existence will be if I am hounded day and night by paparazzi."

"You're probably right about the article and the paparazzi, but how could it hurt for you to tell me—"

"I know I'm right about those gadflies. If you don't believe me, you can ask Oprah or Prince William what it's like to have the media constantly on one's doorstep. I'm sure they know exactly what I'm talking about. I do think I would handle fame better than Elvis Presley does, though."

"Did."

"I beg your pardon?"

"Than Elvis did. He's, um, well, he's dead. He died quite a few years ago. The press can't hound him anymore."

"Shows how much you know."

This was turning into a conversation I never in my wildest imagination pictured being a part of. But why did that surprise me? Daily dialogue with a ghost was my new norm. I wished I could shake my head until my brain settled back into the old norm.

"Well, anyway, you're probably right that you would handle the press better than Elvis."

"Yes, I've grown very wise over the years. Television has done that for me," she said.

"Oh, I'm sure. And how many years are we talking about?"

"I don't like the doubting tone of your voice and I don't like your insistence on asking personal questions this morning. Why don't we return to our original topic? Your subconscious reason for wearing that skirt, which is a tad too tight across the beam. I find that far more interesting."

"We won't return to the topic of my skirt for two reasons. First, the only decision it indicates is the conscious choice I made between showing my knees and pulling on yesterday's blue jeans. And second, I can sidestep personal discussions as easily as you. The difference is that I'm aware of sidestepping them and know why I do." I almost bit my tongue in half to keep from adding that I owed that awareness to critical thinking skills and a memory, neither of them saturated with ten thousand hours of television psychobabble. I wasn't above letting my own hurt feelings show, though. "Also, I'll thank you not to make comments about my beam, which is not too broad and which my skirt fits perfectly. Far from being too tight, there is even room for my phone, my favorite pen, and a tissue in the pocket. And now, if you'll excuse me, I'm going to unlock the door, because it's time to open the shop."

I snapped the dead bolt open, picturing how many times Granny's fingers had turned it more calmly. Part of her morning ritual, no matter the weather, no matter her mood, had been to push the door open, take a deep breath, and look up and down the street. *Even if no one else is out and about and ready to shop, I'll invite the morning in,* she'd say.

So I flipped her old needlepoint sign to its "open" side

and pushed the door open to continue her tradition and restore some equilibrium to my haunted existence. I closed my eyes and took in the deep breath, but when I opened my eyes and looked left, it was all I could do not to yelp. Geneva's face hovered inches from mine, staring at me. A bone-deep chill traveled across my back, left to right, and, there, out of the corner of my right eye, I saw her misty hand come to rest on my shoulder.

"The differences between us," she whispered, "are smaller than you like to think. Those four dead people need us."

Chapter 7

Geneva ruined her exit when she failed to enunciate the word "poor," making it sound as though she'd said "four" dead people. Or maybe that was just my ice-cold ears; I was having trouble getting past her sinister whisper and ghostly embrace. I felt as though I'd spent the last half hour underdressed in a haunted subzero freezer. Debbie bustled in, ready for her usual Tuesday-morning shift, while I was still shivering.

"You're not coming down with anything, are you?" she asked, stopping short when she saw me with my shoulders hunched and rubbing my hands to rewarm them. "I'm still waiting on a couple of the girls to lamb, and I don't have time to catch a breath, much less a cold."

I shook my hands out and squared my shoulders. "Nope, I'm healthy as a cosseted Cotswold."

"Good." She turned abruptly and went to put her jacket and purse away.

Even though Debbie had told Ardis she would be in, I'd half hoped she would call and say she'd changed her mind. I wasn't entirely adept at running the shop by myself yet, but by midmorning there were usually two or three TGIF members knitting and gossiping in the comfy chairs grouped here and there around the shop. Almost any one of them could set me straight or at least help me muddle through until Ardis came in at noon.

"You know, Debbie," I said when she came back out front, "if you wanted to skip today, no one would blame you."

"My bank account would. Tuesdays are my half days, anyway. It won't be a big deal. By the way, good morning. I didn't say that when I saw you shivering. You freaked me out for a minute."

"Just a sudden chill. Nothing to worry about. You aren't worried about being away from the farm, though? About reporters trampling all over or disturbing the sheep? What if they leave a gate open?"

"The press is more interested in a handsome fugitive and a beautiful woman dead in each other's arms. Saying it happened under a tree east of Knoxville is about as close as they've come to pinpointing the location. But the sheriff said he'll have someone out there all day, anyway, and it turns out it's my cousin Darla. She's a little green at being a deputy, but she's had a few sheep of her own ever since she was in 4-H, so the girls will be in good hands. Besides, if UPS and even GPS have trouble finding the farm, I'm not too worried about CBS."

"Good point. And you've got the dog. Bill, right?"

"Yeah, he's my boy. He'll nip at any stray newsmen's heels and keep them in line if Darla can't."

"Did he bark Sunday night or yesterday morning when, er . . ."

"No, his crate's in my bedroom and he slept like a baby. The house is a hundred and sixty years old and the walls are solid brick. We don't hear much when the windows are shut. But you don't think if he *had* heard something I could have done something, do you? That I could have stopped or saved or . . ."

"No, no, really, I don't." Rats. This was one of the hard parts of investigating—asking what seemed like a small droplet of a question and then watching as the implications of it sizzled and upset or horrified someone. Pest-infested textiles were so much easier to deal with than people. Especially people—or ghosts—I cared about. "No, Debbie, I'm just glad you've got him out there with you. So how are *you* doing?"

"I'm fine. I'm fine. Mabel dropped twins last night." She looked more frazzled than fine, despite her twin avowals. Her usually neatly braided hair was pulled back in a loose ponytail. Blond wisps were beginning to escape. "Mabel's a sheep," she said.

"Yeah, I thought she probably was. Did you get *any* sleep last night?"

The string of camel bells on the door jingled, interrupting Debbie's yawned answer, and two women came in, one older, one younger. I didn't recognize either of them, and by the way they looked around, exclaiming over the burst of colors that met their eyes and getting their bearings, it was clear they were newcomers to the shop.

"Let us know if we can help you find anything," I said.

"Needlepoint supplies?" the older woman asked.

"Sure, follow me."

It would have been easy enough to tell them "upstairs, front room on the right," but it was better customer service to take them there. That also gave me a chance to glance around for Geneva. She sometimes liked to sit on the stairs or perch on the newel-post. I didn't see her, though, until I returned to the front room. She was hovering by the two comfy chairs near the front window. When she saw me, she motioned me over.

"Oh dear." I sighed. Debbie was nestled in one of the chairs, the cat curled into a skein of ginger fur in her lap, both of them sound asleep.

"Did you know Debbie used to entertain Will Embree out at her place?" Geneva asked.

"Where did you—"

"Wait, wait, don't answer," Geneva said. "We have incoming from two directions. Two from behind and three more at the door. Oh goody. Look who it is."

The bells jingled as the door opened, and at the same time I heard the first two women coming back from upstairs. One of them was describing an antique loom, a customer after Granny's own heart.

I turned to greet the new arrivals and saw why Geneva was so pleased. Shirley and Mercy came through the door flanking a younger woman who could only be Mercy's daughter, Angela. Geneva found the twins endlessly fascinating. They fascinated me, too, but more in the way an itching, red rash does. Even though we'd parted on semifriendly terms the previous afternoon, I had trouble following through with the warm greeting I'd started. Still, I was able to muster a plausible smile.

It was wasted. The twins were arguing and didn't return my greeting. Geneva circled them a few times, empty eye sockets wide. I didn't really care that the Spiveys didn't seem to notice me standing there, but I was very glad they weren't aware of Geneva's attentions.

The other two women cut short their loom discussion when they came back into the room. Their hands were empty; no needlepoint supplies. A pity. The younger one gave me the kind of wave that indicated they were happy browsing and they started leafing through the pattern binders near the sales counter. I would have been happier helping them leaf, but I turned back to the Spiveys.

To my surprise, the twins weren't togged out in identical outfits. They also weren't wearing their usual sweat suits. Taking a chance on making a snap psychobabble fashion judgment, I decided that could be a good sign. They both wore pressed khakis, but one's blazer was lemon yellow and the other more of an orange sherbet.

The upgrade from garage-sale casual was almost encouraging and certainly interesting.

What wasn't surprising was the fact that I'd never met Mercy's daughter, Angela. True, the twins were Granny's cousins, but they were a dozen or so years younger than Granny, and they'd never been close. Patchy images of Shirley and Mercy appeared throughout memories from my childhood. But whenever I tried to envision a girl with either of the twins or even trailing behind them, probably looking agonized or embarrassed, I got nothing. Any memories or awareness of Angela's existence, if they'd ever been there, were gone as though eaten away by a moth.

Vanity made me want to say that Angela was in her early forties rather than her late thirties. The only evidence I was going on for that assumption, though, was her mother's estimated age, the lines creasing Angela's low forehead, and her cheeks, which were probably once round and rosy but were heading toward jowly. According to Ardis, Angela had a tattoo. That wasn't so unusual, but the only detail Ardis revealed was that the tattoo was on a part of Angela's anatomy she didn't ever want to see any closer. That didn't really tell me much. I could think of a lot of places on a lot of people I didn't want to see any closer.

As I approached them, Angela gave me a halfhearted smile and then broke eye contact. She looked profoundly unhappy, but I couldn't tell if her unhappiness stemmed from being in the shop or being dragged there by her mother and aunt. She looked cowed and uncomfortable, like a teenager under duress to attend and perform. From the way she pulled at the cuffs of her blouse and tugged her skirt, she wasn't in her normal comfort zone of dress, either. She was tugging on a herringbone pencil skirt.

"Maybe the two of you are twins, too," Geneva said in my ear, "separated at birth."

My herringbone pencil skirt was no longer my favorite.

"Hers is not as tight across the beam as yours," Geneva said, continuing to study Angela. "Although hers required more yardage in the first place. She also has a tiny runner in her left stocking."

The Spiveys *et fille* stopped in front of Debbie.

"What's wrong with her?" the twin in the lemon yellow jacket asked. She pointed at Debbie but looked at me. Debbie and the cat continued sleeping soundly.

"Just a little bit of exhaustion," I said.

"You're either exhausted or you're not," the lemon yellow twin said. "It's like being pregnant. You can't be just a little bit. She isn't pregnant, is she? That can account for a lot of exhaustion, let me tell you."

Angela had started inching back from between the twins, but she stopped and gave the yellow twin a scathing look. "Ma, her husband died three years ago. Of course she's not pregnant. Be decent."

Talk about being decent, it was only then that I remembered that poor Angela had been widowed a few months earlier. I'd never met her husband, either, but that shouldn't stop me from offering my condolences. Even though I'd had a bone to pick with him before he died. Before he was killed.

My goodness, what a lot of sad and unpleasant things had happened in this town recently. I dropped into the chair next to Debbie's, wondering if I'd made the right decision in packing up my apartment in central Illinois, where the only real disruptions in the flat cornfield of my life had been the occasional blizzard or tornado.

"And now what's wrong with you?" Shirley asked me.

"She must be exhausted, too," Mercy said. "Let the

poor thing rest. Angie, sweetheart, why don't you show Kath what a go-getter you are? Be an angel and go see what you can do for those customers waiting so patiently at the counter."

I was back up out of the chair like a shot and racing to beat Angie to the customers. I should never have let those khakis and pastel polyester blazers fool me. Soon after Angie's husband died, the twins had mentioned that she would need a job. They'd been testing the waters then, and I hadn't bitten. Now they were angling more seriously and that's why all three of them were here.

But I didn't zip past Angie on the way to the counter because she wasn't headed there to demonstrate her customer service skills. When I tagged the counter first, the camel bells on the door behind me jingled. I turned around just in time to catch a glimpse of Angie's unhappy, herringbone-clad beam disappearing down the street. Mercy squawked and started after her, but Shirley held her back with a grip on her shoulders. She also whispered something in Mercy's ear. That could have looked sisterly and consoling. It didn't. It looked sneaky and suspicious.

"Your shop is even more exciting than we'd heard," said the older of the two women at the counter. Her good humor came through with the warmth of her voice and showed in the creases at the corners of her eyes. She was probably in her mid-fifties but must have gone silver years earlier. Her thick hair was cut even with her jawline and she wore it tucked behind her ears, a pair of sunglasses acting as a headband. She made business casual look more chic and trustworthy than the Spiveys did. Also more expensive. No poor little polyesters had given their lives to put the clothes on her back.

"And we had no idea Blue Plum was so photogenic," the younger woman said, patting a large, compartmented bag slung over her shoulder. She was tall and sleek, even in cargo pants and Dr. Martens boots, and her dark hair was long and sleek to match. She looked as though she'd be equally at ease dressed for a tango with a rose clenched between her smiling teeth. The age difference between the two women might make them mother and daughter, but there was nothing about their features or coloring to suggest they were.

"There's great small-town atmosphere here," the younger woman said.

"You think?" I couldn't help asking.

While both nice, normal, very-pleasant-to-have-in-the-shop women confirmed that opinion with comparisons to other small towns they knew and loved and couldn't pass by, I watched Geneva following the twins and mimicking their movements. They examined the Icelandic wool, stroking and squeezing the various shades although it was unlikely they planned to buy any of it. Mercy held a couple of the skeins under her nose and sniffed them as though testing the bouquet. Geneva pretended to sneeze. I opened my mouth to remind Geneva to behave herself but caught myself and returned my attention to the paying customers.

"Your scarf is beautiful," I said to the older woman. "Raw silk?"

She had the scarf wrapped around her shoulders in one of those twists that look so artistic and effortless and thrown together for the occasion and that would take me half an hour to figure out. It was a lovely thing, wide and loosely woven, in a range of shimmery blues and greens. Granny would have loved it and the way she wore it.

"It's silk and something else I've forgotten. Don't tell my sister. She wove it and she's told me what the other stuff is too many times already."

"I promise I'll only tell her she's very talented. Is she local?"

"No, I'm pretty sure you're safe." The woman laughed. "She lives in Minnesota. I know she'd love your shop, though."

"Thanks. Did you find what you were looking for upstairs?"

"I just needed a quick fix," the photographer said. "I don't really have time for needlepoint these days." She patted her camera case again.

"But I was wondering if you could make a couple of recommendations," the scarf woman said.

"Sure. As you can see, we have a wide variety of yarns, threads, needles, and notions. Pretty much, if it's related to fiber or needlework, we've got it, and we also do special orders when we can. Or if you need help with a pattern or a particular project, we do that, too."

I smiled some more. They exchanged looks.

"Well, now we feel bad," the photographer said. "All your wonderful wares and services and what we're really hoping is that you can tell us the best place to eat lunch."

"And can you give us directions to a B and B, if there is one?" the scarf woman said. "We're on a tight schedule today but maybe we can make it back in the morning to do some shopping. You can help me find something for my sister's birthday."

"Oh. Sure, of course." I nodded away my disappointment. The local yarn shop wasn't the most obvious place to seek dining and lodging information, but I knew there were travelers and whims of all kinds. "Lunch is easy," I said. "Nobody can beat Mel's on Main. Mel has everything from vegan to a daily meat and two veg, plus the best homemade bread and pastries. Go left out our door and it's toward the end of the block. Your nose won't let you get lost."

"Perfect. I think we saw that on the way in. And a B and B?"

"I'm not as up on places to stay. I know there's a motel out on the four-lane, but ask at Mel's. Someone there will know about B and Bs."

"Sounds good," the scarf woman said. She started to say something else, but the photographer slipped in ahead of her.

"Pictures are okay, aren't they? Sorry, Sylvia." She touched the other woman's arm. "I didn't mean to interrupt, but the light looks perfect out there right now." She turned back to me. "If I want to get pictures of the front of the shop, of any of the shops, that's not a problem, is it?"

"If we don't see tourists taking pictures we don't know how to act."

"And the same goes for freelance journalists taking pictures?"

"Um, sure. As far as I know."

"Super. I'll meet you outside, Sylvia. I want to catch the courthouse with that blue, blue sky." She turned with an "Oh, hi, sorry," as she dodged the twins.

Mercy followed her to the door and watched her angle across the street. Shirley kept her eyes on the woman named Sylvia, who was still standing at the counter. Geneva draped herself around one of the ceiling fans, which I'd forgotten to turn on with the lights.

"Are you both journalists?" I asked.

"More like trying to be," Sylvia said, sounding apologetic. "Hi, I'm Sylvia Furches." She held out her hand and I shook it. "I hope you don't think we were trying to mislead you."

I hadn't until she brought it up. "I'm Kath Rutledge."

"It's a pleasure to meet you, Kath. And that was Pen Ledford. We're taking a class at the community college in Asheville. We have a final project we need to do, and when Pen heard about the, well, about the trouble here yesterday, she was keen to take a run over the mountains to see what we can dig up. I think she has 'scoop' on the brain. She's full of energy and ideas." She smiled and wiggled her fingers near her ears to illustrate all that energy percolating out of Pen. Then she folded her hands and leaned closer. "Did the murders happen in Blue Plum?"

"Near here," I said, wishing not for the first time that lies would roll off my tongue convincingly. Settling for being nonspecific would do in a pinch, though. Sylvia and Pen could find out more, easily enough, without my being their source.

"It was shocking news, wasn't it?" Sylvia said. She sounded genuinely distressed but kept her voice low and serious. Maybe she'd learned to erase signs of titillation in her journalism class. "I remember reading about the situation, the paper protests, several years ago. Embree was his name, wasn't it? Pen is more up on the details than I am.

I didn't bother to answer. Of course she knew his name was Embree.

"And then what happened yesterday. Terrible." She shook her head. "It was at some kind of farm, wasn't it?"

I nodded noncommittally and darted a few glances to locate the twins. They were looking through the rows of button drawers, making as little noise as possible. Browsing the buttons put them in a good position to hear everything being said at the counter. So far, though, they hadn't offered to fill in the gaps I was leaving. I wondered how long that would continue.

"You couldn't give me directions to Cloud Hollow, could you?" Sylvia asked.

"Me? Gosh, no." That sounded more polite than "absolutely not" or any of the more emphatic variations that sprang to mind. But if Sylvia and Pen knew enough to stop at the local wool shop for directions to Cloud Hollow—by name, no less—did they also know who owned Cloud Hollow and her connection to the Weaver's Cat? Depending on whom they'd already talked to, they might. Or maybe not, if they needed directions to the farm. Maybe the Weaver's Cat was their first stop. At least they didn't seem to know what Debbie looked like. Maybe they didn't know her name yet, either.

"You've never been out there?" Sylvia asked, bringing my zigzagging thoughts back into focus. She was still trying for mildly curious but was no longer pulling the wool over the wool shop owner's eyes.

"Honestly, Sylvia, you wouldn't want my directions even if I could remember them to give you. *I* can't even follow them. The one time I was out that way I almost didn't make it back alive I got so turned around. Crossing the river, recrossing the river, re-recrossing the river. It was a nightmare. And the roads? Whoo. Full of twists. Full of turns. And GPS doesn't even know the place *exists*." I should have gone with the rude refusal. Stomping her request flat might have kept me from blathering on, something I'm prone to do when trying to compensate for not lying. Even the twins turned around and stared when they heard me driveling on.

Sylvia considered my overblown answer, head tipped, eyes infinitesimally skeptical. Then she smiled and shrugged and looked over at the twins, making me realize that she was aware of their interest all along. The wily twins were quick to turn away, though, and she didn't catch their rolled eyes.

"Good Lord, you are pathetic," Geneva said from her perch on the ceiling fan. "My jaw droppeth."

"No need to blush, Kath," Sylvia said kindly. "I think you're probably a very good and loyal friend."

She left the shop, leaving me to wonder what kind of friend she'd call me if she knew I was tempted to turn the ceiling fan on full blast to see if anything jaw-dropping happened to my friend up there.

The camel bells got a workout over the next few minutes. The Spiveys left on Sylvia's heels, but only after Mercy winked at me and Shirley touched a forefinger to the side of her nose. If they assumed I knew what either of them meant by those gestures, they assumed wrong. I wasn't sure whom I pitied more, Sylvia and Pen, Debbie and her sheep, or myself and the shop, if the twins were teaming up with the wannabe journalists.

As soon as the bells quit quivering behind those two, they jingled again. That proved to be one jingle too many for Debbie's nap. She woke with a start and an exclamation, startling the cat as well as the next customer. This was no ordinary yarn shop customer, though. This was a woman in a tailored, charcoal gray pinstripe suit, a silk blouse, and three-inch heels. She stopped just inside the door and put her hands on her hips, one shoulder slightly forward, as though she'd been practicing since girlhood for the chance to pose like Wonder Woman. She also didn't beat around the bush.

"Which one of you is investigating Shannon Goforth's murder?"

Chapter 8

"Keep that cat away from me," Wonder Woman said, her throat sounding tight and her voice brittle. She was already flushed and breathing hard when she came through the door. Adding fear, allergies, or dislike of cats to that mix wasn't improving anything.

The cat, of course, took her words as an invitation to come on over and say hi. The woman moved away, putting a display table between them. The cat blinked at her and teased by pretending to follow. She fell for his trick, backing farther away and ready to protect her ankles, but he faked her out by leaping onto the table and appearing at her elbow. It looked to me as though he wiggled his ginger eyebrows at her, but that might have been a trick of the light.

Debbie, looking refreshed from her nap, scooped the cat into her arms. "Kath is the one you want to talk to," she said. "This guy can stay here and help me take care of customers. Why don't you two go up to the study, Kath? That way you'll have complete privacy."

I looked at our visitor. She needed calming more than she needed a three-flight climb to the attic in her heels. "The kitchen should be quiet. I'll make tea."

Geneva loomed over my shoulder as I filled the kettle at the sink. "I'm glad your subconscious doesn't talk to you the way hers does. She's making me nervous."

I glanced over my shoulder at the woman. She'd pulled herself together and stood at the kitchen table, arms crossed. She looked like an aggressive young executive, but maybe that was the way she held herself together in times of crisis. Or maybe it was her lacquered, unnaturally bronze hair and her lethally pointy shoes. I was glad she hadn't kicked the cat.

"I'm Kath Rutledge, by the way."

"I know who you are."

"Oh. You didn't seem to know when you came in."

"And then your coworker identified you." The woman made no move to sit and didn't tell me her name.

"She's a tough one," Geneva said. ""Why don't you soften her up by offering cute sandwiches or tea cakes?"

"Because there aren't any," I said.

"Excuse me?" The woman asked.

"Er, I'm sorry there isn't anything to offer you with the tea. Will you excuse me for a moment? My phone's ringing."

Her eyes didn't quite believe that. There hadn't been a peep from a phone.

"Um, it's vibrating." I turned my back and blushing face away from the guest and the ghost, pulled the silent and twitchless phone from my pocket, and pretended to check the display before putting it to my ear. "Geneva, hi. No, it's not a good time to talk." I kept my voice low, getting into the role, eyes on the floor as though listening. "Sure, sure, let's get together later and compare notes. Sounds good."

"Pssst."

I looked up. Geneva hovered six inches from my nose.

"Aren't I a genius for inventing telephone communication with the dead?" she asked.

"Pure dead genius. I'm hanging up now." I pocketed the phone and turned back to the woman. "Sorry to keep you waiting. I'll just get the tea and you can tell me why you're here."

"I turned the kettle off," she said. "I don't like tea. I'm going to say what I came to say and then I don't have any more time to waste. I'm needed at the office."

"You don't want to sit?"

"No."

She wasn't growing on me.

She looked around the kitchen, taking in the well-worn cupboards and counters, the bundles of dyestuff hanging from hooks, and the wall covered with exuberant projects from our beginners' classes. I particularly liked the swarm of T-shirts pinned to the bulletin board that a Girl Scout troop tie-dyed with Kool-Aid. From the lift of her lip, Ms. Executive Suit didn't agree.

"I had you figured wrong," she said, giving me the same critical going-over she'd given the kitchen. "I thought you were some kind of private detective."

"Who are you?"

"Carolyn Proffitt. I work at Victory Paper. I was Shannon Goforth's assistant."

"Oh my gosh. I am so sorry for your loss. Are you sure you don't want to sit down?"

"How do you picture sitting down being of any help to me?"

"You're right, it couldn't be. Of course."

"I came here to tell you the facts. Will Embree killed Terry Widener two years ago. The police have always known that. And now they know Shannon was afraid of him. He was calling her and it scared her."

"How do they know that?"

"Because I told them."

"How did you know? Did she tell you?"

"I heard her pleading. I heard her tears. I heard her say 'I'm afraid.' "

"You overheard her talking on the phone?"

"To him!"

"But did she tell you it was Will Embree? Did he have a phone with him out there in the woods? I'm just trying to make sense of this."

She hesitated, then slammed again. "I've told the police, and the only other thing I'm telling you is that it will kill Shannon's mother if you stir up a bunch of nastiness. *She* knows he killed her. *I* know he killed her. *The police* know he killed her, and . . ." She ran out of breath at that point and burst into tears.

"Sweetheart," Geneva said in a pretty decent imitation of Sam Spade, "you need to work on your grilling technique."

Chapter 9

Carolyn Proffitt's visit left me feeling subdued but not cowed. I scrounged in a drawer for a notepad and wrote her name and the little she'd told me about herself, then added three bullet points: *phone calls*; *fear*; *motive for visit—altruistic?* I looked at the list, wrote *facts* across the bottom, and slipped the paper in my pocket. While I scribbled, Geneva bubbled with excitement over her new role.

"I will be a wonderful grilling coach," she said. "I'll rush right up to our detective office and sit down at our detective desk and I will try to remember all the best *Dragnet* episodes for you to study. Joe Friday is extremely competent. He is always interested in facts, too, and I think even you will be able to learn something from him."

Debbie had put some happy tunes on the CD player while I was away. They were more innocuous than happy, but at least not slow or somber. Turning on the background music was another thing I should have done before unlocking the door. Absentmindedly, I pulled the paper back out of my pocket and added a note to include the ceiling fans and music in my shop-opening routine. Debbie looked up from winding some of the Icelandic wool into balls. The only customer in sight was an older man leafing through a binder of sweater patterns.

"Everything okay?" Debbie asked. "Where's . . . ?"

"Everything's fine. She went out the back door." Nodding at the customer, I added, "I'll tell you about it later."

Hearing my voice, the man turned and smiled. He was older than I'd first thought. His thinning hair was so white it was almost invisible, and he was almost as thin himself. The skin on his face and the backs of his hands was taking on that delicate, papery look of beyond seventy. His wrinkles and age spots pushed him past eighty. He was upright and clear-eyed, though, and his white beard and moustache were clipped with precision.

"You're Mr. Berry, aren't you?" I asked. "You are! Oh, I haven't seen you in years."

"Kath. Look at you. Ivy's little sprout. The world changed in the blink of an eye, didn't it? You're all grown up and Ivy's gone, but I see she lives on in your smile and bright eyes."

"And Granny always warned me about your smooth tongue."

"She broke my heart." He shook his head and I could believe she had. "I was on my boat when I got the news," he said. "I am so sorry. After your grandfather died, if I'd had my way, she would have come away on that boat with me. Did you know that?"

I thought of the times she'd mentioned him in passing and clucked her tongue. "I'm not sure she ever thought you were serious."

"I might have been, if I'd thought there ever really was a chance. She was happy enough going out for the occasional meal, a contra dance now and then, an evening stroll. But she wasn't about to leave her pots and kettles of dyes or the Weaver's Cat for two or three months at a time to sail with an old coot. And I wasn't about to give up my boat. Besides, she said she had all the yarn she needed in her life and didn't need one more." He laughed and I knew I was supposed to laugh, too, because I remembered hearing Granny say it and chuckling afterward.

"Ah," he said, "you don't know the joke, though, do you?"

As I shook my head, the camel bells jingled and half a dozen chattering women flocked in.

"Your hands are full now," he said, "but will you have supper with me Thursday night?"

"I'd like that."

"Good. Shall we say seven, then, at Mel's? I'll bore you with the legend of Yarn Berry and we'll lift a glass of Mel's best house red to Ivy."

"I'll look forward to it."

"I will, too.

"So who are you buying all this beautiful Icelandic wool for?" Debbie asked as she put the balls of oatmeal, toast, and coffee-colored yarn in a bag for him. "Here you are talking about Ivy and making a date with Kath. Do you have another lady friend stowed somewhere on that boat of yours?"

Her questions and remarks clunked as they fell into our otherwise gentle exchange, but Mr. Berry showed no sign he took offense.

"I'm going to knit a sweater for my brother," he said. "He's even older than I am and has trouble keeping warm. Keeping warm and keeping friends are two things I find to be increasingly important these days. It was good to see you, Kath. See you Thursday."

"Remove foot from mouth," Debbie muttered when he'd gone. "I know better than to make assumptions. Or to make dumb comments if I do make assumptions. Ivy and Ardis have told me often enough."

"You've never met Mr. Berry?"

"Heard of him but never met him. That's one of the

problems with being part-time. I'll go see if I can help those women in the other room."

She was unhappy with herself, but there was no time to talk her out of it. A tour bus had arrived, docking at the curb like a cruise ship on wheels. Passengers debarked, ready to raid shops up and down Main and on all the side streets as well. The bus moved off to park behind the courthouse and we stayed busy the rest of the morning, so I didn't have a chance to tell Debbie what Carolyn Proffitt had said. By the time Ardis arrived to take Debbie's place shortly before one o'clock, Debbie was in a hurry to get home, so I let her go.

That afternoon, in between customers, I did tell Ardis, and I showed her my notes.

"I like your suspicious mind," she said, "also your attention to the details of opening the shop, but questioning motives sounds like a good way to open an investigation."

"But maybe Carolyn just rubbed me the wrong way. First she was bullying, then she was crying, but maybe she's right. Maybe she talked to Bonny. Maybe Bonny's reconsidered and doesn't want anything stirred up."

"Kath, honey, do you have any idea how many projects our customers start in any given week? A month? In a year? And what percentage of those projects do you think end up being finished? Think of all the space in drawers and at the backs of cupboards and on the top shelves of closets that is relegated to the likes of 'You Can Crochet This Tonight' or 'Easy Sweater in a Weekend' or 'Heirloom Embroidered Christmas Stocking for Your First Grandbaby.' I have no doubt we could clothe the starving children of India with the yarn and floss gathering dust and moth eggs in the forgotten and ignored corners of Blue Plum. But, Kath, honey, know this: You will not find a single UFO in Bonny's house. Bonny finishes what she starts. She does not give up. She does not let go. Do you understand what I'm saying?"

"You lost me at UFO."

"Unfinished object," Ardis said. "Bonny hasn't got a one. And she isn't going to consider the investigation into Shannon's death finished until she has answers to those questions furrowing your brow. I'm sure they've occurred to her, too. She's no dummy."

"Tell me about Bonny."

"Do know the house up on Fox with the elaborate gingerbread, the one they call the Showboat Gothic?"

"That's Bonny's? I love that place. It's like woodwork embroidery."

"That's the one. Bonny and Calvin started out in one of those rural subdivisions. Dogwood Acres, I think. Then Bonny came into some money. They bought the place on Fox, planning to turn it into a B and B. Things didn't go according to plan, though, and now Bonny's there all alone."

"Poor thing, she's having it rough. First she loses her husband and now her daughter? How long ago did Calvin die?"

"Worse than that," Ardis said. "He ran off with the interior designer they hired to renovate the place."

"Brother."

"And of course that's another reason Bonny isn't going to let this rest until she has her answers. Shannon was her entire focus after Calvin took off."

"I'm going to have to be careful when I talk to her again. Poor thing." The "poor thing" could apply to both of us; I wasn't looking forward to disturbing a grieving mother, even if she *had* asked me to find out what had happened. It seemed an awful lot like poking an angry mother bear with a stick. Maybe I should take Geneva up on her offer of Joe Friday lessons.

We had a final spurt of late-afternoon business. Then, while we counted down the till, I told Ardis about the wannabe journalists and the Spivey visits of the day before and that morning.

"Spiveys," Ardis said, shaking her head.

"I don't think Carolyn Proffitt is the twins' source, though. Carolyn didn't use the word 'stalker,' and they didn't think the stalker was Will. I think there's someone else Shannon confided in." I jotted that on a scrap and added it to my pocket.

"That's why you're the brains of this posse," Ardis said, nodding at the pencil in my hand. "I'd be more likely to take anything the Spiveys say and run it down the garbage disposal. These other two, now, Ledford and Furches? There are some of both families in the area."

"Pen Ledford and Sylvia Furches, yeah. They acted like they'd never been here before. But they knew more than they let on. Maybe they lied about their names, too."

"And none of them bought anything? That's typical of the twins," Ardis said, "but it would have been nice if the wannabes had greased our counter with a modest angora or alpaca purchase. I'll give them this, though. They're showing more initiative than the professional news crew from Knoxville. The Knoxville bunch parked their van behind the courthouse early this morning and acted like the natives might be contagious. They interviewed Sheriff Haynes on the courthouse steps; then they had a pizza delivered to the van and they haven't set foot outside since. I heard all that from Ernestine when I ran into her at the bank. Did these other two sound smart enough to find Cloud Hollow?"

"I tried to discourage them, but sure. They'll find it or they'll find someone who'll tell them."

"Spiveys."

"Maybe. But Debbie's cousin Darla was on duty out there today."

"And Debbie can take care of herself. And as for the budding journalists and the Spivey blight, we'll just have to wait and see what misery they sow or reap."

Chapter 10

Thursday evening, Mr. Berry and I arrived at Mel's from opposite directions on the dot of seven. He walked toward me with a clipped, almost jaunty step as though he heard parade ground music in his head. He was average in height and average in looks, but he wore his blazer and khakis with such an air that, with his white moustache and beard and his thin face still tan from however many months on his boat, I could imagine a director casting him as an ancient soldier or sailor, upright in every sense of the word. In fact, when I'd last seen him, probably ten years earlier, he'd played the sea captain in the Blue Plum Repertory Theater's production of *The Ghost and Mrs. Muir*. I could also believe, as he walked toward me, that he thought of himself as classic movie leading man material. David Niven or Gene Kelly.

He held the door for me and I stepped inside, inhaling as much of my favorite atmosphere as I could while maintaining some semblance of decorum. Since meeting Geneva, I'd decided that if I were lucky or unlucky enough to linger as a ghost, I wanted my haunt to be Mel's on Main. Surely inhaling the aromas of that café for eternity would be heavenly. Unless inhaling without tasting was closer to the opposite, but I was willing to take the chance. Tonight the aromas on tap were crusty cheese, roasting sweet potatoes, and the ever-present hint of melting chocolate.

"What's Red doing over there?" I knew that question came from Mel and she was referring to me, even though my eyes were closed, the better to luxuriate in the bouquet of French Onion Soup Night at Mel's on Main.

"Falling in love, I think," Mr. Berry said.

"She's blocking traffic," said Mel. "Sorry, folks. She just completed a ninety-day sensory deprivation experiment and it might be dangerous to restimulate all five of her senses too soon. Are you receiving sound yet, Kath? If you are, then let your nose bring you on over here and let these good people out to enjoy the rest of their evening."

I opened my eyes, startling an elderly couple standing uneasily in front of me. I apologized for holding them up and opened the door for them. They edged past with uncertain smiles and a tentative wave to Mel.

"It's kind of an unwritten municipal policy that citizens try their best not to make the tourists nervous," Mel said. "You might want to keep that in mind now that you've seen the light and become one of us."

It was *my* policy to ignore Mel's pot-calling-the-kettle-black statements. If we had a falling-out, she might not cut off my café habit, but why take that risk? Although that café habit, acquired since relocating to Blue Plum, probably had something to do with the weight gain Geneva had so helpfully mentioned.

Mel was fortyish, bright, and intense. Her hair was bright and intense, too. Her current style was short spikes dyed mustard yellow. Her normal look included a pencil stuck behind each ear and several more in the bib pocket of her mustard yellow apron. Taken altogether—the spikes, the pencils, the strength and honesty in her eyes, and the prickles in her direct personality—there was no doubt that she meant to make a success of her café and catering business or that she would stand beside any friend who needed her.

"What kind of salad do you recommend tonight, Mel?" I asked.

"Roasted radish, beet, and carrot. Here, take a look."

"Ooh," was all I could say.

"The gorgeous vegetables, a bed of spinach and romaine, a hint of balsamic, fresh thyme, cracked black pepper, a grind of sea salt, and a smattering of pecans halves lightly sautéed in olive oil and dusted with curry powder." Mel kissed her fingertips.

We placed our orders and took a table at the window.

"We'll watch the great big world of Blue Plum pass by," he said as he held my chair. "And although I'm making a joke about the size of Blue Plum, I do think it's one of the nicest towns on the face of this earth."

"You've done a lot of traveling?"

"I'm an old pirate. I love the water and I've sailed the seven seas."

"That sounds like a line from a song."

"Close. It's a line from a story I used to perform. You didn't know *that* about me, either?" He shook his head. "Sad, sad. I can tell Ivy didn't talk about me nearly enough. A sure indication I should have spent more time here. That you still think of me as Mr. Berry is another. Please, it's John."

"Not Yarn?"

He laughed. "The legend, yes. It really isn't much of anything. Believe it or not, Yarn was my mother's maiden name. She was Rose Eleanor Yarn, she became Rose Yarn Berry, and she named me John Yarn Berry. She always told me Yarn was a variation of Arne and meant sea eagle, and I suppose that might be true. And maybe between that and growing up in landlocked, backwater

Dry Creek Cove, Tennessee, I was destined for the three things I love best."

I knew I was supposed to ask. "What are they?"

"Sailing, storytelling, and knitting. My mother was a great knitter. She knit anything and everything we needed. If we'd lost the roof off the pig shed in a windstorm, she would have sat right down and knit us a new one, and more pigs to go under it. She had no girls, though, so she passed her love of knitting on to me along with her maiden name. I was the apple of her eye until I broke her heart and left to join the navy. She died while I was at sea, too." He was quiet for a moment, then smiled sadly. "She had a wonderful sense of humor. Ivy reminded me of her."

A waitress brought our dinners—piping hot French onion soup with browned and bubbling Gruyère for me and a slice of fresh tomato tart with a side of the roasted beet salad for John Yarn Berry—and two glasses of a local winery's cabernet.

"To absent friends," he said, raising his glass, "wise and warmhearted. To Ivy McClellan, our dear departed."

It may have been more than two months since Granny's death, but there were still words and gestures that closed my throat, and I found I wasn't immune to hokey toasts, either. The glint of tears in John's eyes and our simultaneous reaching for tissues and blowing of our noses helped get me past it. Then, while my soup cooled to a safer temperature, I told him some of my ups and downs since Granny's death and about my decision to keep the Weaver's Cat.

"Do you enjoy being at the helm?" he asked.

"I'm really more of the cabin girl."

"You'll grow into it. Don't doubt yourself. Ivy never doubted herself or you."

"Sometimes, in the middle of the night, what I worry

about more is that I'll grow out of it instead of into it. That I'll get tired of small-town life, small-business headaches, the lack of professional stimulation . . ." I stopped and thought about that. Out of all my worries, in all the world, that wasn't one I'd put into words to anyone else. But that wasn't true. There were quite a few worries I hadn't put into words to anyone else. Worries about the existence or nonexistence of secret dye journals. What those journals meant if they did exist. The weird sense of transferred emotions I felt from time to time when I touched a sleeve or shoulder. But, first and foremost, the worries about seeing and believing in a ghost. I shook my head to dislodge those last words before they had a chance to leak out. John was kind and easy to talk to, but I wasn't about to share too much with him.

"You know that's a perfectly legitimate worry, though," he said.

"What is?" My words and worries about ghosts hadn't leaked out after all, had they?

"Outgrowing Blue Plum. I won't tell on you, though."

"Oh good. Thanks. Ardis has enough on her plate without having to worry about me jumping ship, too. What about you, though? From what Granny said, you leave and come back and leave again. I don't even remember the last time she mentioned seeing you. How long have you been away this time?"

"Guilty as charged," he said. "Personal experience is exactly how I know your worry is legitimate. Coming and going—quite often with the emphasis on the going—is how I've kept my mental balance. It might work for you, too. Have you thought about taking the occasional consulting job out in the bigger world?"

I told him I had and that I wasn't sure I was ready for that kind of balancing act yet. He seemed willing to talk about why I was reluctant, but by then my soup was cool enough and we'd spent more time talking about me than made me comfortable. Instead I dove into the perfect brown soup, felt like smacking my lips, and asked about his brother.

"Ambrose," he said. "Mean as snakes. Maybe one of the reasons I left in the first place. But the farm and I are all he's got and, except for the boat, he's all I've got. I'm selling the boat, did I tell you that?" He drank the last of his wine and stared out at Main Street growing dark. "I'm sorry I missed Ivy's funeral. I've definitely been away too long this time."

I didn't ask again how long that was. He hadn't answered the first time, and I knew what it was like to be asked questions I'd rather ignore.

The next morning, Debbie was waiting for me at the Cat with the latest issue of the *Blue Plum Bugle*, hot off the press and fresh off the front stoop.

Chapter 11

If the font the *Bugle*'s editor used wasn't called Screaming Headline, it should have been. I could have read it if Debbie held the paper up across the street. The point size left room for only three sentences on the front page. The first two were merely sensational. "Tragedy in Blue Plum" and "Motive Cloudy in Cloud Hollow Calamity." The third was the whopper. "Gun Belongs to Missing Security Guard."

"Has anyone ever told you your face is easy to read?" Debbie asked. "Even Ernestine wouldn't need a magnifying glass to see the questions racing through your head."

"Do you know this guy, Eric Lyle?" Lyle was the missing security man. He worked for Victory Paper.

"Never heard of him," Debbie said, "but I'm ready to hear he's guilty. I knew that gun didn't belong to Will."

"Why didn't we hear about him or the gun sooner?"

"Good question," Debbie said. "Maybe the *Bugle* scooped everyone else?"

"Or they don't have a good source of insider information."

According to the *Bugle*, the gun we found with the bodies, a Smith & Wesson Chief .38-caliber revolver with a two-inch barrel and holding five bullets, belonged to Eric Lyle. I pictured the reporter proudly getting the gun's description exactly right. Eric Lyle worked as a night security guard at Victory Paper. He was thirty-two. There were photographs of all three—Shannon Goforth, Will Embree, and Eric Lyle. Smiling pictures, probably personnel shots from the company for Shannon and Eric. Will's picture showed a younger, softer-looking guy than the man than I'd seen under the tree in the field.

"They can't find him," Debbie said. "Eric Lyle. He's missing. Did you read that part? If that isn't incriminating, I don't know what is."

Eric Lyle was last seen the day of the deaths, Monday. He clocked out of work at six that morning. He spoke to the day-shift security supervisor coming on duty. He waved to the man at the gate on his way out. He bought gas at a convenience store along the highway. They had a positive ID on the store's security tape. He used his credit card for the purchase. Neither he nor the car had been seen since, and there was no further activity on the credit card.

Out of the corner of my eye the blue-gray spider's web shawl on display near the front window appeared to ripple and Geneva shimmered into view behind it. The effect was weird because the insubstantial shawl was more solid than the ghost. Geneva yawned, stretched, and sighed as though bored beyond tears. She drifted over to see what held us in thrall.

Debbie shivered as though someone had drifted over her grave, and that was enough to get her moving and refocused on the workday ahead. "You go ahead and read the article," she said. "I'll take care of the cash register and get the place ready to open. There's another article rehashing the old mess with Victory Paper. It might be more accurate than what the Knoxville and Nashville papers dredged from their files."

I held the *Bugle* out so Geneva could see it without

buddying up too close. Even if she couldn't literally breathe down my neck, having a ghost reading over my shoulder gave new meaning to the word "claustrophobia." She didn't do any more than glance at the paper, though, before complaining.

"I liked the other picture better," she said. "Where is it?"

"What other . . ." I smothered the rest of that with a "hmm" and a throat clearing.

"These pictures are boring. When you look at the other one, you see a whole lovely, tragic story. Maybe it's inside. Turn the page."

I whispered "Hush," then called after Debbie, who was already busy with the cash drawer. "You're sure you don't mind opening by yourself?"

"Nope."

"I'll take the paper to the kitchen, then, and get out of your hair."

"Take your time. Absorb it. It's good background material for the investigation."

I spread the A section of the *Bugle* on the kitchen table, separating the three sheets so the lead article, its continuation on page six, and the Victory Paper article from page three were all face up. Besides the pictures of Shannon and the two men, there were pictures of the paper plant and the river with the second article, but no other photographs. I looked at Geneva.

"It must be on the back side of a page," she said. "Let's turn them over."

There wasn't really any "us" in Geneva's "let's" because she wasn't the kind of ghost who could move or manipulate objects. I hadn't thought about it until then, but that could be a source of her occasional depression. Spending eternity taunted by pages one couldn't turn or—more to her taste—televisions one couldn't turn on or channels one couldn't flip, would be hellish. Another source of frustration for her was how slowly she thought I responded to the blithe suggestions she made that started with "let's."

"Turn the pages! Turn the pages!"

I turned the three sheets over, but only the new superintendent of schools smiled out at us from page four. She was flanked by stories about roadwork and new sewer connections. Page five had ads and miscellaneous items of county news. I flipped the pages back to the articles and the photographs of Shannon, Will, and Eric.

"When did you think you saw another picture?" I whispered. There'd been articles in all the big-city dailies on Tuesday and Wednesday. They'd run the same photographs of Will and Shannon, though, and nothing more.

"It's not what I *think*. It's what I *know*. It was in the paper. I saw it."

I shrugged. "Sorry."

"There are two whole sections of the paper you haven't even touched." She pointed at the two sections I'd put aside.

"Those are sports and human interest stuff."

"Open them! Open them!"

"Calm down." I opened them, turning the pages slowly so she could see them, telling myself *I* was calm, as well as sweet and accommodating. Also telling myself I only imagined that I wanted to snap each page open and slam it down on the table, although I was finding myself hard to believe. Section B contained four pages of community organization and school sports news. I was especially sweet and didn't say, "I told you so." Section C was nothing but classified ads. When I'd turned and displayed all the pages, I turned my empty hands palms up. "Sorry, it's not here."

"I saw it." She billowed a time or two—an unnerving sight that made me glad she couldn't move objects. Or throw them. She was obviously convinced she'd seen the photograph, and she was obviously getting more frustrated and upset.

"Where did you see it?" I asked. "Where were *you* and where was *it*?"

She stopped billowing. She stopped moving altogether and looked more dead and disturbing than if she'd shrieked and flown at me.

I hesitated before saying, "It wasn't in *this* paper, was it."

She stared.

"How long ago did you see it?" I tried to keep my voice low and even because she didn't like questions that stirred up her memories. She didn't like it when I questioned those stirred-up memories, either.

She continued staring and I felt my shoulders creeping toward my ears in case of sudden ghost implosion. But then she appeared to give herself a shake, as though coming out of a trance. The effect was more as if a watery reflection riffled.

"I only wish I'd listened to my mother," she said, "and always kept a clean hankie in my pocket."

"Sorry, what?"

"You have no idea what it's like being forever without one, especially when there is so much to weep and wail about."

"Um, is there any way I can help?"

"No. But don't worry about me." She sighed. "I will tax my strength by describing the missing photograph for you and then I will melt away into a dusty corner and sob."

I started to interrupt her—there were no dusty corners in the Weaver's Cat unless she meant to sob in the farthest corners of the rafters in the attic—but she was playing her role to the hilt and no protest from me was going to stop her.

"I will sob and mourn," she said, "because they were so beautiful and romantic, even in their tragic death. The picture shows them laid out, lying head to head in that grassy meadow, their eyes staring up into the sky as though they looked beyond the passing clouds and all the way to heaven. And he was so proper in his suit—serge, I think it was, though I'm not certain. And she was lovely and demure in pale dotted lawn—pale except for the ghastly bloodstain seeping through her bodice. And she had a ribbon with a cameo at her neck and the hair escaping her snood curled sweetly at her temples. Chestnut. That's a good name for the color of her hair. And it was sad the way it still shone so in the sun.

"The shotgun lay beside them. They could not have used it themselves. Not and lie there as they did, as though their bodies were composed for the photographer. It is a shocking picture and not one you would forget if you had seen it. It tells a shocking story and my tears fail to wash either the picture or the story from my memory. I do not know what the world is coming to when the lives of two such true sweethearts are so cruelly ended. At least the photograph spares us the dreadful colors of their death. It was far worse seeing them there in that gory spring grass."

It was my turn to stare. "Geneva, what are you talking about? I thought you were describing a photograph. But did you see . . . what are you remembering?"

"Horror." She said it with bleak simplicity, all color fading from her voice. "I will go weep now." And she faded away, too.

It wasn't payback for Debbie's falling asleep Tuesday morning that kept me in the kitchen, but I sat there longer than I should have. First, trying to clamp down on the images Geneva had left to haunt me. Unfortunately, I didn't see how there was anything I could do right then either to make her feel better or to somehow sort out her story. If it even was her story. But from her telling of it and from her reaction to the telling, that surely wasn't just some television episode she'd absorbed and internalized.

But even if it was a fabricated memory, I didn't need those disturbing images in my head mixing with and clouding the disturbing images already there. So I dusted off a technique I'd used for dealing with troubled textiles when I wasn't able to give them immediate attention. The technique was to isolate and plan—seal the problematic item away to protect it and surrounding pieces, then develop a plan for diagnosing and solving the issues discovered. That worked well when dealing with filth of undetermined origins or stains or mold. Maybe I could make it work for memories of murder, too.

That settled, memories compartmentalized (I hoped), I made a pot of strong coffee and finished reading the lead story in the *Bugle*. Debbie was right about it raising questions.

Autopsy results, in addition to showing that Shannon died several hours before Will, also showed she was pregnant. Funny that Debbie hadn't mentioned either of those twists when she handed me the paper, but maybe she hadn't absorbed much past the part about Eric Lyle's gun. And where was Eric Lyle? What part did he play in the Cloud Hollow tragedy? Gunpowder residue was found on Will's hands. What if Will killed both Shannon *and* Eric before killing himself? But then where was Eric? In his car at the bottom of Lake Watauga? But why bother to dispose of him? Why kill either of them? Who died first? Was the whole thing a horrible chain reaction—

literally *boom, boom, boom*? Between questions like those crashing around in my head and the effort it was taking to keep Geneva's story from leaping back out of its box, I felt a massive headache brewing that no amount of caffeine was going to fix.

And I really had to look at Geneva's story again. That couldn't have been just a performance. She'd begun with her usual melodrama, and certainly her weeping was true to form, but fading away quietly like that at the end was not her usual shtick. She was convinced, and convincing, that she'd seen a newspaper photograph of a double murder. Worse, it sounded as though she might also have been there and seen the bodies. But where? Except for the green grass, her description matched nothing at Cloud Hollow. And *when* had she seen the bodies? Before or after she died? Had she stumbled across the scene? Witnessed the crime? I rubbed my temples and the back of my neck, troubled by putting words to another thought. Was Geneva that bloodstained young woman?

Surely not. Although I was new to the world of believing in ghosts, I was pretty sure they couldn't change their clothes and hairstyles after death. The watery, blurry ghost haunting me wore her hair loose, not neatly captured in a snood. It was harder to tell about a ribbon with a cameo around her neck, but I didn't think she wore that, either. More to the point, there didn't appear to be a ghastly bloodstain across her bodice. But maybe bloodstains don't make the transition to the afterlife? But then where did all the stories of bloodstained ghosts come from? That was a very strange line of thought for someone schooled in chemical analysis and the scientific method. I decided I'd reached my quota of weird for the day and it was time to go pull my share of real-world retail weight.

Before leaving the kitchen, I cocked an ear but didn't hear Geneva weeping. *And that's what happens when you give in to being haunted,* I told myself, shaking my head sadly. *Listening for a ghost's sobbing becomes ordinary.*

"I was right, wasn't I?" Debbie said when she saw me. "Eric Lyle is the one. He killed them."

That wasn't the best topic of conversation for setting a happy mood in the shop, but she was alone at the counter and I didn't hear floorboards creaking or customers chattering anywhere else. Rather than cause friction by disagreeing with her about the certainty of Eric Lyle's guilt, or by suggesting other possibilities, I dodged the current murder altogether.

"Have you heard anything about another double murder around here?"

Prefacing that question with a time frame would have been a good idea. Judging from Debbie's eyes and mouth flown wide, and her hand suddenly pressed to her chest, I'd almost given her a heart attack. The camel bells on the door jingled as she blinked, breathed, and recovered her voice.

"What do you mean, 'another double murder'?" she asked.

From the look of his set jaw, his flinty, suspicious eyes, and the hand resting on the butt of his revolver, Deputy Cole Dunbar was interested in knowing that, too.

Chapter 12

Deputy Cole Dunbar wasn't an idiot, and he had good instincts. Neither of those attributes worked to improve our relations. Even though I tended to be a polite, nonconfrontational person, one with a reasonable sense of self-preservation so that I didn't call him Clod to his face or to anyone else, he sensed it anyway.

"Two bodies weren't enough for you?" he asked. "You're back in town a few months so you need to celebrate by finding a couple more?"

"You are an insensitive clod." So much for being polite. Back in town a few months and I'd already blown my cover. Calling him *a* clod wasn't the same as calling him Clod, though, so I could still pat myself on the back. "And why are you keeping track of how long I've been back in town?"

"As a sworn peace officer, it's my duty to keep track of movements in and out of town. Forewarned is forearmed. You were here for several weeks following the death of your grandmother. You left to pack up your belongings in Illinois. You moved them here, and here you seem to be staying. Not so hard to keep track. And, as I recall, while here during the initial few weeks, you racked up a pretty good body count."

Sentetious clod.

"It's also my duty to follow up on information received, so I will repeat Ms. Keith's question. What do you mean, another double murder?"

I looked over at Debbie. She was sitting on the stool behind the counter quietly crying. "Oh, Debbie, no, it's nothing." I grabbed the box of Kleenex from the end of the counter and took it to her. Touching her tentatively, I was relieved to feel nothing, and I put my arm around her. "There hasn't been another murder. It was some old story I heard. I think. I mean, I heard it and I think it's old. Aw, now, it's going to be okay."

"Ahem," Clod said.

"Normal people don't actually pronounce the word 'ahem,' Deputy. They cough or clear their throats. What are you doing here, anyway?" So much for being non-confrontational and having a reasonable sense of self-preservation. I stopped myself and held up a hand. "Sorry, I'm sorry, can you wait just a moment, please?" I breathed in, breathed out, worked at letting the annoyance slide past. He was a lot of annoyance, but it was good practice. "Sorry, Deputy. Off on the wrong foot. Is there something we can help you with this morning?"

He had the flinty, suspicious eyes again. Or maybe they'd never warmed up in the first place. "I'm looking for Joe."

"Why are you looking for him here?"

"Isn't he here on Fridays?"

"Afternoons." Debbie sniffled into her Kleenex. "Friday afternoons."

I tamped down a moment of annoyance with Debbie for giving Clod that information. So what if he was looking for his brother? Interesting, though, that he had to *look* for Joe and couldn't just call or text him. It made me wonder. If Joe caught wind of the fact that Clod was looking for him, would he stick to his Friday-afternoon schedule or go find someplace that needed to be fished? And given the opportunity, would I provide the notifying wind? I felt a conspiratorial smile sneaking past my guard. It put me in a sunnier mood.

"You might actually be able to help me, Deputy," I said.

He darted glances at the skeins and balls and scarves and needles and knitting and weaving surrounding him. His eyes went from flinty and suspicious to alarmed and suspicious. That was a curious improvement.

"I mean with this story of an old murder."

He relaxed back into his own element, cocking one hip and nodding for me to continue. I told him the sketchy details, removing Geneva's melodramatic grace notes and keeping an eye on Debbie to make sure she wasn't freaking out.

"Where'd you hear this from?" he asked.

"A woman. I'm not sure who she is."

"Where'd it happen? How long ago?"

"I don't know."

"Victims' names?"

"No, I . . ."

"Well, you know, Ms. Rutledge, it's kind of hard to pin something like this down without a few of the things we call 'facts.'"

"Why? Because you've had so many sensational double murders in Blue Plum you can't keep track?" Clod might know how to ooze condescension, but I know how to pour on the sarcasm.

"Because they make it easier to search records and archives," he said.

"Which is why I asked if you'd ever heard about it. I thought if you had, then you might be able to supply some of the missing facts. I hoped your knowledge of crime in the area might provide an entry point for locating and accessing further information. But you haven't heard of it, so you can't help, so thank you anyway." I moved down the counter away from him and tried to look busy with a pair of scissors. He followed.

"What's your interest in this old story?" he asked.

I folded a piece of scratch paper and started snipping. "Same reason I don't like leaving a movie before the credits are over."

"Because you're into useless trivia?"

"Because I like to know how things work from start to finish."

"Could be. Or it could be you're plain nosy." He nodded. "Yeah, well, Ms. Nancy Drew, I can understand that. I do think making paper dolls like you're doing there is a better hobby than hunting up old murders, but even that's a safer hobby than chasing around after real bad guys. I'm glad to see all your handicrafts here are keeping you off the streets."

I held up what I'd cut. It looked like a string of paper ghosts. I tucked them in my pocket to show Geneva later and started on a string of paper deputies. Still, I couldn't help flapping my mouth. "You mean like instead of asking questions about a missing security guard? Or about the gun owned by that security guard that was used to shoot and kill two people? Or why the owner of the field where the deaths occurred didn't hear anything about the security guard, who is possibly at large and dangerous, before that information showed up in the paper four days later?"

Clod gave me a narrow-eyed glare before ignoring my questions and turning to Debbie. "Ms. Keith, what time will Joe be in this afternoon?"

"Fast and Furious," she sniffled.

"Is there a translation for that?"

"Four o'clock sit and knit," she said.

"Pffft." On his way to the door he stopped. "Ms. Rutledge?"

"Hmm?" I held up the string of deputies I'd cut, refolded them, snipped off their heads, and smiled at him. "Was there something else?"

"The library has old newspapers on microfilm and the historical society has a photograph archive. The archive is open by appointment. You'll find the number in the phone book."

"Oh. Thanks."

He touched the fingertips of his right hand to the brim of his Smokey Bear hat, which he cloddishly hadn't removed when he came in, and left. Debbie gazed after him, her head atilt, her eyes soft and moony.

"I don't think he was trying to insult you when he called you Nancy Drew," she said. "He probably isn't allowed to share information about ongoing investigations with civilians. I've always thought he was kind of cute. And don't you think what he said about the shop keeping you off the streets was funny and sweet?"

Debbie and Clod? I pegged him for early forties and she was early thirties. But why not? I decided I liked her better when she was egging me on to beat the cops at their own game, though. And did I think he was cute, funny, and sweet? No, I thought he was insufferable and his sweet aspersion sounded like a challenge.

Granddaddy had made the TGIF workroom by removing the wall between the two back bedrooms on the second floor of the Weaver's Cat. He'd sanded the wide-plank floors and filled one wall with built-in bookshelves. Over the years, under TGIF's care, a hodgepodge of Welsh cupboards grew along the other walls as storage space for materials was needed. Sturdy oak tables for projects took up most of the floor, but room was always kept at one end for a circle of comfy chairs. They were mismatched and well used.

TGIF, as a whole, met on the second Tuesday evening of each month. Those meetings consisted of a hospitality half hour and a short business meeting followed by a program of general interest. Throughout the programs, members worked on whatever portable projects they brought with them. They knit, crocheted, spun, tatted—anything they could do quietly with fibers while they listened to presentations on everything from the ancient art of nålebinding to the techniques judges use to grade raw wool to the care and feeding of silkworms. Once, when I was down visiting Granny, I'd done a program for them on how to safely clean and properly store antique unmentionables. I demonstrated on a pair of crotchless pantaloons, always a crowd-pleaser.

The membership of TGIF also divided itself into half a dozen or so special interest groups that met on various weekly schedules. There were the Wild Wednesday Weavers, the Saturday Spinners, Friday Fast and Furious, and other less alliterative offshoots. Friday Fast and Furious was a group devoted to challenges and community service. Their goal that year was to knit or crochet one thousand sweet little hats and donate them to the county hospital for newborns and hospitalized infants. That meant, because we averaged seven active members per meeting, that we should each produce a hat every 2.92 days. I was the slacker of the group.

Friday Fast and Furious didn't limit their community service to fiber and textile arts, though. They were the group Ardis had encouraged me to ask for help untangling the mysteries I encountered when Granny died. The members of Friday Fast and Furious were the posse, although I still shied away from thinking of them as *my* posse, with me as the intrepid leader of the pack.

"Good, here's the horse's mouth now," Mel said as I joined them that afternoon. Her mustard spikes looked electrified.

"Nice to see you, too, Mel. Hi, Ernestine, Thea."

Thea, straight from the library, and Ernestine, her thick lenses polished to a gleam, were already sitting, needles flashing. They nodded and smiled. I took the flowered wingback across the circle from Mel and irritated her by fussing with my needles and rosy pink wool, then putting them down and getting up to help myself to a cup of coconut tea and a scone from the plate and carafe she'd brought with her from the café. One of them had put a CD in the communal boom box—instrumental bossa nova, which was surprisingly good knitting music, accommodating both the fast and the snail-paced. It was less stressful for me, anyway, than the crescendo of the *William Tell* Overture, which invariably left me panting and looking for stitches that had galloped off into the sunset.

"Is Joe here?" Ernestine asked, peering around in case she'd missed him or mistaken him for something else.

Debbie came in and sat next to Ernestine. While Ardis and I took turns minding the shop or attending Fast and Furious, Debbie never missed a meeting if she could help it, even though she had Friday afternoons off and could have headed home. She said that as much as she loved the farm and wouldn't think of giving it up to live in town, and as much as she loved her animals and thought they were more intelligent than some people she knew, the sheep never had gotten the hang of pulling up chairs and settling in for a good, long chat. She made herself comfortable and picked up the thread of conversation.

"Did I hear you asking about Joe?" she asked Ernestine. "I talked to him in the kitchen a few minutes ago. I thought he said he'd be here. But then I saw him getting in his truck, so I guess not."

"Did you tell him Cole was looking for him?" I asked.

She pulled three sky blue hats from her workbag and added them to the week's collection. "Yeah, I did. Maybe that's where he's gone."

Or maybe that was *why* he was gone. I hid a smile in a bite of scone. "Mmm, what is this, Mel?"

"Pear ginger." Mel was putting the finishing touches on a tangerine-colored hat. She'd previously contributed cherry-, lemon-, blueberry-, and plum-colored hats and a dozen green ones in shades ranging from iceberg lettuce to curly endive. "What's the plan?" she asked.

I put my tea and scone down and didn't pick up my knitting. "Following threads. I've been collecting a few, pulling them from here and there. Some of them aren't so easy to tug. Some of them are twisted."

"Murder is twisted," Ernestine said.

"And we're going to untwist it."

Thea sat back, looking pleased. "Watch out, Blue Plum plods, the game's already afoot and my money's on Kath."

"Except?" Mel asked. She was the only one watching my face. "Spill it, sister. We're all friends here."

"I want to be sure about something, about what Thea just said. Are we treating this like a game? Because if we are, then that isn't right. Thea, I don't mean that as a criticism. But we can't be gleeful. I keep thinking of Bonny out there in Debbie's field telling us that her daughter deserves respect. You agreed with her then and you were right. She does. They both do, so this can't be a game, but are we making it into one?"

"Long-winded," Mel said, "but a fair question."

"And here's the answer," Thea said. "I never said I

think it's a game. That was only me Thea-fying a classic quote. It was only that and my natural buoyancy, and I haven't tried to rein that in for years and I'm not about to start pulling the reins now. But I'm not laughing at what happened and I don't take it lightly."

"Okay," I said. "Good. That's what I thought. I just wanted to be sure."

The background chatter of needles was comforting. How they all kept knitting through gossip or drama was literally beyond me. My knitting skill wasn't nearly the caliber of the rest of the Fast and Furious. I left my needles on the arm of the chair, not wanting an unplanned hole showing up in my rosy hat, and not sure what reactions my next questions would bring. Or, come to think of it, how Geneva would critique my technique in asking them. I glanced around for her. She usually enjoyed Friday Fast and Furious. But she wasn't anywhere that I could see.

"Focus," Mel said.

"Sorry. Okay." But I'd been worried about her since she'd disappeared after describing the horrible murder scene that was still so vivid to her. Mel was right, though. Focus. "Okay. Do any of you think we ought to talk about what happened last time?"

Needles clicked industriously. The others looked at me, at one another. Debbie didn't. She studied her stitches. Then she asked quietly, "Or what almost happened to us? I told Cole Dunbar you should be arrested for endangerment."

She had. Thank goodness Clod knew how to identify the real bad guy in a tense situation. But if Debbie still thought the accusation stood, I had to wonder why she was so keen now for me to lead them off into who knew where or what.

Rather than answer her, I took a sip of tea and waited.

"Ernestine says that what you really did was save us," Debbie said.

"But?" I definitely sensed a "but" in there.

"But there is no end to the season of mourning," Ernestine said.

"No," Thea agreed, "*but* it doesn't have to stop us from moving forward."

"And we can't let anyone get away with murder," Debbie said.

Ernestine reached over and patted Debbie's hand, then went back to knitting.

There were more nods, mine included.

"Right." I nodded again, hoping that would somehow make what I said next easier for Debbie to hear. "One of the threads I've been following, the first one, in fact, is this: *Is* anyone getting away with murder in this case?"

The soft clicking of needles continued. Except for Debbie's.

"We need to follow *all* the threads, tug on all of them," I said to her. "See where they go. Keep an open mind. Not just look for evidence that supports the way we want the story to play out. And we need to be prepared for some of the threads to lead to unpleasant surprises."

"Or danger," Ernestine said, eyes bright and wide behind her thick lenses.

"Danger?" Ardis appeared, puffing, in the doorway. She propped herself with a hand against the jamb, catching her breath from climbing the stairs too fast. "You know what I say to the measly concern of danger?"

"Been there, done that?" Thea asked.

"Too trite," Ardis said. "This is better. We are women who have stared down the barrel of a gun."

"Exactly," Ernestine said with great satisfaction. "Exactly."

"And sometimes the danger is in the complications," Ardis said. "Cole Dunbar is downstairs looking stern and starched. He says he needs to speak with Debbie and I don't think he's planning to discuss dyed-in-the-wool color palettes."

Chapter 13

Ardis had sent Clod on a wild-goose chase to the basement, taking pleasure in telling him Debbie might be down there weighing walnut hulls or onion skins. She said the effort it cost him to keep his forehead from wrinkling and his jaw from slackening and a "say what?" from slipping out of his prissy mouth was well worth her puff up the stairs.

"But what do you think he wants?" Debbie's voice immediately sounded ten years younger. Her eyes were huge, their sleepless shadows standing out on her pale face. How had I failed to notice how fragile she'd grown since Monday?

"Come on," I said. "I'll go with you and we'll find out."

Before we reached the workroom door I heard Ardis say, "She's Ivy all over again, isn't she?"

Thea answered with an unrestrained "Yee-haw," and I couldn't help wondering how soon I'd regret the impulse that made me hop up out of my comfortable chair to act as shield or sword. It turned out to be as soon as I saw Clod Dunbar standing at the top of the stairs, arms crossed and unamused. Apparently he hadn't enjoyed his detour to the basement.

He wasn't happy, but he did have a smidgen of humor. He nodded toward the TGIF workroom. "Sounds more like a rodeo in there than your frantic and flabbergasted knitting circle or whatever you call it. Ms. Keith, I need to speak with you. Is there a private space, an office or some such, that we can use?"

Debbie looked at me, at Clod, and back at me but said nothing.

"May I ask why you need to speak with Ms. Keith now? You were here earlier. You couldn't speak to her then?" I kept my voice light, low, even, and as far from strident or demanding as possible.

"I know what you're up to, Ms. Rutledge," Clod said. He also went for low and even, but his delivery was marred by the look of long-suffering on his face.

"Then you're one up on me, Deputy," I said, upping my ante by adding friendly and familiar to my tone.

"I sincerely hope I am, although I will not count on staying that way. Ms. Keith," he said, turning to Debbie, "I have one or two questions I need to ask you. I assure you I will be civil and there is no need for Ms. Rutledge to accompany you in whatever capacity she thinks she's acting."

Ardis popped back out of the workroom, having most likely been just inside listening. "The study will work, don't you think, Kath?" she asked. "You girls go on and take Coleridge up there. There really isn't any other space where you can be sure you won't be interrupted. Now, if you will kindly move aside, Coleridge, I have a business to run downstairs and I can't stop here and chat with you any longer."

She made a shooing gesture that Clod obeyed with a polite nod but wary eyes. Ardis, in addition to matching his height and breadth, had been both his third- and fourth-grade teacher. According to her, that experience permanently imprinted itself on his psyche to her benefit. At least while she was present and looming.

"Thanks, Ardis. Come on," I said to Clod and Debbie, "The study's a good solution. I'll take you up."

"That's kind of you, Ms. Rutledge," Clod said, "but I'm sure we can find the way ourselves. Your expert guide skills won't be necessary."

"Maybe not my skills, but my key if the door is locked." I brushed past him and trotted up the stairs. The cat met me at the top in the open, as always, doorway.

"Meow."

"Hello, you." I rubbed the cat between his soft ears, delighting in his answering purr. What a sweetheart. He twined around my ankles, wrapping me further around his little paw, and chirruped at Debbie coming up the stairs behind me.

"He prefers it when you call him by his name," a lugubrious and colorless voice sighed from somewhere in the study. It was an interesting ghost phenomenon that the sounds Geneva made gave me only a general direction for her but usually not an exact location. I was glad to hear her, though, even if she was complaining. Again.

"You were unbelievably rude about calling him Dirty Harry," she lamented, "so I thought you could try calling him Sergeant Friday instead. It might inspire you."

"I thought you said the door was locked," Clod said almost on top of her moan.

I was able to answer them simultaneously. "Oh no, really, I don't think so." Then, for Clod's benefit, "I'm pretty sure I said *if*, Deputy. *If* the door was locked. And isn't it super that we found it open? I'll just get the light for you and clear these piles off the chairs and you can make yourselves comfortable. Debbie, honey, you come sit in Granny's rocker."

Geneva huddled in a corner of the window seat doing her best impression of a damp dishrag. She didn't say anything more to me, not even a muffled "hmpf," and I couldn't tell if she noticed when the three of us crowded into the room or if she registered my proximity when I pretended to look out the dormer behind her.

"Ms. Rutledge?" Clod said.

Geneva's silence and the fact that she didn't lift her head to stare with woeful eyes were definite measures of her despondence. She usually showed at least some curiosity in visitors, but even when the cat leapt into the window seat and mewed at her she didn't answer, and I saw no ripple of recognition or interest.

"Ms. Rutledge," Clod said as though he thought I hadn't been paying attention for some time. "I am talking to you."

"You don't need to shout, Deputy. I'm right beside you."

"And you don't need to do anything else useless for us. Thank you for showing us how to climb the stairs and enter an open doorway. Please close the door behind you; then go back down the stairs and do not linger near the keyhole."

"I wouldn't dream of trying to listen in, and I won't take offense at that remark, either. I'm sure your manners are overburdened by the stress of your investigation. Eavesdrop on your conversation? Good heavens, no. There's not a *ghost* of a chance that I would do any such thing. Perhaps *someone might do that*," I said, speaking toward the window seat, over my shoulder, as I headed for the door, "but no, not I."

Clod, being the essential clod he was, slammed the door behind me.

"Evicted?" Ernestine clucked sympathetically when I returned to the TGIF workroom.

"That's okay," Thea said. "We'll make Debbie tell us what happens. That's what friends are for."

"That's what tunnel of fudge cake is for, too," Mel

said, "bribery. If Debbie doesn't talk, I'll whiff one of those babies under her nose until she gives in."

"Good idea, Mel." I dropped back into the flowered wingback, confident in my backup plan. If Debbie felt bound by conscience or misplaced loyalty to the authorities, I felt sure my fly on the wall would have listened in and would be eager to tell me all.

"So, Nancy," Thea said, sitting forward, "what's our next step?"

I picked up my knitting and gave her a look.

"Okay, okay," she backtracked. "I missed the memo about no allusions to Nancy Drew. Completely understandable, though. The image is too immature. How do you feel about Miss Marple? Too long in the tooth for you? At least she knits."

"Jane Marple is my favorite," Ernestine said. "Next to V. I. Warshawski."

The rosy pink preemie hat hanging off my needles was beginning to look more like a shower cap, and I saw that I was gripping the needle in my right hand as though it were a pencil waiting for inspiration. Poor little hat. I sighed and laid my knitting mess back down. "I'll be right back."

I went across the hall and came back wheeling the reversible whiteboard-corkboard we used for classes and demonstrations and now, for the second time, for organizing questions about a crime. The first time I'd used it for that purpose had been at Debbie's suggestion.

I closed the door quietly—though tempted to slam it to show Clod two could play that game—and wheeled the board to a position the other three could see without craning their necks. Also into a position where I could flip it to the corkboard side when I heard Clod thumping back down the stairs. Ernestine took her glasses off, polished the lenses on her sleeve, put them back on, and peered at the board. I picked up the marker and put it back down.

"Hold on a sec." I went over and turned up the volume on the bossa nova. If Clod could worry about an eavesdropper at his door, I'd play *that* game, too, by making it harder to hear *us*. "Okay," I said, rolling my shoulders, ready and facing my posse. "I lied earlier. I haven't collected just a few threads. I've got a whole ball of them."

Chapter 14

"We might as well include the questions we've all had rattling around in our heads since Monday," I said. I wrote, *Why were Shannon Goforth and Will Embree in that field?* on the whiteboard and then half a dozen more questions, one below the other:

> *Did they arrive together?*
> *When?*
> *How?*
> *Did Will kill Shannon?*
> *Did he kill himself?*
> *If he "could never kill anyone," then how could he kill himself?*

"Those are tip-of-the-iceberg stuff," I said, "or they're—"

"The starter end of a ball of yarn," said Thea.

"Yeah, that's what they are. And you know how sometimes when you pull on the starter end and hope it'll all unwind beautifully from the center, but instead you get yarn barf? Well, stand back, because here it comes. I've heard from two sources, the Spivey twins and a woman named Carolyn Proffitt, who says she was Shannon's assistant at Victory Paper, that someone was stalking Shannon. Carolyn Proffitt says it was Will. The Spiveys say it was someone else." I wrote *Was someone stalking*

Shannon? on the board and below it *Was it Will?* "But if it was Will, how did he manage to do that while supposedly hiding out in the national forest? And how about all these questions?" I wrote:

> *Eric Lyle—where the heck does he fit in?*
> *Where is he?*
> *Why is he missing but not his gun?*

"Wait, go back," Thea said. "You didn't write down the one about how Will Embree could stalk and hide at the same time. But if he was good at hiding, he was probably good at stalking, too."

"But if more than a few people knew he was stalking, then how much hiding was he doing?" I wrote all that down and discovered I'd gotten carried away. Ernestine was probably happy, but I'd written my questions too big and was almost out of room. I felt as though I was percolating, and I must have looked like it, too.

"Keep it together," Mel said. "I've got pen and paper here somewhere."

While she dug madly through her knitting bag, I dug back through my memory for something I'd heard about Debbie . . . something—Geneva had said it. She asked if I knew that Debbie used to entertain Will out at her place. I hesitated, then squeezed two more questions into the space at the top of the board:

> *How much does Debbie know about Will's recent movements?*
> *How recently was Debbie in contact with Will?*

I looked the board over. I'd been right. Yarn barf. We needed organization. We needed a bigger board. *What time was Shannon killed? What was Will doing from the time she died until he did? Did anyone see either of them or talk to them earlier that morning? Did anyone hear the shots? Whose baby was Shannon having? Who is the Spiveys' source?* I rubbed the back of my neck, feeling my brains doing the bossa nova at double time.

As I turned around to see if Mel had found her pen and paper, the door flew open. Foiled by my own cleverness—I hadn't heard Debbie's light feet running down the stairs over the jazzy music I'd turned up. She was clearly upset—probably over something cloddish Clod had said or asked—and she'd flown back down the stairs looking for refuge or understanding. Looking for friends. She pulled to a stop when she realized we were all staring at her. Then I, slick operator that I was, telegraphed what we were doing and my guilty conscience by looking from her to the whiteboard and back. And then Clod arrived and I should have flipped the board and closed the scene with crossed arms or a challenge. But I needed lessons in that kind of quick, confrontational thinking.

Clod stared at me. That was uncomfortable enough. Debbie's eyes were now focused on the whiteboard. On the two questions sailing across the top of it above all the others. *How much does Debbie know about Will's recent movements? How recently was Debbie in contact with Will?* From the look on her face, the headline for the whole board might as well read, *Is Debbie Involved in Murder?*

"Debbie, I . . ."

She made a sobbing noise—sounding less human even than Geneva—turned, and ran. I would have gone after her, but Clod slid over to fill the doorway.

"I expected more of the knit-one, knot-two, yank-it-out going on in here," he said. "I take it you're the ring-leader of this cabal?" He nodded his chin at me.

I didn't say anything and didn't ask him where he'd

learned the word "cabal." Probably in third or fourth grade. He wasn't listening for an answer, anyway. He was finally enjoying himself.

"Next time you'll want to put your board *here*, on this side of the room." He used the sort of large, repetitive gestures airport personnel perform when directing jumbo jets to their docking gates. "And facing *that* side of the room." Again with the repeating gestures, this time with both hands directing all eyes to me. "Oriented that way," he said, "so the casual passerby won't be upset by the unexpected and inane." He smiled, gave a sarcastic salute, and strolled away.

"Stupid, stupid, stupid," I muttered at myself.

Thea, subdued, took the eraser and started to clean the board.

"No!" I grabbed the eraser from her. "No. We can't quit."

Neither Ernestine nor Mel said anything. Thea didn't offer arguments. They all waited while I studied the floor, my fingertips and the eraser bouncing off my lips.

"Debbie's reaction," I said, thinking it through and still looking at the sturdy, wide planks of the floor. "We don't know for sure what her reaction was about, which questions she was reacting to. We can guess, but her reaction is another reason we need to investigate. It indicates something. And that damage is already done. We can't go back." I started rewriting what Thea had wiped away. "We can't quit. Debbie will see that. We'll make her see that. And phooey on whatever Dunbar thinks of us. And really, at this point, how can it hurt to go on?"

"All righty, then," Mel said. "I'll go make the tunnel of fudge. Bribe or peace offering—either way, it works."

Ardis agreed to drive with me to Cloud Hollow to make amends to Debbie. We knew we couldn't afford to lose her as an employee. More important, we couldn't afford to lose her as a friend. It was close to eight when Mel called to say the cake was cool enough to transport. She met us at the door of the café.

"Want to come with us?" I asked.

"Sorry. Early to bed for me in order to make tomorrow's sweet rolls rise." She handed the cake to Ardis. "And this," she said, handing me a bag. "Cinnamon raisin bagels. Fresh. Her favorite."

My nondescript Honda had never smelled so good. The concentration of warm chocolate and cinnamon aromas did wonders for my own concentration, too. Despite the dark and the twists and turns through woods and around hills, we went wrong only twice. Ardis was kind and didn't blame me for that or for the reason we were heading out there.

"Investigations turn a harsh light on everyone involved," she said. "I think I read that somewhere. And every question on the board was legitimate. After she's thought about it, Debbie will see that. And we need her to see that because we can't do without her at the store."

"Dunbar was right, though. I should have been more careful about where I put the board."

"But Debbie asked you to reinstate the posse and investigate, didn't she?"

"Before we left the farm Monday morning. She and Bonny both did."

"Then she'll understand. Besides, Cole must have said something or asked her something that upset her. Something happened that made her run out of the study and barge into the workroom like that. Do you suppose he upset her on purpose? So she would run down the stairs and he'd have a chance to sneak up on you?"

That was far-fetched, but Ardis was stirred up.

"Doggone it. I think he did upset her on purpose," she

said. "And I've a mind to speak to him about that kind of behavior in a law-abiding business the next time I see him. Good Lord! Did you see that car on the side of the road?" She twisted in her seat, a hand to her heart, but we'd already gone around another curve.

"Barely."

"I've a mind to speak to Cole about that, too. Overnight parking shouldn't be allowed on these narrow roads. It's a hazard after dark."

We found Debbie's drive soon after, and I turned in, thinking of her alone out here with her sheep and Bill the dog. She'd told me on the morning of the dye workshop that she grew up on Cloud Hollow farm. She was proud of its being one of Tennessee's recognized Century Farms—land owned and worked by the same family for at least a hundred years, and in her family's case almost two hundred. She meant to keep hold of the farm, keep it going, and hand it down to the next generation. I supposed I could understand that fierce loyalty and the hold the land had on her. But with no near neighbor's lights winking in the dark as we crunched down her long gravel drive, I was glad the place I felt most attached to had streetlights and sidewalks and friends next door.

We pulled in behind Debbie's pickup in a widened area between the house and the outbuilding she and her late husband had built to be her dye studio. We hadn't gone inside the house or the dye studio on that interrupted workshop morning, but I'd admired the lines of each. The studio was a single-story frame structure that could easily be mistaken for a cute guest cottage. Its steeply pitched roof gave it the look of a small saltbox out of New England more than something belonging on an east Tennessee farm.

The two-story house was the original farmhouse, built by Debbie's some-number-of-greats-grandfather in 1832.

She told us the bricks were made onsite with clay dug from the banks of the Little Buck. The bricks' red had mellowed over the scores of years and now gave the impression the house had sprouted and grown along with the oaks surrounding it.

We climbed out of the car, not sure what kind of reception to expect appearing uninvited after dark, but the light spilling across the porch from the windows on either side of the front door gave us hope. The evening breeze shushed through the new leaves on the massive oaks as we climbed the front steps. Bill barked, once, inside. Ardis took the bagels, letting me bear our offering of tunnel of fudge.

"What if she's getting ready for bed?" I said, wondering why that hadn't occurred to me before.

"Only Mel goes to bed this early. And if she is, then there's more for us."

"Mel called," Debbie said when she opened the door.

Bill the border collie's welcome was less guarded, but Debbie took the cake when I handed it to her, and the two of them ushered us back to the kitchen, where plates, forks, and a cake knife were already waiting on the table. When we sat down, Bill went to his bed in the corner, not far from Debbie's chair. He lay with one white foreleg extended as though showing off his genteel paw.

Ardis took over serving the cake, saying she knew neither Debbie nor I would cut big enough pieces. Her idea of the ideal size was a slab. I remembered Geneva's unflattering comments about my perceived weight gain and bravely sacrificed my self-image to our quest for renewed harmony. Debbie helped that along by plying us with more sweet tea than I usually drank in a week. Refilling our glasses seemed to make her happy, though, or at least kept her busy.

She updated us on new mother Mabel and the twin lambs. They were getting along well. We complimented Bill on his excellent manners and remarked on the red geraniums filling the windows on both sides of the corner where he sat. Bill's smile was wider and looked more genuine than Debbie's. The small jokes and pleasantries we passed were real enough, but Debbie didn't bring up the questions she'd seen scrawled on the whiteboard and we didn't ask about her interview with Clod. Ardis carried most of the conversation.

"I don't believe I've set foot in this kitchen since one spring when I had to bring your uncle Harmon home from school after one of the Dillow boys got hold of him. I won't tell you what the results of Lester Dillow's attentions were while we're still eating. That would have been about forty-five years ago, though, and if I remember right, the kitchen looked exactly the same back then. Although I believe your grandmother grew African violets instead of geraniums and you have more up-to-date appliances. I love your red microwave and toaster."

Debbie shrugged one shoulder. "I've always loved this kitchen."

"Of course you have, hon. You look right at home in it. Your grandmother did, too, and you favor her when you pull your hair back in a braid like that."

"Ardis is right," I said. "The kitchen suits you."

It did. It was a cheerful time capsule I wouldn't have expected to find in a house of that era. I knew people who took such kitchens and dragged them back to a pseudo-authentic, antique country look or pulled them forward and primped them into something sleek and contemporary. But sometime around the middle of the last century, when Debbie's family discovered yellow countertops, aquamarine cupboards, and peach chiffon linoleum, they'd latched onto them and hadn't let go. The anachronisms of the room made me smile. It was a modern kitchen wrapped in a 1950s color scheme inside an antebellum farmhouse.

"And now that I've admired your kitchen, may I also admire your bathroom?" I asked.

"Down the hall on your left. Sometimes the door sticks." I thought I heard her add, "And watch your head," but the sweet tea had a louder voice than Debbie's and I didn't stop to ask.

I found the door in a dark-paneled wall, both of them painted in some bygone decade with a beautiful example of faux walnut grain. The bathroom was tucked in the space under the stairs, so the head warning had been real. After watching mine and after washing my hands, I found out the sticking door was real, too. It took some wrestling and a shoulder butt before it popped open, and I was breathing hard but proud of myself for not quite panicking when it finally did. I felt like a character in a children's book tumbling back into real life after visiting some other world.

The sounds of Ardis talking and laughing in the kitchen and Debbie softly joining in were welcome and calming. They were the sounds of our small breach healing. Rather than interrupt, I stayed for a few minutes in the hall.

As I listened to the riffle of their voices, I ran my finger over the ripples of the faux grain, imagining the craftsman creating that illusion with gliding strokes of color. The panels on the opposite wall were equally beautiful, and I wondered what other architectural details and treasures the house held. The voices continued murmuring in the kitchen, so I stepped farther down the hall and peeked into a darkened doorway.

And saw nothing, of course, because darkened doorways usually lead to darkened rooms. But as I turned to go, a point of light flashed and caught the corner of my eye. I turned back to the room, not sure where to focus, and saw the light again. But not in the room. Out a window opposite the doorway. Through another window in the dye studio. Someone with a tiny flashlight was sneaking around. My heart forgot all about not panicking.

Chapter 15

I flew into the kitchen and caught Ardis on the tail end of a story about mothballs and squirrels. She looked up when I skidded in, grabbed the edge of the table, and leaned toward them, eyes no doubt goggling.

"Somebody's in the dye studio," I whispered, almost breathless. Too breathless maybe. They looked more worried about me than about what I was trying to tell them. Why was I whispering, anyway? The prowler couldn't hear me.

"Sorry, hon," Ardis said, "I heard a few consonants in there, but the rest of it sort of disappeared. Take a breath and say it again."

"Somebody's in the dye studio. I saw a flashlight."

That was all Debbie needed. She forgot all about being withdrawn or hesitant, scraped her chair back, and called Bill to her side. He was instantly alert but didn't bark.

"I'll call 911," I said.

"Go ahead," she said, "but I'm not waiting."

"What are you going to do?" Ardis said. "You can't think you're going out there." She got up and was able to take up enough room that Debbie couldn't squeeze past.

"I'm going to find out who's out there in my studio and what they think they're after."

"Don't be ridiculous. That might be Eric Lyle." Ardis

put her hands on her hips to make herself even more of a barricade.

I didn't hear the rest of their argument because the 911 dispatcher was asking me to repeat myself. I covered my other ear and squinted, as though that would improve reception or help the dispatcher process what I was saying. I told her again what was happening and she asked me to repeat it one more time, slowly, assuring me she was only following procedure so that she was clear on the exact conditions of my emergency and could relay details accurately as the situation unfolded. I closed my eyes entirely and had some unfriendly thoughts she didn't deserve.

"Listen," I finally said, "it's just a few things you have to be clear on. Intruder? Yes. Gun? Very likely. Murder? Here, a few days ago. Situation? Very dangerous. Got that? You can repeat it all you want, but I have to go." Then I hung up. I felt bad about being short with her and for saying there might be a gun when I knew no such thing, but if that brought a good guy out here faster, one who *did* have a gun, then I wasn't going to beat myself up over it. And then I saw there really was a gun. Debbie was standing by the back door with one.

"A rifle?" I squeaked. "Where'd that come from? How'd you get around Ardis? Ardis? What's going on?"

"She got down and crawled under the table," Ardis said. "Good move, Debbie. Now, please tell Bill he can stand down." Bill held Ardis in the corner with a firm eye and a low noise in his throat.

"He's fine where he is," Debbie said calmly. "This isn't a rifle, Kath; it's a shotgun. It belonged to my husband. Don't worry. I know how to use it and I always keep it safely locked away until I need it. Like now. I'm taking it outside with me and it's going to help me find out who's in my studio without my permission."

"That's stupid." As if blurting that to someone holding a gun was particularly bright. All she needed to do was point the thing at me and I would let her go anywhere she wanted.

In fact, all she did was vaguely wave it at me and I didn't challenge her. She told Bill to stay, leaving Ardis cornered and unhappy. But she didn't tell me to stay and, although I had to keep myself from screaming as though I were charging into the jaws of a forlorn hope, I followed her out the door and into the night.

"If it is Eric Lyle, what do you think he's looking for?" I whispered in Debbie's ear. A mistake. She was so intent on sneaking quickly and quietly across the darkened farmyard to the studio that she hadn't noticed me following her. And she was more keyed up than her calm voice had suggested.

"Ee-eee-eee," she started to say. Only part of it escaped, though, before she clapped her hand over her mouth. She turned to me with big eyes. "Are you crazy? Don't ever sneak up on someone holding a gun."

"Good idea," I whispered. "Why don't we go back to the house before we surprise whoever's in there, who might *also* have a gun and be a cold-blooded killer. We can wait for the cops. Maybe it'll be Deputy Dunbar who comes."

Her only answer to that was for her eyes to go from big and alarmed to slitty and cynically dismissive. We stood on the studio's porch, an extension of the concrete slab, our backs flat against the wall between a window and the door. I tried to hear movements inside but the place was too well insulated. I heard more rustlings and twig snaps in the dark night surrounding us than coming from the building. Debbie turned and started toward the door. Before she inched too far, I put a hand on her shoulder. Another mistake.

"For cripes' sake," she whispered fiercely. "What?"

"Shouldn't we have a plan before you jump in there with your gun blazing?"

"I'm not going to shoot anyone."

"What if he shoots you?"

"Tch." She turned away and started moving before I could ask my other pressing question—what if he shot me?

She continued to inch, which told me she wasn't entirely sure about barging into the studio. I continued listening for sounds coming from inside, trying to tell myself I wasn't rooted to that spot with the bone-rattling fear that bullets might start flying past my ears or through them.

Too bad I was so logical and convincing. In no time at all I had myself believing I was doing something much more important than standing there shaking. I believed I was using skills honed to an expert level during my previous experience of finding someone sneaking around where he didn't belong—namely, sneaking around in the cottage where I'd stayed after Granny died. Said expertise then led me to conclude that any movements currently transpiring in the dye studio couldn't be heard because they were as stealthy and low-down as they came. And that's when I realized I had a pretty good idea of who was inside and I peeled my back from the wall and sprinted after Debbie.

"Now what?" She was really having trouble keeping her reactions to a whisper at that point.

I looked past her. The door was very slightly ajar. Good.

"Where's the light switch?" I whispered in her ear.

She put her hand on the doorframe and mimed reaching inside at that height.

"Okay. Good. I'm ready." I bounced on my toes, feeling the fizz of the righteous vigilante in my blood. "Let's do it. Let's throw the door open, flip on the light, and just plain surprise the hell out of him. Come on. Before the cops get here and steal our thunder. We'll do it on three."

Debbie gaped, obviously not so into this scenario as she'd let on. I stepped around her.

"One, two, and the heck with three." I slammed the door open and flipped on the lights, expecting to surprise Joe Dunbar, our friendly neighborhood burglar-of-all-trades, with whom I was really annoyed because I thought he'd given up this pastime.

He was surprised, all right, only it wasn't Joe and it wasn't a he. It was the younger of the two journalism students from Asheville. The one with the camera. Pen. And she was going to make one crackerjack photojournalist someday. She had guts and good instincts and she didn't scream or freeze when Debbie came in after me with the shotgun pointed straight at her. She snapped a picture.

Chapter 16

"Hands up," Debbie snapped at Pen, "camera down."

Those commands did make Pen freeze. Maybe in confusion. I decided to help her out.

"Put the camera on the table, Pen. Then put your hands in the air."

Pen, standing to our right at the far end of a solid work island, had a look of "really?" with a touch of the sardonic to it on her face. She followed through quickly, though, when Debbie diagrammed the instructions with brisk precision, aiming the shotgun at the camera, the table, her hands, the ceiling, and back at the middle of her chest. I let Debbie keep Pen's attention and moved forward to lean an elbow on the island at the opposite end from Pen, going for a serious, in control, just-a-bit-menacing look.

I was torn, though, because Debbie's studio was calling to me. The labels on jars and boxes wanted reading; the bundles of dried dyestuff hanging from hooks and nails wanted pinching and squeezing. There were cupboards to open and shelves to explore. Kettles, tubs, dippers, and stirring rods waited, ready for vibrant colors to engulf them. I smelled chemicals, plants, and wool. I'd always loved rummaging through Granny's dye kitchen, and a circuit of Debbie's whole studio wouldn't take long. The space was only about fifteen feet by twelve.

But I couldn't ignore the confronter and the confrontee before me.

Debbie was looking down the length of her shotgun at Pen. No doubt she was seeing a tabula rasa with a bull's-eye on it. She hadn't met Pen and Sylvia the morning they'd inveigled their way into the shop and my good graces. She and the cat had been snoozing in the comfy chair.

"You know her, Kath?" Debbie asked, nodding her chin at Pen without taking her eyes from her.

Pen turned a hopeful smile my way. If she hadn't been dressed in head-to-toe black, with her long hair tucked under a black knit cap, I might have smiled back. As it was, I wondered if she were taking Special Ops 101 in addition to her journalism class, and I was almost surprised she didn't have shoe polish smeared on her face to complete the look.

"Nope," I said. "Can't say that I do."

"Yes, you do," Pen said. "You called me by name."

"You came in the shop once. That hardly counts as knowing you."

"So who are you?" Debbie stepped closer.

"I'm Pen. Pen Ledford. Penelope."

"What are you doing here?"

"Research."

"I bet," Debbie said. "What kind of research? Into what? And what makes you think you can break in here and sneak around to do it?"

"Oh, well, see, it's for my final project. I'm filling in local color. Interviewing folks, taking pictures, poking around here and there. That kind of thing." She kept her hands raised but waved them to show how much of "that kind of thing" she was accomplishing. "You've got a nice setup here, by the way. Some of your equipment's pretty interesting. Sharp knives, pruning shears. I like the poisonous chemicals, too. And that huge marble mortar. Or is that the pestle? I never can keep those two straight. Which is the one that looks like it could be used as a bludgeon?"

"What are you talking about?" Debbie asked.

"For my class project I'm writing about that murder-suicide thing, and I thought if I could soak up some atmosphere by coming out here I'd have a chance of getting a real scoop, you know? And I've got a pass here somewhere, if you want to see it."

"A what?"

"I think it's in my pocket. And it's a legit press pass. Well, almost, anyway. Class ends next week, though, and I really need to finish this up. And with the stuff I've already got, and after tonight, I'm pretty sure this will get me an A." Pen jabbered on, eyes wide and innocent. But there was a hint of something like satisfaction or cynicism tickling the corners of her mouth.

"I don't think that's the way a press pass works," Debbie said, nose wrinkled. The barrel of the gun was beginning to droop, and she looked as though she'd like to scratch her head.

"I can show you the pass if you want to see it," Pen said. She started to lower her hands.

"Keep your hands up, Pen," I cut in, "and keep your gun up, Debbie. Don't let her stun you with her twaddle. Of course that's not the way a press pass works. You must think we're a couple of idiots, Pen. Talk about insulting. And where's your buddy? Where's Sylvia? I thought you were working on this project together. Are you two splitting the research or are you cutting her out of your scoop?"

That's when I wondered about the flashlight. The bobbing, probing light that had alerted me to her presence. Where was it? Not in her hand. Not next to the camera on the island. It sure wasn't tucked into the waistband of her snug black superspy pants.

"Where's the flashlight, Pen?"

Pen didn't answer any of my questions. She didn't move or shift her weight. There was no infinitesimal flick of her eyes to the area of floor we couldn't see behind the nice, solid, four-foot-wide, six-foot-long work island. Pen stood still, her face blank. And she was quiet. Too quiet.

"Oh, for heaven's sake," I said, figuring out what was going on and instantly furious. "You have got to be kidding me. Nice try, Sylvia."

"You mean there's another one here?" Debbie asked.

"Yes," I spat, and I stormed around the end of the island knowing I'd find Sylvia crouched behind it. Probably in a matching head-to-toe snoop suit. And probably with a voice-activated snooper spy recorder. She'd be smiling at me cordially on the outside and snickering on the inside. "Darn it!"

"Where?" Debbie asked.

Nowhere.

"Darn, I was sure she'd be here." But as hard as I stared at the floor behind the island, Sylvia wasn't there. Double darn. When would I learn that my instincts for surprising people red-handed were pitiful? Although . . . although there was a double-door cupboard on that side of the island. "Aha!" I yanked the doors open—and terrified an entire stack of enamel pots and another of plastic tubs.

"I could've told you no one would fit in there," Debbie said over my shoulder.

"I was so sure," I muttered. "Whoa, wait a second. What are you doing over here? Where's . . . darn it!"

We were victims of my own misdirection. Debbie had followed me around the island and now Pen was gone.

So was the camera. Debbie looked at me, spirits sinking and shotgun drooping. She swore more colorfully than I had and started for the door.

"Don't bother, Debbie. We won't find her in the dark."

She swore again.

"But I *did* see a flashlight," I said. "So where is it?"

"At this point, who cares? It was probably something like this, though." Debbie pulled her key ring from a pocket and I walked over to see something no bigger than one of her keys. "She probably tucked it in a pocket or up her sleeve."

"The light I saw was bigger than that." By then we were both sounding petulant.

"This is brighter than you think. Here." She flipped the overhead lights off. "See? All you do is squeeze it. It's plenty bright. You could sneak around anywhere with one of these."

She flashed the light toward the window in the end wall, then lit up the stove and sink along the back wall and played it over the island. I was about to grumble agreement when the hair on the back of my neck prickled and I was aware of movement in the dark near the open door behind us.

"Hands where I can see them, and freeze!"

Debbie's micro flashlight, while adequate for the casual cat burglar, was nothing compared to the industrial explosion of light Deputy Dunbar blasted into our eyes. I knew it was Clod behind that nuclear torch only because I recognized his barked order. He'd barked it at me another time when it also hadn't been necessary. To be fair, he was doing his cop thing, following his stiffly starched cop training. To *me*, his adherence to cop procedure cemented my opinion of him as a knee-jerk clod.

My eyes were still dazzled, so I couldn't see the look

on his face when he realized whom he'd bagged, but I did expect to hear some sort of swallowed oath or at least a groan when he recognized us. I didn't. I also expected him to quit shining the light in our eyes and he didn't do that either. He drilled the blazing beams farther in. I screwed my eyes shut and put my left hand on the island because my head was starting to swim.

"Deputy, for God's sake, will you take that light out of our eyes? Please?" I refused to cringe in front of Clod, but I might have been whining by then.

A voice fortified with honeysuckle offered respite. "Turn your back to him, hon, and the light won't be in your eyes anymore."

"Oh yeah, good thinking, Ardis."

"Don't move," Clod snapped.

"Sorry, too late." I made the mistake of looking at him over my shoulder and received another blast of light.

"Put that flashlight down, Cole Dunbar," Ardis said. "Can't you see these girls aren't who you're after? Here, give that thing to me."

I heard a scuffle, a grunt, an indignant "well," and a low growl. The grunt was Clod and the "well" had to be Ardis. The growl sounded like Bill, the border collie, giving his opinion of Clod. I agreed with him. Someone was smart enough to flip on the overhead lights. I turned around. Ardis stood with one hand on the switch and the other behind her back. She scowled at Clod. Clod was not a healthy shade of any natural color.

"Hey, Bill," Debbie said. A happy tail whapped my shins. "How did Ardis get past you, huh, big boy? How'd you let that happen?" She still had the shotgun in the crook of her arm as she bent to rub his ears.

"I believe I was a dog whisperer in a previous life," Ardis said. Her face softened as she watched Debbie with Bill. "It just took finding the right words and the right tone of voice and then we got on like a house on fire."

An ear-piercing whistle popped our little bubble of pleasantries.

"Stop talking. All of you," Clod said. "Stop. No talking. No moving. Ms. Buchanan, return my flashlight." He held out his hand.

"Do not turn it back on," Ardis said. She looked down her nose at him and made him nod before she brought the flashlight from behind her back and handed it over.

"Ms. Keith," Clod said, turning to her. "You will slowly and carefully put that shotgun on the floor and step away from it."

"Best do as he says, hon," Ardis said. "No telling how long we'll be here otherwise."

Debbie shrugged. "It's not even loaded."

"It's not?" I said. "Yow. We came out here with a gun that wasn't loaded? We jumped in here and accosted a person or persons unknown with our bare hands and an empty shotgun?"

"Well, really, you're the one who did the jumping," Debbie pointed out fairly enough, "and you seemed to know what you were doing, so I just went with it. But you"—she turned on Clod—"what took you so long getting here? We had the prowler cornered and she got away. Oh, sorry." She'd inadvertently pointed the shotgun, still in the crook of her arm, at Clod. "I'm sorry. I'm putting it down. It's down. There. And now I'm being quiet." She backed away from the shotgun and folded her hands. "There."

Clod stood, eyes closed, pinching the bridge of his nose between a thumb and index finger. That wouldn't be part of his meticulous cop training, but it seemed to help him cope. Ardis started to say something. Feeling uncharacteristically kindly toward Clod, I shushed her with a finger to my lips.

"So the prowler got away." Clod opened his eyes and gave me a sour look. "Considering Ms. Rutledge is involved, that sounds about right."

"Hey!"

"Hey, yourself, Ms. Rutledge."

"I wasn't saying hello."

"No, but it's always a pleasure running into you in the course of an official inquiry. Your involvement generally saves me time. There's less chance of there being an actual perpetrator and quite often no facts to sift through. That means there isn't so much to put in a report and I can go home early. I like that."

"You are such a negative person. You need to work on that. And for your information, I know who the prowler was. Her name is Penelope Ledford. Hair to the middle of her back, straight and dark. Tall. About like this." I held my hand above my head. "Slim. Late twenties to early thirties. Dark eyes. She's taking a journalism class at a community college in Asheville. It's the same class an older woman named Sylvia Furches is taking and I bet her car was parked out there on the side of the road just before the curve. So there." That last part slipped out, but I meant it, so I let it lay.

"And what was she doing?" Clod didn't show he was impressed by my recitation, but he looked less pained and more cop-like.

"Sneaking around in here with a flashlight," Debbie said. "Kath saw the light from the house."

"Do you keep this place locked?"

"Always. Door and windows both. Unless I'm in here."

"Who has keys?"

"I've got mine right here." She pulled out the key ring with the tiny flashlight and separated out a door key and held it up.

Clod nodded and sidestepped Ardis to study the door and frame.

"What about your neighbor across the river?" I asked when Debbie jammed the keys back in her pocket and didn't say anything else. "Remember? You said she was going to drop off the spare when we were locked out on Monday. And, oh, gosh, in all the confusion, maybe she left it for you, but you forgot to look for it, and then Pen found it."

I joined Clod at the door. "I don't see any gouges or scratches, so it probably wasn't jimmied. So maybe she did have the key. Unless she had lockpicks. Or can you really open a door like this by slipping a credit card in there? I've always wanted to try that. Would you be able to tell if someone did that? Is that officially called loiding, or is that only in books? But you know, Debbie"—I turned back to her—"if Pen found the key and she still has it, you should probably get your locks changed." Maybe I was overexcited. I wasn't usually such a chatterbox. I moved back and stood next to Ardis. She patted my shoulder and mouthed, "Good job."

"Thank you," Clod said. Whether he was thanking me for offering my insights or for closing my mouth and stepping out of the way, I couldn't tell.

"Adrenaline," I said, feeling compelled to apologize. "Caffeine and sugar, too. Too much cake and tea too late in the day. Mind if I run back to the house?"

"If you can wait another minute or two, I'd like to clear up a couple of quick things and then we can all be on our way," Clod said.

"Hmm. Okay."

"Ms. Keith," he said, turning to Debbie, "I take it you did find the spare key? And you let yourself in and retrieved the keys now in your pocket?"

"Yes."

"Did you return the spare key to your neighbor?"

"Um."

"You didn't. You found a hiding place for it here."

She nodded.

"If it's gone, Ms. Rutledge is right and you should get your locks changed. Do you know what this woman was looking for?"

Debbie shrugged and bent to rub Bill's ears. I was willing to give her the benefit of the doubt and say she was tired or depressed by then, or overwhelmed, but if I'd had training in police interview techniques, I might have thought she was hiding something. I looked at Clod. He watched her, his head tilted very slightly. If I'd had training in Clod interpretation techniques, I would have said he thought she was hiding something, too.

"Ms. Keith? Any ideas?"

Debbie straightened and looked Clod in the eye. "No."

I wanted to jump in at that point and ask Clod if *he* had any ideas. I wanted to find out what the two of them had discussed in the study. And I wanted to know why Debbie's attitude toward Clod had changed. Why was she looking at him like a sheepdog facing down a threat instead of like a mooncalf the way she had earlier in the week?

Lucky me, though. I didn't need to ask about their conversation in the study because I had my secret weapon. My personal surveillance system—my fly on the wall in the form of a nosy ghost in the attic—would fill me in later.

Clod studied the three of us, settling his gaze on me. I

did my best to keep any secret smiles concerning secret surveillance systems off my face. Also not to stare at the twitch he seemed to have developed around his left eye. He started to open his mouth, maybe to finish clearing up his couple of things by asking me another question or two. But he'd missed his chance to be quick—I was almost beyond desperate. I shoved him aside and scampered for the house.

Chapter 17

Ernestine, Thea, and Mel all called me that night. Each was anxious for a report on our visit with Debbie, though each expressed a different reason for her concern. Ernestine worried that Debbie had no ready shoulder to cry on if she was still upset and needed one. She also wondered if we'd found out what exactly had prompted Debbie's tears that afternoon.

"Was it because of the last few questions you wrote on the whiteboard, do you think? Or was she already crying when she came banging into the room? That's one of those details my sorry old eyes miss."

"I think she was already upset. I don't know if she was already crying."

"You should write everything down that happened tonight," Ernestine said. "Any new questions, too."

Wise Ernestine. When Thea called, I'd located a mostly empty spiral notebook and was absorbed in re-creating a timeline of the events since we'd walked out into that field. I could transfer everything to my laptop later, but for now I liked the idea of using one of Granny's notebooks the way she had to keep track of ideas and to map out a project. Thea's interruption was brief. She said she wanted to be sure Debbie wasn't angry with any of us, that she didn't want the equilibrium of Friday Fast and Furious disturbed, or the pleasant atmosphere in the shop.

"I know what a feud can do to an organization," she said. "You might as well take a piece of muslin in both your hands and give it a good rip."

"She was angry when Ardis and I left her, but at Pen Ledford, not us. Maybe at Deputy Dunbar, too."

"Okay. Good."

After I hung up, I found myself chewing on the end of my pencil and wondering if I was right about the focus of Debbie's anger. Pencil chewing was an old cogitating habit I didn't like and thought I'd broken myself of during the last semester of graduate school. Maybe I just hadn't done much deep thinking since then. I wiped the pencil—then went and washed it; then I made a few notes about anger and Pen Ledford.

It was getting late by the time Mel called. She said she'd woken up and couldn't resettle until she knew how the tunnel of fudge cake turned out.

"You should be arrested for supplying stuff like that," I said. "It was the only thing besides her dog that made Debbie smile."

"That's all I need to know, then."

"You don't want to hear about the rest of the evening?"

"No need. Not if you all were able to eat, enjoy, and remember the cake. Where cake trumps, hope lives. I'll hear the rest tomorrow." Mel disappeared into a yawn and disconnected. I suddenly wished I had another piece of that cake.

Deputy Dunbar had essentially sent us packing, holding a stare-down with Ardis until she finally blinked. She'd slammed her way back into my poor old car to show him how she felt. He'd waited and watched until we drove away, as though he didn't trust us to leave. Why that mattered so much to him I couldn't imagine. Debbie had stood next to Dunbar, unsmiling. But she'd thanked us for coming and she'd said, "See you at the Cat tomorrow."

Sweet Ernestine called with one last question while I was brushing my teeth. "Tell me honestly what you think, Kath. With all the burglars and murderers running around loose out there at the farm, don't you think it might be a good idea for me to drive on out so Debbie has someone to keep her company overnight? Really, it wouldn't be any trouble."

"That is so thoughtful, Ernestine." I was glad I didn't have to try to lie. It *was* thoughtful. It just wasn't in the best interests of anyone else on the road. "Deputy Dunbar was going to arrange for Debbie's cousin to go out there again. The one who's also a deputy."

"That's all right, then," Ernestine said.

"I think so." Besides, she had Bill and her shotgun. Maybe she'd loaded it after Clod left.

My brain certainly felt loaded. Overloaded. Between the excitement at Debbie's, the string of debriefing phone calls, the bucket of tea that I'd consumed too late in the day, and my tendency to analyze, guess, overanalyze, and second-guess any given situation, it wasn't a night made for restful sleep. Burying my head under my pillow didn't fool any of my demons, either. Problems and possibilities paraded back and forth between my ears. Solutions posed themselves, then immediately prompted more questions, and then those questions turned around and flipped every solution on its head.

Sometime around four I woke with a start, surprised I'd been asleep at all. Nothing going on in my head at that point made any sense, and I knew I must have been dreaming and fallen into a nightmare. I dragged myself out of bed and went to find the notebook and try to pull my snarled thoughts into some kind of order. The notebook was on the kitchen table where I'd left it, and I sat down there to capture on paper the loose ends of three particular thoughts—three actions, three possible lines of inquiry the posse could take.

But the atmosphere in the kitchen—the early hour, the pool of dim light spilling in from the dining room giving me just enough to read or write by—the scene only needed . . . I got up and tossed a few ice cubes in a tumbler, splashed in a couple of fingers of water from the faucet, and sat back down. Put my feet up on the table, tilted the chair on its back legs. I was slaphappy by then and had no trouble picturing a trench coat instead of my pajamas and a slug of whiskey in place of the water. If only I knew the right private eye lingo and had a fedora riding low on my forehead. At least I had the dame part covered. There were plenty of dames in the picture . . . but my mind was wandering. Focus, focus, focus. There were three things to write in the notebook.

One: Find out more about Eric Lyle, Pen, and her pal Sylvia. It would take some digging and a few phone calls. It was a job for someone with research skills and ready resources—it was a job for Thea the Loud Librarian. Good. She'd love it.

Two: There was bound to be more gossip buzzing around out there about Will and Shannon. We'd heard some at the Weaver's Cat and should listen for more, but Mel's café might as well be dubbed the crossroads of Blue Plum. She saw and talked to—and overheard—a broad cross section of people. She could be our eyes and ears. Good. She'd love it.

And the historical trust potluck. How could I forget that? I'd never been to one, but from what Granny used to say, I could expect hot dishes, hot gossip, and hot tempers. Apparently members of the trust—civic-minded souls devoted to preserving Blue Plum's history and promoting its future—weren't always in accord. Even over simple decisions like choosing what color hollyhocks to plant behind the courthouse. Granny had considered the annual meeting one of the social and entertainment highlights of the year. Good. Who wouldn't love that?

What number was I up to?

Four: Debrief Geneva. We needed to know what Debbie and Clod had talked about. It was something that upset her enough that she ran from the study. She'd also stopped gazing at Clod with moony eyes and telling me he was cute or funny, but that was a development that might be good, bad, or merely coincidental because she'd come to her senses, as anyone might who knew and spent any amount of time with Clod.

So where did that leave us? We'd soothed Debbie with the tunnel of fudge, but the full frontal assault we'd planned hadn't happened because of Pen. How annoying. So was that a waste of a good assault cake? Or would the soothing effect linger and could Ardis and I just come right out and ask Debbie what was going on, ask her if she was holding something back, if something had changed since she'd asked me to investigate? After all, we did work together. We were friends. And open, honest communication should be the way to confront problems among friends. If there were problems. And if one didn't have a ghost up one's sleeve. If . . . But . . .

But the pencil and paper had done their jobs. I was nodding off. The numbered list before me was like a blanket thrown over the smoldering remains of my nightmare. I could go back to bed. A plan was in place. Action and forward movement could continue.

Except . . . a blanket on a smoldering fire? Was that really such a good idea? A blanket could smoke, catch fire, combust . . .

With that disturbing picture in my head, I was almost afraid to crawl back into bed. I did anyway and gave myself up to sleep and dreamed of a wet blanket in the shape of a damp, dismal ghost wearing a fedora.

The alarm rang a few hours later, too soon for my sleep-deprived brain, but the sunshine let me shrug off my lingering worries. After tucking a bowl of oatmeal under my belt—Granny's opening salvo guaranteed to invigorate any morning—I took a brisk walk up and down several hills, then headed for the Cat to start the day, set my plans in motion, and find out what Geneva had heard.

Only to discover my personal surveillance system was on the fritz. My ghost was ailing.

Chapter 18

I wasn't sure a ghost *could* take ill, but Geneva definitely was not her normal miserable self. When I ran up the back stairs to drop my purse in the study before opening the shop for the day, she was crouched in the window seat, just as she'd been the previous afternoon. She didn't answer when I said hi. She was unmoving and unmoaning.

"Look what I made, Geneva." I held up the chain of paper ghosts I'd cut. I'd taken a pencil and given them round eyes and mouths like cartoon ghosts.

She didn't say anything or make any kind of noise, pitiful or dismissive or otherwise. Even a shriek or a wail would have been a heartening improvement. But there was no riffle in her foggy shape to show she'd even looked. I stood the paper ghosts on the desk. Maybe she'd catch sight of them later.

I hadn't known her for many months, but I thought I'd experienced her full range of moods and moping. She'd sniveled and cried, complained and gone into silly snits, blustered and stormed. She'd disappeared for a few days at one point and I'd been surprised by how much I missed her. But even then she'd reappeared, doing what I took to be a Greta Garbo imitation by saying she'd only wanted to be alone. She didn't do a good Garbo, but at least she'd come back. This bleak frame of mind she'd slipped into was different and it worried me.

"We had kind of an exciting thing happen last night," I said. "Debbie and I caught a prowler out at her place."

No flicker of interest.

"It was one of those two women who were in the shop that morning the twins came in with Angela—the morning of the Unfortunate Incident of the Twin Pencil Skirts. Do you remember?"

No snort of laughter or derision. No comment about broad beams.

"In fact, the twins followed those two out of the shop." Rats, I should talk to Shirley and Mercy. Find out what they'd seen or heard. I couldn't bring myself to make a note of that, though. Besides, if I asked, then they'd know I was interested in Pen and Sylvia, and somehow that didn't seem like a good idea. They had a knack for collecting information. It was getting the information back out of them in one piece that was the trick. That and keeping personal information out of their reach in the first place. Generally speaking, the less the twins knew or were involved in my business, the better I liked it.

I could ask one of the posse to tackle the Spiveys. But in my professional life I'd never liked passing off the nastier preservation problems to colleagues if I wasn't willing to poke around at them myself. Besides, anyone else asking the Spiveys anything about Sylvia and Pen would start questions turning in the Spivey collective mind and might put them on to the fact that there *was* a posse—inklings of which they already had. If its existence was confirmed, they would want to join—by hook or by crook or conniving. And that was out of the question.

So on to the question I really wanted to ask. "Geneva, I've been dying to know . . ." That was unfortunate phrasing, but she didn't react so I stumbled on. "When

Deputy Dunbar and Debbie were up here yesterday afternoon, after I left and he shut the door, what did they talk about? Was he asking her questions or did he tell her something that upset her?"

No answer.

"Because I think it was something significant. A *vital clue*." Adding a touch of melodrama couldn't hurt. "And think about it—if you tell me what you heard, you might be the one who cracks the case. You'll be Geneva the Ace Detective." I framed those words with my hands and held them up so she could admire her accomplishment.

Nothing. But was there nothing because she couldn't remember or because she'd sunken into a virtually catatonic state?

Speaking of cats—the cat came into the study, having enjoyed the breakfast I'd tipped into his bowl in the kitchen. He brushed against my leg, then jumped to the corner of the desk nearest the window seat and blinked at me. He turned and blinked at Geneva, then tucked himself into a handsome meatloaf shape and started his motor. Geneva gave no sign she knew he was there. Then I did something against my better judgment.

"Sergeant Friday," I said, addressing the cat, but at the same time checking for a reaction from Geneva out of the corner of my eye. There wasn't any. "I hope you know I really don't want to call you Sergeant Friday. Or Dirty Harry." The cat continued to purr and lifted his chin for me to rub. He didn't care what I called him. Geneva remained a statue. "Friday, you seem comfortable enough with ghosts. What do you know about them? What does it mean when one is here but not here at the same time? That sounds like a riddle, doesn't it? I don't like riddles, Friday. They make me anxious. I'm worried about our friend here."

The cat tipped his head and looked at me with half-closed eyes.

"Okay," I admitted. "You're right. I'm anxious and I'm worried and I'm also edging toward angry for no good reason I can think of. But how am I supposed to figure out what's wrong if she won't talk to me?"

There was no change in Geneva. The cat went on purring. His purr was a wonderful noise I still marveled to hear after all the years of being hissed at or ignored by Granny's cats. Unfortunately, although the text of his purr sounded warm and fuzzy, it was wordless and unenlightening. Cats and ghosts. Two of a kind. There was no counting on either one of them to solve my problems for me.

"Well," I said, trying not to let all the miff and concern I felt color that one word, "time to open the shop. You're both welcome to come along if you want. Otherwise I'll be downstairs if you need me." No reaction from Geneva. I sighed. "Okay. I'll see you later."

The cat blinked, possibly thinking I'd left off rubbing his chin too soon. But he took my dereliction with his usual grace, deciding the interruption was a good time to relocate for a cozier nap on the cushion in the window seat. He yawned and stood, then shivered his tail and made the leap. At the last minute his tail flicked the chain of paper ghosts. The ghosts tipped and fell so they lay on their backs, their blank eyes staring up at the ceiling.

Seeing their penciled-in eyes and mouths, both round with surprise, jogged a memory. What was it Geneva had said when she'd described the bodies she remembered? *Their eyes staring up into the sky as though they look beyond the passing clouds and all the way to heaven.*

I glanced over at Geneva and jumped. When had she lifted her head to look at me? *Her* blank eyes stared into mine—eyes so bleak and hollow it felt as though they looked past my confused thinking and cloudy emotions and all the way to my unnerved core.

"Geneva? *What?* What is it? What's wrong? What can I do?"

Nothing but her stare. Frustrating, creepy ghost.

Why was she even sitting there in the window seat? Why didn't she moan and disappear? Billow and then vanish until she worked through whatever griped her? Fade away and stay away until her trouble drifted out of her shadowy memory and she could complain that she had no idea what I was nagging her about if I tried to remind her? Obviously there was still a lot I didn't understand about the care and feelings of ghosts.

But in peering more closely at her, in my own cringing way, I realized there wasn't anything in her stare that felt menacing. There wasn't any threat in her dejected posture. And she *did* remain visible. She was there, damp and depleted, looking at me. And that gave me a small measure of hope—a ghost of a hope.

I almost snorted at that thought, but I wasn't feeling *that* comfortable with her behavior. Plus I didn't want her to think I was laughing at her. Maybe it was her natural inclination to keen and wail over the troubles paralyzing her, but she was holding herself in for my sake. Maybe this was her way of asking for help. And if all of this had to do with her horrific memories of that earlier murder-suicide, then there *was* something I could try to do to help.

"Okay, tell you what." I packed as much positive, upbeat, "altogether now, we can do it" into those words as I could muster. "It's Saturday, so the shop will be busy, but if I can get away for a break, I'm going to run over to the library, do some research. Cat, I'm sure you'll think you need another nap by then, but Geneva, um . . ." My upbeat faltered. I knew I might regret this later, but I made myself smile and pressed on. "Geneva, if you want to come with me, you can."

Chapter 19

Ardis and Joe Dunbar arrived simultaneously not long after I had the shop up and running for the day. Ardis came in the back singing, "Oh, What a Beautiful Mornin'." Joe came in the front door with two steaming take-away cups in his hands and a newspaper tucked under his arm.

"It is," Joe said, agreeing with Ardis when she'd flung her arms out on the last note. "I was over in Unicoi and watched the sunrise from up on top of Beauty Spot."

"And I watched it with my eyes closed from under my pillow with the shades drawn," Ardis said. "Sleeping late is a beautiful way to start any day. I didn't get where I am by traipsing all the way to Unicoi to watch the sunrise. What were you doing over there?"

"Bit of this and that. Here, I thought you two might like coffee." He handed us each a cup.

"You're a doll," Ardis said. "I slept so late I didn't have time to make any. You're sure you don't mind?"

"That's why I brought them."

"You're a very sweet liar, too. I know you brought one of these for Kath and the other for yourself."

I could feel her looking at me out of the corner of her eye, wondering how much an offered cup of coffee might mean. She could wonder all she liked. I might wonder, too, and for all I knew, so might Joe. I'd never given him any particular encouragement toward anything beyond a getting-to-know-you-type friendship. That murky baggage thing was taking some getting used to.

"Be a dear, though," Ardis said, holding her cup under her nose and closing her eyes, "and when you run back to Mel's for your own cup, see if she has any cheese bagels and bring me one?" She took a noisy sip. "Mmm, straight to my caffeine tooth."

"Bagel for you?" Joe asked, looking my way.

"No, the coffee's fine. Thanks."

"Back in a few, then. I'll just leave this here." He took the paper from under his arm and set it on the corner of the counter.

Ardis opened her eyes when she heard the camel bells signal he'd left. "I don't really need the bagel, but I wanted a chance to talk to you in private first. Now that you've slept on it, what's your take on all of that out there at Debbie's place last night?"

Right then I was more interested in the newspaper Joe had so casually left on the counter. Too casually? Why bother to leave it? Was it suddenly too cumbersome to carry around with another cup of coffee and a bagel? Hmm. Two could play at casual. I pulled the paper toward me. It was the *Asheville Citizen*. Not one I usually read.

"I think we need to find out where the other journalist was," Ardis was saying. "Whatever she was up to might be more ominous than what the one we caught was doing. Whatever *that* was. It might be like that Sherlock Holmes case about the dog that didn't bark. I think her absence from the scene of last night's crime means something sinister. Are you listening?"

"Halfway." I was also leafing through Joe's paper, but I interrupted that and told her about my middle-of-the-night brainstorming. "I wrote down a few notes and some questions it would be good to follow up on. I'll add yours. Do you think Mel and Thea will mind if I ask them to do a few things?"

"You mean *assignments*?" Ardis asked.

"We can call them that if you want." She'd made "assignments" sound exotic and dangerous. Also possibly foolish. I hoped I wasn't getting anyone into anything we'd regret.

"I most certainly do want to call them assignments," Ardis said, almost licking her lips. "And you should, too. Hon, if you don't mind a little constructive criticism, move beyond the 'might be' and 'maybe.' You passed that stage days ago."

"You could be right."

"I *am* right. And when you give out the *assignments*, don't leave out Ernestine. You know she'll want one, too. And Debbie. They all want to contribute. Can you e-mail their assignments to them? Or text them! I don't have one of those fancy phones, but now I really think I should get one. Instant communication. Instant answers. Tiny camera. Video! The only thing they're missing these days is phasers you can set to stun. And wouldn't *that* be useful. Then again, maybe you should speak to everyone in person. That might be safer. What do you think?"

She didn't wait to hear what I thought. She was in high-excitement mode. "And what's *my* assignment? Wait—I know—my assignment *is* Debbie. Perfect. We did well last night and she'll be here for her shift this afternoon; you can count on that. But . . ."

Her hands flew, carving out the scenario playing in her mind. It was a good demonstration of why she wasn't just a favorite player at the Blue Plum Repertory Theater, but was also the permanent, much-valued volunteer director. While she elaborated on her plan, I scanned the business section of Joe's paper.

"... But I should see if I can get Debbie to tell me what she's holding back from us. Don't you get the feeling there *is* something? Well, and it's not just a feeling. I *know* there's something. And I know she'll feel better once she gets it off her chest. I need to be gentle, though. That's paramount. And don't you love that word? Paramount. It reminds me of all those Hitchcock thrillers. But I will be gentle; I promise you that."

"Sounds perfect," I said, flipping through the sports section. "You'll be all honeysuckle and kid gloves. Resistance will be futile."

"Exactly. What have you got for the others to work on?"

"Listening in on gossip. Looking for information about the wannabe journalists. I don't know, though. That all sounded good in the middle of the night. It's kind of lame in the light of day."

"Gussy it up, then. It's all in the makeup and costuming. If you call it surveillance and research, you aren't gossiping and being nosy; you're skillfully employing tools of the information-gathering trade. See what I mean? From lame to legitimate in one easy vocabulary lesson. So then, besides operating Brain Central and analyzing our findings, what will *you* be doing?"

"Hmm? Oh, I guess I'll go ahead and text the others."

"Good. Get the ball rolling."

"And I thought I'd go to the library over lunch. I've got some other, uh, research to do."

"Hush-hush?"

"Mm-hmm."

"Good. Mum's the word on my end and I'll tackle Debbie while you're gone. That way it won't look like we're ganging up on her."

"Good plan. I think you're right; there's something going on with her ..." I didn't want to be more specific than "something." More specific was moving in the direction of "suspicious." And beyond "suspicious" lay "suspect" and I really didn't want my mind traveling that far. I continued flipping through the paper, flipping past my increasingly uneasy specifics . . . "Yeah, it'd be great if you can get Debbie to . . . hold on a sec." Hah! I *knew* I'd find something in that paper. There was a two-page spread in the features section, complete with color photographs. "Oh my goodness. This is . . . I'm not sure what this is." I couldn't help smiling, though.

Ardis was about to snatch the paper from me when Joe came back sipping another coffee and carrying a bag big enough to hold half a dozen bagels. He saw me with the paper and caught my smile. Ardis caught his *and* mine and she smelled conspiracy.

"What are you two in cahoots over?"

"Nothing," I said, letting her take the paper. "It's the first I've seen or heard of it."

Her glance went to the photographs, then to the headline.

" 'Where There's a Will'? Oh good Lord." She groped for the stool beside her so she could sit and read the article more carefully.

The piece was part interview, part travelogue, featuring a guy I'd run into a time or two named Aaron Carlin. Carlin wasn't just an example of local color; he was saturated in it. I'd never seen him without a smile or an offer to help. I don't think Ardis had ever actually met him, but she knew his family's reputation for being an antisocial backwoods clan with a history of starting fires. She was not a fan of the Smokin' Smoky Carlins.

In the article, Aaron claimed to know the locations of the various hidden caves and hollows where Will Embree had lived in the national forest—knew them because, he said, he'd been Will's personal backcountry guide and led him to them. The photographs showed Aaron in various atmospheric locations—surrounded by the dense foliage of a rhododendron hell, standing at the beginning of a passage between two towering, moss-covered boulders, walking along a narrow trail, and pointing out a dubious dark opening at the base of a shadowed bluff.

"Is this so-called piece of journalism the work of those two women?" Ardis asked. "Maybe that's what the second one was up to last night. Talking to a ne'er-do-well and tapping out useless drivel on her keyboard while her partner was snooping."

"No, I don't think it's them," I said. "Not unless they're using the pen name Carson Otterbank. Check the byline. That can't be a real name, can it?" I looked at Joe.

He shrugged. "I've heard worse."

Oops, he had, poor guy. Ardis had told me "Joe" was a name he gave himself sometime during his school years to get away from the shudder-inducing name his academic parents had given him. There were a few people around town, Ardis among them, who still called him Ten—short for Tennyson, full name Tennyson Yeats Dunbar—but not many could get away with it. His brother, Clod, also had a hefty name to contend with, but he'd fared better. Cole—short for Coleridge—wasn't such a bad name, and Blake as a middle name was doable. But there wasn't much anyone could do with either Tennyson or Yeats. Poor guy.

"Good Lord," Ardis repeated. "Whyever would the editors think it was a good idea to interview a Smokin' Smoky Carlin? And you two think this is funny?"

"Not funny, but kind of fun," I said. "Interesting, anyway, after you've met the guy. It's a human interest story," I said.

"Mm-hmm. If ever there was one."

From my quick perusal of the newspaper article, the reporter, Carson Otterbank—it wasn't clear from the byline or the article whether Otterbank was he, she, or they—had spent several days in Aaron's company, hiking the national forest, following the trail of Will Embree, and hearing stories of Will's two years in the wilderness.

"Tall tales, I don't doubt," Ardis said, folding the paper and handing it back to Joe, "and we can only hope that Bonny doesn't see this or hear about it."

"A man has a right to his own story," Joe said mildly.

"Are you talking about Will Embree or this particular Carlin?" Ardis asked.

"I'd say both of them and everyone else, too, don't you think?" he said.

"And letting each person have his or her own story is part of the reason you're so keen for us to investigate Will and Shannon's deaths," I said. "If you stop and think about it."

She did think about it. Ardis was good that way—willing to look at more than one side and willing to make changes. She thought and she nodded and she put her hands flat on the counter. "You're right again. It surely is part of the reason. And it's why we can't do anything without making an effort to be scrupulously fair-minded. So *I* will make an effort to lay aside my unkind and quite likely biased thoughts about *this* Carlin. No matter how well deserved they might be. Now, Joe, hand me over a bagel and tell me—can you find this Carlin for us?"

The question caught Joe off guard. While Ardis had talked herself through her concession to the possibility that not all Carlins were flaming sociopaths, I'd watched his face. It shifted from interested to questioning to catching on.

"What are *you* two up to?" His voice was drifting toward uneasy.

"Exactly what you think we are," Ardis said. "Nothing more than what's right. And that's exactly what you always try to do, too. You know it and so do I. And we need your help on this. The rest of Fast and Furious are already in."

"Carlin isn't all that easy to find." He opened the bagel bag and held it out for Ardis to choose from.

"Ah, asiago peppercorn. See, you *are* a good man."

He pulled a short stack of paper napkins from his shirt pocket and handed one to her. She lifted a bagel from the bag and laid it in the middle of the napkin on the counter in front of her. It looked like an offering.

"If Carlin is hard to find," she said, folding her hands, face as serene as Buddha's, "then start with something easier, hon. You still have ties to Asheville?"

He gave a minimal nod, a more minimal shrug.

"Good. Find Otterbank."

Chapter 20

I'd never known someone who ambled half so well as Joe Dunbar. There was a lazy grace to his long legs, and ambling off into the morning, the afternoon, the sunset—wherever they went—seemed to be what they did best. His legs might have studied Clint Eastwood Casual at some finishing school for mystery men. True to form, after making no promises, except to see us that night at the potluck, he ambled on out of the Cat. Ardis put a hand on my arm.

"I hope I didn't overstep there, Kath."

"Hmm? Overstep what?"

"Giving him that assignment without consulting you."

"Joe has ties to Asheville? What ties?"

"He lived there for years, hon. He's quite well-known."

Really? So much I didn't know about long, tall, ambling Joe.

"Hon? About sending Joe to find out who this Otterbank person is?"

"Oh, no, don't worry about it. It's not like I really know what I'm doing." Wasn't that the truth.

There was a lot I didn't know that day. For instance, I didn't know what to expect from Debbie when she came in for her shift. She'd been on an adrenaline roller coaster all week—holding it together for the most part, but with an erratic swing or two along the way. Not that I thought I would do any better if I found bodies and burglars and was badgered by boorish Clod Dunbar.

On the other hand, it wasn't as though Debbie had gone through those experiences alone; I'd been there, too. And I had been alone when I interrupted a burglar not so many months before and when I'd found a body. I hadn't had anyone to share the screams and heart-thumping horror with. Although maybe in comparing our reactions I was feeling a tad juvenile just now. And really, I hadn't been all alone. I'd had Geneva. But I could honestly say that discovering *her* was a horror that I shared with no one else. Period. But as soon as that thought said "boo" in my head, I tried to erase it. Geneva was histrionic and somewhat annoying and not entirely without creep factor, but her existence was complicated and she wasn't truly a horror. She was a ghost and she couldn't help that.

Debbie was subdued when she did arrive shortly before noon, and she looked about as tired as I felt. She had on one of her long skirts and a lightweight sweater in a pretty soft yellow. I looked down at my blue chambray tucked into my khakis and felt ordinary and uninspired.

"You look as pretty as sunshine, hon," Ardis told her. "But that was some storm we had out at your place last night, wasn't it?"

Debbie's response was curt and corrective. "It didn't rain."

"Well, no, hon, it didn't."

"Then maybe I misunderstood. I thought you said it stormed." Debbie's eyes were wide and bright. The snap to her words and set of her chin gave her away, though, and I decided I wasn't patient enough to stick around playing games of disingenuous misunderstanding.

"Now that you're here, Debbie, I'm going to dash over to the library," I said, thankful for Ardis' brilliant plan to let me disappear while she gently wrestled out of Debbie whatever it was she was hiding. If Debbie was going to be prickly or snarky, I liked that plan better and better. "I'm glad to see you're no worse for the wear after last night, storm or no storm." Another good plan would be to avoid confrontational or glib exit lines.

Debbie's eyes went from wide and willful to blazing. She checked for customers browsing too close and leaned in with a harsh whisper. "Why didn't you tell me about that woman and her friend snooping around here? You should have warned me. What else do you know that you aren't you telling me? And what have you told the others that you haven't told me?"

It would have been easy to throw her hissy fit back at her and ask what she was keeping from us, but I stuck to the plan. Ardis was definitely better suited for handling those questions and this flare of temperament, and we didn't need the public drama and trauma of a major blowup in the store. Besides, I had enough of that in my private and paranormal life with Geneva the diva.

I raised a placating hand and shook my head. "Nothing. There's nothing, Debbie."

"I asked you to find out what happened. I didn't ask you to turn me into the number one suspect!"

Debbie's voice was still low, but a few heads were turning by now. One woman, with studied nonchalance, moved closer. Ardis took over.

"Fiddlesticks, hon," she said, putting her arm around Debbie. "Kath isn't keeping anything from you or anyone, except maybe Cole Dunbar, but that only makes good sense. And don't you know by now that Kath isn't about anything if she isn't about good sense? Why, she spent the wee hours of this morning turning the wheels in her head and she's got a plan and assignments for all of us in the posse so we can help. Kath, honey," she said, turning to me, "before you run off to the library, tell Debbie about the progress you've made and what you'd like her to do this afternoon."

"Oh, well, um . . ." I thought fast and put a finger to my lips, tipping my head toward the closest customer. "Let's hold on to the progress report for now, but Debbie, if you can, I'd like you to keep an ear out in the store . . ."

"Surveil the premises," Ardis cut in. "Take note of everything pertaining."

"Notes, yes, notes would be great and . . ." I tried to gauge Debbie's response. She didn't look impressed by that assignment. "And also, I'd like your impressions of everyone you know or have met who's involved, from Will to Pen Ledford. Write it all down. I want the impressions from you, and I'll get Thea onto facts, and then we'll see what meshes and what doesn't and what we can pick apart. So impressions, okay? Can you do that?"

That assignment did spark an interest, and Debbie turned the last of her vehemence on Pen. "I don't know much about that sorry woman, but I'll bet she knows something. Or she thinks she does, anyway."

"Hon, we all think we know things," Ardis said.

Something else I didn't know that day was if I'd known what I was doing when I invited Geneva to go along with me to the library. Maybe I'd banked on her continued lack of response to anything I said or did. She hadn't acknowledged the invitation when I asked her and still didn't say anything when I ran up to grab my purse. But when I heard the cat trotting down behind me, I looked back and she was drifting down the stairs behind the cat.

They followed me into the front room, he looking

happy and ready for a jaunt, she like a patch of congealed fog. She drifted over to the mannequin near the counter, sinking as she went, until she ended in a pathetic swirl of mist curled around its base. She would have added the perfect touch to the display if the mannequin had been modeling a deerstalker and one of those classic Sherlock Holmes coats with the short cape. Instead it wore an argyle vest in eye-killing shades of orange, magenta, and lime green and also had on a knit cap with giant pom-poms that were supposed to be earmuffs but looked more like mutant raspberries. Ardis had dressed the mannequin in that getup and I'd thought about suggesting a less unusual combination. She knew the business, though, and by noon we'd already sold six copies of the vest pattern and a dozen for the hat.

At the moment Debbie was at the end of the counter, hunched over a legal pad and writing notes at a feverish pace, slashing underlines onto the page here and drilling punctuation marks into it there. Ardis sat on the stool behind the counter, going over invoices and making encouraging noises that sounded more like she was egging her on. The cat watched a pair of teenage girls pawing through the sale bins, each swaying to her own plugged-in music. Geneva, except for her eyes staring at me, looked like a circle of ghostly quilt batting. Couldn't she at least blink?"

"Something wrong down there, Kath?" Ardis asked, her eyes following my scowl to the base of the mannequin.

"What? Oh, no. Just thinking. Isn't there a quote from somewhere about fog and cats?"

"Sheep," Debbie said without looking up. "There's a really depressing poem called 'Sheep in Fog' by Sylvia Plath."

"I'm sure there is, hon," Ardis said, "but I think Kath

is more likely remembering the Carl Sandburg poem. 'The fog comes on / little cat feet. / It sits looking / over harbor and city / on silent haunches / and then moves on.' I made all my students memorize it. You should have read some of the rude parodies they wrote and thought I didn't know they were passing around."

"Will memorized 'Sheep in Fog.'" Debbie dropped her pen onto the legal pad and leaned her elbows on the counter and her chin on her fists. "I hadn't thought about it before, but there was a time when he was really into Sylvia Plath and Anne Sexton. Did you know they both committed suicide? Maybe that was something he always had in the back of his mind."

"And if he did, then there wasn't much you or anyone else could do about it," Ardis said.

Debbie shook her head. "I don't know if I believe that."

"Oh, hon."

Ardis and I each reached a hand to Debbie. Ardis touched her cheek. I put mine on the shoulder of her soft yellow sweater.

"Did you love him?" I asked.

She jerked away from me with an unintelligible noise and looked around—for an escape route, I thought. Then I realized she was looking to see if anyone else in the room had heard my question or her shocked reaction. But the only customers in the front room then were the two teenagers, and they were still at the sale bins, still listening to their personal soundtracks.

"Never mind, never mind," I said in a rush. "Don't pay any attention to me." Where had *that* question come from? Nothing like walking up to an emotionally shaky friend and applying a good old sucker punch straight to the gut. Great interpersonal skills, Kath. "Debbie, I'm sorry."

Except . . . of course I knew where the question came from. It came from my fingertips touching her sweater and that weird transference of emotions . . . the way it had happened when I touched Will and Shannon and the way I'd been zapped by the intense hatred when I touched Bonny. Except this emotion was muddier. There was love, yes, but also . . . ambivalence? Uncertainty? I couldn't tell. But why now? Why, when I hadn't felt Debbie's emotions any of the other times I touched her, did I feel them now? Why did I *ever* feel them? Was it something to do with the types of fibers my fingers touched? Or with the intensity of the emotions involved? I didn't like it and I didn't want to stop and think about it. None of it made sense.

"Forget I said anything, Debbie. Ignore me. You don't have to answer that."

"Yes, I do." With some effort, her voice produced normal sounds again. "Look, I've been upset. I think you can understand that. But I asked you to find out what happened and you need to ask questions and *I* understand that. So I do need to answer. Did I love Will? It doesn't matter. It just doesn't matter. Will loved Shannon. She was the world to him. When she died, his world ended."

I looked at Ardis. She'd been caught off guard by my question, too. Her glance flicked back and forth between Debbie and me, and she looked ready to leap in with another hug if leaping or hugging was needed or could help.

Debbie was calm, though. Her eyes, voice, and hands were steady. Ardis was right about her and I'd seen it for myself. Debbie knew how to take care of herself. She was tougher than she looked or sometimes sounded. She obviously believed in the single-mindedness and finality of Will's love for Shannon. But she hadn't really answered my question, and in fact, it *did* matter whether she'd loved him. Did she really not see that? Didn't she know how suspicion worked? Or lovers' triangles? Or women scorned? Or the pedestrian mind of Clod Dunbar?

And if I were really cut out for the grilling life, maybe I could ask prying and antagonizing questions without tripping over my tongue, turning into a nervous wreck, or turning tail and running.

The cat twined in a circle around my ankles, then looked up and blinked at me with the sweetest smile. It's possible it wasn't really a smile and he was just busy applying another layer of cat fur to my pant legs, but I chose to interpret the combination of actions as meaning, *My friend, you're doing fine. Just go for the smooth and everything else will slide on in to home. You and me, we are the cat's pajamas.* Believing that's what he meant gave me strength.

Then I looked at Ardis and saw Geneva's hollow eyes staring at me from over her right shoulder.

I yipped, which scared the cat. The cat leapt straight up onto the counter, which startled Debbie. Debbie, obviously not as calm as I thought, screamed, which sent Ardis—eyes as wide as Geneva's—into mother-tiger-to-the-rescue mode.

"Did he scratch you?" Ardis demanded. She turned to the cat, hands on her hips. "Did you scratch her? We will have none of that, buster, because if we do, we will have none of you. Is that clear?"

"Mrrrph?" said the cat.

"No, no, it was my fault," I said. "I thought I stepped on him." I leaned down and put my face close to his—a move that would have earned me a stripe across the nose from any of Granny's cats. "Are you okay, sweetie?" I asked. I hadn't known I could make such a goo-goo voice.

He butted his forehead against mine, then flopped on his side with a loud purr.

"Well," Ardis said, "so long as he's clear on that."

The cat turned partially onto his back and waved a paw, inviting her to rub his belly, which she was happy to do. Debbie joined in the reconciliation love fest by smoothing the fur between his ears. It was cat bliss.

"I think Buster is pretty clear on how things are around here," I said.

"Oh my, did I just name him for you?" Ardis asked.

"Ab-so-lute-ly not," Geneva said, enunciating each syllable with ponderous thunder. "I would rather kill myself than call him Buster."

That seemed unnecessarily harsh. "Um, no," I paraphrased, eyeing Geneva uneasily. She still hovered behind Ardis' shoulder. She didn't look any less dismal or droopy, but she was slightly denser and more cohesive, if those were the right words. And pretty cranky. "No, he isn't really a Buster, I don't think. I'll keep working on it. But thanks, anyway, Ardis."

Ardis shivered and pulled her sweater more snuggly around her.

"Can we go now?" Geneva asked. She had all the dampening enthusiasm of a spoiled and bored child.

Chapter 21

"I wasn't sure you'd come with me," I said into my cell phone as we crossed the street toward the courthouse. "I wasn't sure you were ever going to talk to me again. Are you going to be okay out here, though? Do you really think it's a good idea?"

Trying to carry on a conversation along the way probably *wasn't* a good idea considering I still slipped up occasionally. But she *was* with me, and that was an improvement, even if she did turn her hollow eyes toward me with a look that might as well have said, *Don't know. Don't care. Don't want to live.*

"Don't run into that pole—oh . . . oh well." She passed right through a utility pole without a bobble. She certainly didn't hurt the pole. "Do you want to talk about what's bothering you? It might help."

She raised her shoulders and dropped them with a barely audible sigh. If she'd had pockets, her hands would be buried in them and she'd be kicking along the pavement in a dejected hunch.

"Okay, well, you can tell from the way I blundered into that question with Debbie that I'm not the best at touchy-feely emotional stuff. I try, but . . . wait a second. Speaking of touchy-feely, do you know anything about other spoo . . . um, other paranormal stuff?" I was so busy looking at her to see if that sparked any interest that *I* almost walked into the mailbox outside the bank. What a pair we were. The dangerous duo out for a blunder down the sidewalks of Blue Plum.

Some tourist boys dragging behind their tourist parents snickered and I heard one of them say something about not being able to walk and talk at the same time. Geneva wasn't talking anyway, so I decided I might as well put the phone away.

"The library's a few blocks down," I told her. "I'm going to hang up now, but stay close, okay? I don't want to lose you out here." Or anywhere, I realized as I dropped the phone back into my purse.

I was a tad nervous now that we were out in public—open-air public as opposed to the contained public of the Weaver's Cat. Geneva had traveled with me a few times by car between the cottage where we'd met and the shop. And I knew enough not to worry that a sudden gust of wind would carry her vaporous presence away. But before relocating to the Cat she hadn't been *anywhere*, hadn't left that tiny cottage for who knew how long. She certainly didn't know how long she'd been cooped up there. Being housebound or shop-bound for weeks or months—let alone a dozen or so decades—would bore most people to death. Although, come to think of it, maybe that was why the confines of the cottage hadn't bothered Geneva.

The bright morning had turned into an afternoon of gray clouds with only fleeting patches of sunshine, dreary one minute and dazzling the next. Much like Geneva on a more typical day. I wasn't used to seeing her in direct sunlight and the effect was interesting. In the sun she faded to the point where she wasn't much more than a collection of dust motes. But not the sparkling kind of motes that make one think of tiny tinkling fairy bells. Hers were just dust—dull, dusty dust motes. I didn't share that observation with her, though. That would have been about as sensitive as telling Mercy Spivey her roots were showing.

The first time Geneva came into Blue Plum with me, she said she vaguely recognized it. But after wafting into the Cat she hadn't expressed interest in looking any further around town. Walking to the library I thought she might see something familiar, something that would catch her eye or jog a memory. Something that would cheer her up. The exteriors and roof lines of many of the buildings hadn't changed for a hundred or more years, so there was a chance. But she paid no attention to anything we passed. She didn't seem to notice the warm patches of sun. And she didn't seem to care that I'd stopped talking to her. Yet she stayed beside me.

The name of the J.F. Culp Memorial Public Library was almost bigger than the impressive block of limestone J.F.'s family donated for the sign—in the shape of an open book—out front. There were some who thought the sign looked more like a distorted gravestone than a book, but as Granny said, there were also some who wouldn't recognize a book if you hit them upside the head with it.

The library's redbrick exterior was designed to fit into the town's historical streetscape without jarring the eye. It gave the general feeling of bygone architecture without mimicking any particular style or period. The interior was supposed to be cutting-edge, or at least up-to-date. To hear Thea tell it, though, the reality of the functionality fell short. *We've got all the inconveniences of late-twentieth-century shoddy workmanship,* I'd heard her say, *and none of the actual charms of the eighteenth or nineteenth century.*

I held the heavy glass door for Geneva. Needlessly. She drifted through one of the sidelights, stopped in the lobby to stare at the drinking fountain, then drifted through the security gate. In the open area in front of the circulation desk she stopped again and drew in a breath. Or not exactly a breath, but she made a sound of sharp inhalation. The weirdness of a ghost emitting sounds of respiration hardly fazed me anymore.

"How many books are there in this library?" she asked in awe. That something finally shook her out of her doldrums and made her utter anything other than a complaint did faze me—so much so that I answered.

"I don't know. Let's ask Thea."

"Ask me what?" Thea looked up from her computer behind the circulation desk, reading glasses pulled down her nose.

Geneva threw her hands in the air. "Now you've done it. Now the loud one will think you're crazy. Pretend you didn't say anything. I've seen that movie with Marian the Librarian, and these women are territorial around their books. Please don't do anything else to get us kicked out. I don't think I've ever seen so many books in one place and I want to look around."

"Ask me what?" Thea repeated less patiently.

"Answer her. Answer her." Geneva shooed me toward Thea, but I turned and watched as she sailed into the stacks looking as full of herself as the figurehead on a ship. On a ghost ship. Grumbling, bossy thing.

"Kath?"

"Answer her!" came a shriek from somewhere in the biography section.

"Have you got a minute?" I asked, turning back to Thea. "Can I ask you to do some research for me?"

"Where does the minute come into it—in the asking part or in the research?"

"The asking. I don't know how easy the research will be."

"Leave that to the expert. What do you need?"

I looked around to make no sure no one else would hear. I heard Geneva humming her favorite dirge-like tune as she navigated the shelves but otherwise didn't see or hear anyone. I lowered my voice anyway. "Information on a few people?"

"What kind of information?"

"Anything you can find."

She nodded. "It's a slow Saturday afternoon. I'll see what I can do. And let me assure you that my professional scruples and my allegiance to the American Library Association prevent me from asking why you want this information, what you intend to do with it, and from alerting others to your interest without your consent. They also keep me from putting any label other than 'people' on the subjects constituting the focus of your request. In the interest of full disclosure, however, I should tell you that if I have the opportunity to take a short personal break this afternoon, it's possible my mind will wander in the general direction of the word 'suspects.'"

"Which might be a leap, but pinning the words 'of interest' onto the back end of the word 'people' is fair enough."

"Cool. Give me everything you already know, no matter how inconsequential you think it is. You never know what tidbit will provide the point of access to research gold. You'll be at the potluck tonight?"

"Yes."

"Then I'll see you there and bring what I've found. What are you bringing?"

I must have looked blank.

"Sorry, my mind flipped to the Food Channel. What *food* are you bringing?"

"Er . . ." I really was blank on that. I'd put off making

a decision, wondering what one should take to one's first Historical Trust Annual Meeting and Potluck, not wanting to overthink it, hoping for inspiration . . . which finally struck. "I know. I'll swing by Mel's and pick up one of her coconut cream pies." Mmm, Mel's pie. It was a beautiful solution in every sense.

"No, that's no good," Thea said. "That'll be cheating and everyone will know it. Come on, you're Ivy's granddaughter. There are potlucks and there are potlucks, but this is The Potluck. Capital *T*, capital *P*. The least you can do is throw together a green salad. With a honey-mustard dressing or something. And put on a skirt."

"Really?" I should have realized there was such a thing as potluck etiquette. But there should be time after work to make a run to the grocery store out on the highway for fresh spinach. And tomatoes if they looked any good. Maybe an avocado. "I wonder why Ardis didn't clue me in."

"She probably thought you knew or she didn't want to embarrass you. But sure. Green salad will be great. People loved Ivy's salads."

"Huh, okay. I guess I'll do that, then."

"Everyone will be glad to see it. Oh, and I've been meaning to tell you. Some of the TGIFs donated money to the library in Ivy's memory."

"Aww."

"Yeah." Thea was actually quiet for ten or twenty seconds. "There's a box of Kleenex to your right. Yeah, Ivy was something special. She lived her life her own way and she touched a lot of lives. I'll send you a letter with the details so you know what books I bought and you can thank anyone who doesn't want to remain anonymous."

"Thanks."

"One book already came in, though, and I especially

want you to see it. It's brand-new, covers all aspects of natural dyeing. Ivy would've loved it. It's full of color pictures, planting guides for gardens, recipes for dyes—the whole shebang—and it's beautifully presented. Like one of those coffee table cookbooks that's part travelogue, part drool inducer, except with fiber and color. It's a real knockout. Not a book you want to drop on your foot."

"I'd love to see it." I looked toward the shelves of new arrivals.

"That's the problem, though. It's so gorgeous it checked out immediately. I should have put a hold on it for you as soon as I ordered it. You want me to do that now?"

"Oh, absolutely. Who checked it out?"

"Librarians never tell. I'm sorry I didn't put it on hold for you to begin with, though. I'll do it with the rest of the books and . . ." She stopped, listened, looked left and right, as I'd done earlier, then lowered her voice even though there still didn't seem to be anyone else in the library. "And I'll bring the dossiers with me tonight."

"Can you say 'dossiers' without compromising your scruples? It sounds spyish and associated with 'suspects.'"

"It's a harmless word meaning file, folder, record, and report in addition to meaning profile. If it had room for any more meanings it would be a portmanteau. I like it. I think I'll start using it more often."

"You can e-mail the information to me if it's easier."

"Better I bring it tonight. Believe it or not, I don't have a computer at home. I spend enough time staring at one while I'm here—and I'm here most of the time, anyway. And my phone isn't smart enough, either."

"But . . ." I pointed at the computer in front of her. I

wasn't following her logic. "From here? You don't ever e-mail from here?"

"Of course I do. And I could. But."

"But what?"

"Why take chances?"

"Are you serious?" Making sure no one overheard my snoopy request for other people's personal information was one thing, but what was Thea worried about? Someone sinister sneaking through the stacks? Danger in the Dewey decimals? Venal volunteers or archfiendish assistants? But she wasn't smiling, so I kept a straight face. "Won't you be using this computer for your research and creating a file and saving information to it? You aren't worried about that?"

"Don't you read the tabloids while you're waiting in line at the grocery store?" she asked. Now she did smile, but she didn't back down. "I can control my end. I'll clear my search history and I won't keep a file. Humor me on this, though. Maybe I'm odd, but sending sensitive e-mails out there into the big bad airwaves or wires or ether or whatever, all on their own . . . Well, things really do go astray and things get leaked and, like I said, why take chances?"

"Okay." Maybe Pen or Sylvia knew how to hack e-mail systems. Or Clod. Or maybe it was less complicated and Thea was simply paranoid. She was doing me a favor, though, so it wasn't worth arguing about. "There's something else, though, if you don't mind. Have you got old newspapers on microfilm?"

"Let me guess. You're looking for the original stories about Will from a couple of years ago, right?"

As soon as she mentioned them, I knew I *should* be looking for those articles, but I hadn't even thought about digging them up. What kind of investigation was I running that I didn't think of such obvious avenues of information?

"Because you know all that stuff is online these days," Thea said. "The *Bugle*'s site isn't the easiest to search, but there's no need to get carsick scrolling through microfilm anymore."

Ah, yes, that's the kind of detective I was—the kind who didn't need to worry about being on the dense and dim side because I had an intelligent, self-starting posse keeping track of the details I let slip.

"Good. So what do you think? Is it worth reading the original reports? Will they shed light on anything that happened Monday? It might at least be interesting to compare the originals with that summary in yesterday's paper. See if there are obvious discrepancies." I grabbed a piece of scratch paper and a golf pencil from a holder on the desk, started making notes to myself, and stopped. "Holy cow. Did the *Bugle* only come out yesterday?"

"You didn't give me a chance to answer your first question, but the answer to that one is yes, only yesterday."

"What *was* my first question?"

"Do I think the original articles are worth reading? It doesn't matter if I do or don't. Someone else does. We had hard copies of the original articles in the vertical file and they're missing. The articles, not the filing cabinet."

"You're kidding."

"Even with security strips and the gate, it happens, and vertical file materials don't get strips anyway. And when there's a major event, like a natural disaster or a celebrity's death, it's not uncommon for someone to suddenly decide he needs to own the special reports or commemorative issues of *Time* or *Newsweek* or someone's complete works on CD or a favorite DVD. It's cheaper, though, to just take the library's copy." She shrugged. "A murder-suicide counts as a major event."

"Someone took the articles as souvenirs?"

"It takes all kinds, doesn't it? It might be a coincidence, though."

"But you're the kind of person who won't use a library computer to send sensitive information in an e-mail, so you don't think it is a coincidence or that they were taken by a souvenir hunter. Okay, well, maybe not. But think about it. It probably wasn't someone trying to cover tracks or cover up anything else, either, because surely no one is dumb enough to think the library had the only copies of those articles in existence. You said it yourself—they're available online."

"But maybe they were taken by someone doing his own research," Thea said, "and the library was the most convenient place to find hard copies."

Pen and Sylvia. Those rats. Maybe that's what Sylvia was up to last night. "Do you have security cameras?" I turned in a circle, scanning the ceiling and corners of the room.

"I wish."

"An alarm?"

"A building alarm? Kind of fritzy."

"Is there any way to figure out who took them? Or who's been in the library this week? Do you at least know when the articles disappeared?"

"Calm down. On figuring out who took them, only a very anemic maybe. Knowing when they disappeared? It could've been yesterday or it could've been five months ago. Anytime between when the last person read them and when I went looking. I do know they were here six months ago when a volunteer inventoried the files. As for who's been in the library in the past week? Do you have any idea how many people are in and out of here on a weekly basis?"

"But if I described a couple of people, tourists, maybe

someone would remember?" I was remembering Sylvia's beautiful scarf.

"It's our policy not to keep records on the materials patrons check out or use in the building, so that's a dead end. But there is that anemic maybe because we keep the archive room locked and the vertical file's in the archive. I haven't unlocked the room for anyone in the past week, but maybe someone else did. And if they did, maybe they'll remember something. We do get a lot of out-of-town types in here on ancestor hunts. But it's a long shot and maybe a tempest in a teapot. Maybe the articles are misfiled or tucked between a couple of cookbooks. Stranger things have happened. I found *Curious George* shelved next to *The Silence of the Lambs* last month. *That* put some icky pictures in my head."

"But you don't think they're misfiled."

"No. Because I looked. And I'm good at looking."

"If they're gone and they weren't taken by a souvenir hunter, then that adds another layer of questions to the questions we already have. And that makes a whole buncha-buncha-bunch of questions." I bounced my fingertips off my lips with the "buncha-buncha-bunch." It didn't help. "Huh. Well . . ." What was my original reason for coming here? "Oh, wait, what about even older papers? Turn of the century and before."

"Turn of which century?"

"Nineteenth to twentieth."

"Which paper?"

"There's more than one?"

"Come on over here." She came out from behind the desk and led me along the wall that divided the public and staff areas of the building. We stopped at a door and she pulled out a ring of keys.

"You might think this is a closet," she said, putting faux snoot in her voice, "but it is the J.F. Culp Memorial

Archival Repository." She opened the door, reached around the edge of the jamb, and flipped the light switch. A bulb hanging from a socket in the ceiling came on. "Notice I didn't have to pull a string to turn that light on," she said. "We're classy. Where do you want to start?"

I didn't like to tell her, but her repository *was* a closet—a roomy janitor's closet, maybe, but no bigger. It was lined with shelves from floor to ceiling on two sides. Three filing cabinets stood against the third wall. There wasn't room for anything but the door in the fourth wall. I eyed the shelves with their boxes and boxes of microfilm and pictured myself getting snarled in the reels and tangled in loop after loop . . . "Is there an index?"

"We're not *that* classy. What are you looking for?"

"A picture someone described."

"Picture or photograph? And before you ask, yes, it makes a difference. Photographs, the way we think of newspaper photographs, weren't around until the 1880s and not common in the *Bugle* until the late nineties and not all that common even then. I know this is true because a fifth grader came in and told me last week and after she left I verified it with my own research so that I'd look good the next time it came up. Who knew it would come up again so soon? I'm so glad you came in and asked."

"Glad I could help."

"Does that narrow the range of dates for you?"

It did and it didn't. What if Geneva's description of the clothing in the picture was confused? Or completely wrong? What if the photograph she remembered wasn't in a newspaper? What if the nebulous memory of lovers lying dead in the grass wasn't hers but came from one of her blessed movies or TV shows? At that point I felt a chill on my neck.

“Can we go now?” a sepulchral voice heavy with grump said in my ear.

“What?” I couldn’t believe it. Thea and I had talked for a while, but not *that* long. She’d been perfectly happy about looking at books. She’d had the nerve to tell me not to do anything to get us kicked out. And now she wanted to *go*? Then I remembered where I was and to whom I’d just responded with such short-tempered annoyance. Oops. I glanced sideways at Thea. She was pretending not to notice my outburst.

“Tell you what,” Thea said, handing me the closet key and speaking gently. “You take your time here. Lock the door when you’re finished. The microfilm reader is along the wall there in the corner. Before you go, though, make sure you give me the information you have on those people you want me to look up. And remember to give me back my key.”

“Sure. Thanks. Um, one more thing?” I shivered and moved away from Geneva. She’d rested her chin on my shoulder and was sighing ponderously in my ear. “Cole Dunbar told me the historical society has archives, too.”

“Yeah. They did a photo-history project a few years back. They put out a call for people to bring in their old pictures and then they made copies or scanned them. If you’re looking for a picture, then that might be your best bet for finding it.”

“Are *they* indexed?”

“You’d hope so, but I don’t know. I’ve never set foot in the place and probably never will. The volunteer who runs it used to volunteer here, and that’s all you need to know about that or I might color your perception of the dear woman. With your background, though, I’m surprised you haven’t gone over there to root through their trunks of old clothes and check how their quilts are hanging. Or are you afraid you’ll come across as the big bwana expert come to tell the small fry what she's doing wrong?"

"Some of that, maybe."

"She'll take it that way, too."

"Great."

A commotion erupted at the book drop. A family had just come in and a small boy wailed as he watched his father and older sister slipping all their books into the return slot. Thea said something that sounded like "bubble time" and was gone.

"*Now* can we go?"

I looked at Geneva, looked at the closet-slash-archives. "Come here," I whispered and crooked a finger at her. "We need to talk." She sulked after me into the small space and I pulled the door mostly shut. "What's with you?" I whispered. "You talk to me and then you *won't* talk to me. You're happy . . . well, no, you're never happy, but then you go totally miserable. You come in here and say you want to look at the books and then suddenly you can't wait to leave. I know you're dealing with issues that I, as a living person, probably can't comprehend. You're dead. Okay. I get that. But it's not like you haven't had plenty of time to get used to it. What are you, a ghost or a sullen, sulking teenager?" I stopped midtirade. "Oh my God. *Are* you a teenager?"

"I don't think that's possible."

"Why not?" It would certainly explain a few things.

"Teenagers sing and dance and roll packs of cigarettes up in their sleeves. They drive hot rods and have bonfires at the beach and play something called blanket bingo. Plus they have names that sound like small pieces of hardware. I've seen the documentaries on television."

"I think those might have been movies."

"Or docudramas. They looked quite realistic."

I was standing in a closet with a ghost discussing *Gidget Goes Hawaiian.*

"I've never been to a beach," she said. "You should take me. I could scare the sharks away so they won't bite your legs off. I've seen those documentaries, too."

I tried to picture her relaxing on a sunny beach, listening to waves lapping the shore, reading a good book, a cozy mystery maybe, or *Private Investigating 101*, idly turning the pages of *Teen* magazine . . . "Oh my gosh. You can't read any of those books out there, can you?"

"How rude. I can read every bit as well as you."

"But you can't turn the pages so you can't read books anymore. That must be like being in . . ."

"Well, it isn't like being in a blanket bingo documentary—I can tell you that."

"Come with me. I want to show you something."

"You're very bossy today." She huffed a bit but she trailed after me out of the closet, tsking and offering her own instructions all the way back to the circulation desk. "Don't forget to turn off the light and don't forget to lock the door. I didn't say *slam* it. We're in a *library*, for heaven's sake."

Thea stood at the circulation desk with a bottle of bubbles in one hand and a bubble pipe in the other. The previously crying child gazed at her with open adulation. I handed her the key.

"Find what you wanted?" she asked between puffs.

"I'll come back when I have more time."

"Okeydoke."

"Where are your audiobooks?"

She blew another cloud of bubbles and pointed. Geneva stayed for a moment, watching the boy pop as many of the bubbles as he could catch, and then followed me past the low shelves of picture books in the children's area to the other side of the room. On the way

I stopped at one of the computer catalog desks and scribbled a note on a piece of scratch paper and took three or four more pieces along.

When we were standing in front of the shelves of recorded books, I held up the note I'd written so Geneva could read it: *Problem solved. No pages.*

There were two ranges of shelves—several thousand titles, easily. It was paradise for the page-turning impaired. Geneva floated from one shelf to the other, then came to read over my shoulder when she saw me writing another note: *You listened to* The Ballad of Frankie Silver *on my laptop at the cottage. Remember?*

"I felt at home in that story."

Pick one out. I'll borrow it. You can listen in the study.

"Look through them and pick one out?"

I nodded and scribbled. *Summaries of stories on backs.*

"Take one off the shelf, read the summary, and choose?"

Yes! Tedious ghost.

She stared at me, stared at the shelves, stared at me, then flew at the shelves with her arms spread wide. I almost screamed. But caught myself when she passed through the wall and came out again, nary a box tipping.

I shook my head and mouthed, "Sorry."

She sniffed, then watched as I scanned the shelves for authors and titles I recognized. And tried to filter out her helpful suggestions.

"Don't choose only red ones. The blue ones are prettier. This box is fatter. It must be a better book. Or are the words just longer? How do they make these recordings? You should find out and record me. My book would be very exciting and realistic. And I just had a very marvelous idea. I would leave the *k* off the word 'book' and call my book a '*boo!*'" She shouted that in my ear. "Wouldn't that be a wonderful joke?"

Despite wanting to bean her with the unabridged dictionary sitting on the table behind us, I chose half a dozen audios ranging from Charles Todd to *Charlotte's Web*. I stood the boxes on the table so she could read the front and back of each. While she did that, humming to herself again, I quickly jotted down the sparse information I had on Eric Lyle, Pen Ledford, and Sylvia Furches. Then I wondered about adding Carolyn Proffitt to the list. But why? Why should I be suspicious of her? Because she'd irritated me? Then again, how could it hurt to know more about her before believing her story one hundred percent? If I could wonder about Debbie, whom I liked and basically trusted, why not wonder about Carolyn Proffitt's motive for accosting me in my own store and telling me to back off?

"I'll take all six."

I held up two fingers and added Carolyn Proffitt's name to the list.

"I'd like all of them."

I held up three fingers and looked at the clock over the circulation desk. I'd been gone long enough and needed to get back so Ardis could have her turn at lunch. I picked up the list.

"How about half a dozen, then?"

We took all six. It was easier than arguing.

On our way back to the Cat, I pulled out my phone and made a deal with Geneva—before I started one of the audiobooks for her, she would tell me what she'd heard Clod and Debbie talking about. Even if Ardis was successful in getting Debbie to talk, I wanted to hear a third party's take on their exchange. Even if that third party believed teen beach movies were documentaries. Not to mention that she was a ghost. Honestly, if I were to stand back and listen to my own thoughts, I'd believe I'd spent too much time fumigating textiles out from under the regulation fumigation hood.

"You don't want to encourage my cooperation by playing a tiny portion of one small book first?" Geneva asked.

"No."

"Pretty please?"

"Geneva, do you realize what an important role you play in this investigation? And do you know that you're the only member of the posse who can fill that role?"

"Really? Tell me more."

"You're our . . ." I didn't like to say "fly on the wall." She wasn't fond of flies . . . "You're our spy, our infiltrator."

"Infiltrator. I like that. It sounds very important."

"Not just important. Vital."

"I like that even better. I haven't felt vital for quite a few years."

"Good. Do you think you can do one more thing for me? Can you tell me why you weren't talking to me? Why you've been so desolate? Talking really might help."

"Are we friends?"

"We are. And friends help each other."

"Then no, I won't tell you because we are friends. If I tell you, then I won't be helping you, especially when you're trying to go to sleep and you hear things go bump in the night."

"Oh."

"But you want to help me?"

"Yes."

"Then do not ask me anymore and do not remind me and maybe I can forget."

"You don't think it would help to find out . . ."

In an instant she swirled around in front of me, a dangerous sound building low in her throat. I stopped short, but the sound increased as she started to billow. I took a step back.

"You got a wasper in your face there, darlin'?"

I blinked and looked to my left. An old man in overalls was sunning himself on the bench in front of the Blue Plum Bank and Trust. He smiled.

"Waspers don't mess with me none," he said. "They only pester sweet things. You're Crazy Ivy's granddaughter, aren't you? You look just like her."

He probably thought he'd made a friendly observation. Or, more likely, he hadn't thought at all. That's what I told myself, anyway, as I imagined swirling toward him, billowing like Geneva and blasting, *Do not call her Crazy Ivy,* into his thick, unthinking skull. But I held myself back, held it together. If Granny could let the nickname slide past her, I'd try to let it slide, too.

"I'm Ivy's granddaughter, yes." I said it as lightly as I could, although ignoring the nickname and Geneva at the same time was a strain.

"My condolences, then. She's sorely missed."

"Thank you."

"You're welcome," Geneva said.

Although she still hung too claustrophobically close to my face, she'd ceased billowing when the old guy started talking. That was due to her natural nosiness trumping her supernatural spookiness. If she wanted to believe I'd thanked her for the billowing reprieve, instead of him for his kindness, that was okay with me. That she had manners at all was a plus. We left the old man smiling in the sun and Geneva floated next to me the rest of the way back to the Cat.

I realized my stupid mistake about the CDs immediately after she told me the bad news about Debbie's conversation with Clod.

Chapter 22

"What do you mean, you can't tell me what they said? You said you would. We had that whole discussion about how important you are to the investigation."

"Yes, we did. You should start calling me V.I. for Vitally Important."

V.I. for Virtually Impossible. "Geneva, we had a deal. You promised you'd tell me what they said."

"No, I promised to tell you what I heard. And I just did. I heard nothing."

"How did you hear nothing? You were in this room. They were in this room. They talked. Debbie cried. You love crying. What do you mean, you heard nothing?" I clapped a hand over my mouth. I was shouting and anyone in the whole building and the next three over could have heard that. I closed my eyes, pretended I was somewhere else. With someone else. Maybe that I was someone else.

"I was following your instructions," Geneva said.

I opened my eyes. "What?"

"I was quite depressed but still I listened to what the deputy told you, because I adore all the *Law and Order* TV shows and so I always try to be law-abiding and orderly. And I'm surprised you don't remember this, but he expressly told you not to listen at the keyhole and you went on at great length about how you wouldn't and how impolite it would be if anyone did. And even though *you* sometimes fall short, I always try to be polite."

"There is nothing wrong with my memory," I ground out between my teeth, "or my manners. I was trying to tell you that I *wanted* you to eavesdrop."

"How unfortunate, and here I thought you were being unusually clear and precise, so I went away and let them have their privacy. And to be on the safe side, in case I was tempted to put my ear to the door, I put my fingers in my ears and sang like this . . ." Her singing exploded in my head. I have no idea where she'd heard, much less learned, the lyrics to the Rolling Stones' "(I Can't Get No) Satisfaction."

"I know how you feel," she said when she broke off. "I had to screw my fingers right into *my* ears, too. Next time I will choose something more sedate. And in future, when you have vitally important work for me to do, you should try harder to make your instructions more straightforward. Now, I've held up my end of the bargain, so which book shall we listen to first?"

Was there really so much to learn about ghosts, or just so much to learn about this one? She was right, though, drat it. Back in my old life, in the lab at the museum, if I'd issued instructions the opposite of what I meant, my colleagues would have thought I was crazy. Oh dear.

Geneva chose *Still Life* by Louise Penny for the first book. She said she liked the irony of the title. "Do you get it? On the one hand you have the book—*Still Life*. And on the other hand you have me—still dead and always will be. Do you think I'm the first ghost in the world to listen to her book? Perhaps if I enjoy it you should write her and let her know."

I thought it was ironic that she understood irony but hadn't managed to understand my eavesdropping instructions. She hovered annoyingly while I inserted the first CD into my laptop and then drifted around the attic in a euphoric cloud as the narrator started reading. Then I realized my stupid mistake.

She was listening to the first CD. Of nine. There might be fewer CDs than pages to a book, but Geneva couldn't do a thing with either and in just over an hour her euphoria would come to a screeching halt. Quite possibly in my ear while I was discussing wooden needles versus metal or plastic with a customer.

"Geneva?"

"Hush."

I stopped the CD.

"Hey!"

"I'll turn it back on in a second, but I thought I should warn you. The story has nine episodes—"

"Like a soap opera? I adore soap operas."

Of course she did. "Good. You're listening to the first episode. It'll last about an hour. If I get the chance later, I'll run back up here and put on the second episode, if you're still interested."

"Of course I will be. And you can come back every hour to put on the next episode and then the next and then the next... how many episodes are there?"

"Nine, but don't you think it would be more fun to save some for another day? It'll give you something to look forward to."

"I don't need to save them," she said. "We brought home six audiobooks and there are hundreds, if not several thousand, more back at the library, and I look forward to listening to all of them. I am beside myself with excitement, in case you hadn't noticed. If you aren't going to buy me a television, these recorded books are a decent enough substitute. What are you doing? Why are you praying at a time like this? Turn the book back on."

"I'm not praying."

"You're also not turning the book on." She was quiet for a puzzled few seconds. "If you aren't praying, what are you doing?"

"I'm getting a grip," I said through gritted teeth and the tightly clasped hands I held to my lips.

"Am I supposed to know what that means?"

"Geneva, I will try to come back up to put the second episode on for you, but I won't be coming back every hour for the next nine hours."

"Whyever not?"

"You mean besides that being a totally unreasonable expectation? I won't be doing that this afternoon because I'm working. I work for a living. Work comes first."

"Before me." She looked less like a euphoric cloud, but she didn't sound incredulous, so maybe she understood.

"In this case it does, yes. And I won't change episodes for you every hour this evening, either, because I'm going out."

"With a paramour?"

"What? No. To a meeting. To the Historical Trust Annual Meeting and Potluck."

"Will that be fun?"

"I don't know. Fun enough, I suppose. My grandmother liked going."

"I see. And fun comes before me, too." She looked more like dingy laundry hanging on a drooping clothesline every second.

"That's not really what I meant, Geneva. I— "

She interrupted. "Will there be a lot of people there?"

"I guess."

"How many?"

"I don't really know. A hundred? It isn't just going to be fun, though. Thea's doing some research for me this afternoon and she said she'll bring the results with her tonight. And with that many people there, Ardis thinks it'll be a good opportunity to ask questions and listen in on conversations without appearing too nosy. She's probably right. I hope so, anyway."

"Ardis and Thea are going?"

"Yes."

"Debbie?"

"I think so."

"Ernestine? Mel?"

"Yes, look, let's not go through the whole list of people you know, okay? I have to get back to work."

"The posse, though."

"Mm, yeah . . ." I hadn't really thought of it that way.

"But you don't think it's a good idea for me to go?"

"No! No. Sorry, I didn't mean to shout." I was ready to cringe in case she took exception to my shout or to her exclusion, but—will wonders never cease?—she remained calm. Thoughtful even. "I hope you understand."

"I do. You don't want me to go. I understand and I can handle that."

"Good, thank you. After work I need to dash to the store so I can make a green salad to take with me tonight, but I'll stop back here before the potluck and put on another episode for you. How does that sound?"

"That will be fine. Will you turn on my audiobook for me, please?"

I left her content for the time being and went back down to work. She even said she'd come find me when the CD ended and wait patiently if I was with a customer or couldn't get away immediately. It was nice to have her acting like a rational, considerate . . . well, like a normal person. Nice, but odd. When I got the chance, I'd have to search for audiobooks in a format I could download in a single unit like I had for the McCrumb book I'd played for her. Preferably free.

On my way past the second floor, I heard voices and clicking needles coming from the front room and popped in to say hi and see if the knitters there needed anything. There were several women I recognized from around town, though I didn't remember seeing them in the Cat before. And there was Ernestine, thick among them—smiling, knitting, listening, and nodding to whatever they were so happily chatting about. I hated to interrupt them, but Ernestine saw me and excused herself. She shooed me ahead of her out of the room and down the hall.

"Ardis called me," she said when we were out of view and earshot. "She said there were more conversations going on this afternoon than the three of you can keep track of. She said crime is definitely paying and asked me to provide backup. The costume was my own idea." She beamed. "What do you think?" She smoothed her tweed skirt, folded her hands, and assumed an innocent look. Then she grimaced and tugged at her waistband. "I haven't worn stockings for years and now I remember why. Horrible things. Like sausage casings. But worth it, don't you think?"

"Jane Marple?"

"I probably look more like Margaret Rutherford doing Jane Marple, or Elsa Lanchester doing Margaret Rutherford doing Jane Marple, but yes."

"You look perfect."

"And I would hardly be convincing as V.I."

"Who?"

"V. I. Warshawski, dear. Haven't you read Sarah Paretsky's books?"

"Oh, right." For a horrible, surreal second I'd thought she meant Vitally Important Geneva.

"I'd better get back," she said. "One of those women is a cousin of the husband of the woman who cleans for Bonny. She might not really know anything useful, but she has strong opinions about everything she does know. I'll make a full report at our next meeting."

"Are you taking notes?" I wasn't sure that was such a good idea.

She patted my arm reassuringly and whispered. "Not notes. They're too obvious. I borrowed my grandson's solid-state, voice-activated recorder. It's under the knitting in my basket."

She yanked at her waistband again and went back to the front room. I continued downstairs, not sure recording was such a good idea, either. If it turned out that secret recordings were illegal, and someone found out and kicked up a fuss, who was Clod Dunbar more likely to arrest—his former Sunday school teacher in her sweet little old lady outfit, or me?

Chapter 23

For lack of a community center in Blue Plum, or a meeting space large enough and not associated with one or another denomination, the Historical Trust Annual Meeting and Potluck was held in the grade school gym. The first thing I noticed when my thrown-together green salad and I entered—I in my flowery crepe skirt, low heels, and pink silk blouse and the salad in Granny's green glass lettuce-leaf bowl—was the lack of a gymnasium fug hanging in the air. I'd worried about that, wondering how eau de PE would mix with this high-tone potluck. Instead I caught whiffs of fried chicken, baked beans, and hot rolls.

The next thing I noticed was that most of the other women wore pants. In fact, many wore jeans. There were a few skirts and dresses and a smattering of jackets and ties, but they were all worn by people who appeared to be over seventy. Or over eighty. That there were no children and almost no one under thirty didn't surprise me. I'd given my share of presentations to preservation groups and historical societies and knew the demographics involved.

The gym's double doors put us at one end of the room. Rows of tables covered in paper tablecloths stretched to the right. I joined the people bearing their hot and cold offerings to four more tables along the wall to the left. The Spivey twins met me there. They wore capris and matching polyester blouson tops in virtually the same shade of pink as my blouse. I shuddered.

"Green salad," Mercy said. It wasn't an enthusiastic greeting, but it was accurate and brief, so I smiled. She was easy to identify this evening. She'd dosed herself with an extra dash of cologne for the occasion. Up close, the extra dash wrestled with the smell of good cooking. Fortunately for anyone standing within nose-shot of Mercy, the aromas of chicken, beans, and hot rolls were muscular enough to come out on top.

Shirley smiled back at me and nudged Mercy's shoulder with her own.

Mercy cleared her throat. "Yes. How wonderful. We certainly can't have too many green salads." She took the bowl from me and nestled it amongst five or six other bowls on the table.

"Is this your first?" Shirley asked, still smiling.

"Salad?" Not the first at the potluck, anyway. There were actually seven other bowls already on the table—all salads—all green. One or two of them, unless they had avocado or bacon bits lurking under their chopped iceberg, looked even less inspired than mine.

"Your first amp," Shirley said. Mercy's elbow repaid Shirley's earlier shoulder nudge. "Annual meeting and potluck. AMP," Shirley clarified on an intake of breath.

"Yes."

"That's nice," Mercy said. She sounded less happy for me than she did smug, but maybe that was my jaded perception. "Oh, and I'm supposed to tell you that there's someone who wants to talk to you." That sounded less smug than it did ominous, but maybe that was the bared teeth in her smile.

"Who?" I stepped back for olfactory comfort. The two of them stepped closer.

"We'll let you know when we catch up with you later," Shirley said.

"When there aren't so many people around," said Mercy.

Where? I wondered. *In a dark alley?* Even meeting the twins in the middle of Main Street at high noon in full sun gave me the willies. Then I remembered that I still hadn't found out who their confidential source was or asked them if they'd seen or learned anything the day they followed Sylvia and Pen. Such as Sylvia and/or Pen stopping by the library. That meant I should try to be pleasant, or at least polite. But if they planned to catch me later, then pleasant or polite could happen later, too.

"Will you excuse me?" I turned my back without waiting for an answer and spotted Thea and Ernestine two tables down, at the dessert end of the spread. Ernestine still wore her Miss Marple tweeds from her afternoon of surveillance in the shop. Thea looked comfortable in jeans and a sweater. Both their ensembles were delightfully accessorized by the bakery boxes emblazoned with Mel's logo that they held in their hands. Before I reached them, either to see if Thea had information for me or to give her the evil eye, I was waylaid by Granny's old pirate beau, John Berry.

"Kath, you're the picture of Ivy's flower garden."

I immediately felt appropriately dressed and less like snarling at Thea. John, being of that generation, of course wore a coat and tie.

"I'm sitting with Ardis at the far end of the middle row." He pointed and I saw Ardis waving from under the basketball hoop at the other end of the gym. "Will you join us? She's staked a claim to plenty of seats."

"I'd love to."

"Good, I'll see you there. I'm on a mission to round

up enough bodies to fill the rest of the seats. It's our usual potluck ploy."

"Ploy?"

He didn't elaborate, but when I looked over my shoulder toward the twins, he followed my line of sight.

"Ah," he said, and hurried off in the opposite direction.

In the gym's far-left corner, beyond the dessert end of the food tables, stood something I hadn't seen in years—a home-use slide screen. It looked wobbly and frail, its tripod base like the pronged cane of a doddering old man. A laptop sat on a cart in front of the screen, flickering black-and-white pictures on and off the screen. They might have been interesting, but between the warped screen and the gym lights, it was hard to tell. No one watched and no one seemed to care that no one did, so I didn't, either.

The gym was filling up. People greeted and chatted and laughed. The individual scents of chicken, beans, and rolls disappeared into the delicious swirl of other hot dishes arriving. My skirt and blouse no longer looked out of place in the flow of color and gamut of dress. I smiled and nodded and shook hands on my way over to join Ardis, and I realized this was the largest indoor gathering of people I'd experienced in Blue Plum.

There were five rows of tables running the length of the gym, with chairs down both sides of each long row. That made the seats around the perimeter and the two or three closest to it prime real estate. Reaching the seats in the middle of the cozy arrangement was going to require squeezing sideways, careful juggling of plates and glasses of sweet tea, and a certain amount of apologizing.

I wanted to get over to Ardis before anyone else joined her. We'd stayed busy at the Cat for the rest of the afternoon and I hadn't been able to ask her if she'd gotten Debbie to talk while I was at the library. Neither of them had given any clues one way or the other. Debbie hadn't appeared to be either happily unburdened or more on edge than before and Ardis hadn't acted as though she was suddenly in possession of key or revelatory facts. It was possible Ardis hadn't had a chance to talk to Debbie at all.

As I rounded the outside edge of the tables and approached her, Ardis called, "Pocketbook? Hurry."

Alarmed, I rushed over. "What is it? What do you need?"

"Put it on that empty chair," she said, pointing four seats into the interior. "You don't have to sit all the way down there when we eat, but I almost lost that one to the new preacher's wife a minute ago and I've run out of clothes to shed."

"Did you find out anything from Debbie?"

"That can wait. The chair won't. Quick."

I hopped to it, standing behind the valuable chair for good measure, not sure I'd be able to stand up to a preacher or a preacher's wife with as much authority as Ardis had. Tables around us were filling fast. Only a few people were brave enough to ask Ardis if the other half dozen seats sitting empty between the two of us were taken. Thank goodness John arrived with Ernestine on his arm and Mel, Debbie, and Thea in tow. Ernestine moved down the table and settled into the chair next to me, and Thea into the one next to her. Debbie, Mel, and John took the seats opposite, with John across from Ernestine. Ardis remained standing at the head of the table. That left two chairs empty, the one directly across from me, draped with Ardis' sweater, and another down at the end next to Thea.

"I think we have an extra seat here," I called to Ardis. She still concentrated on scanning the crowd and didn't answer, but when I suggested to John that he free up the chair by taking Ardis' sweater from it, she heard and squawked. I sat down, duly chastised.

"Best not let anyone else get hold of that chair," Ernestine said in my ear. "Ardis has this down to a science."

"What's going on?" I asked her. The joviality in the gym was increasing, though, and Ernestine gestured at her own ear. I obliged, leaning closer. "Why does Ardis need a science?"

Ernestine's eyes glowed. "Factions," she said. The word popped out of her mouth with such enthusiasm that Ardis, still standing at the end of the table, heard her and nodded approval.

John looked just as keyed up. "The last time I was in town for one of these," he said, "Evangeline Lavender poured a pitcher of iced tea over Archie Sullivan's head when he refused to back her side in the Cola War. I can't believe I've allowed myself to miss out on all this since then."

"It's just as well, John," Ernestine said. "You're a feisty one."

John slapped the table and hooted in reply.

"Hush," Ernestine said.

"Cola War?" I looked from one to the other.

John pulled himself together, put a finger to his lips, and shook his head slightly.

"He shouldn't have brought it up," Ernestine said. "Bad feelings take so long to die down with some people."

Clearly Granny had left something out, the times she told me about the Historical Trust Annual Meeting and Potluck. "Social and entertainment highlight of the year" was beginning to sound like a pale euphemism. I looked around with quickened interest, wondering what words "social" and "entertainment" stood for so politely but with increasingly obvious inadequacy.

Mel, sitting next to John, looked hypervigilant, probably because she'd spiked her short mustard-colored hair straight up for the occasion. But her posture added to the effect. She sat half turned in her seat, with her back toward John and with one ear listening to Debbie. The other ear, from the tilt of her head and the profile I could just see, was intent on a conversation going on at the next table over. I didn't recognize the couple engaged in that conversation and they didn't seem aware of Mel listening to them.

John took no offense at Mel's turned back; he'd turned his toward her. He did a good imitation of a meerkat, sitting tall, neck stretched, eyes moving from person to person down the length of table beyond me. Counting? Looking for someone? Memorizing faces and names?

Ernestine leaned toward Thea to her left. Thea eyed the same conversation Mel was listening to and described the scene for Ernestine, but too quietly for me to hear more than a few words, one of which was either "dimension" or "dementia" and the others "demolition" and "ordnance." Rethinking it, I hoped that last word was "ordinance" rather than "ordnance."

Listening out of context in that direction was proving alarming, so I turned to greet the people sitting to my right—but found only backs and shoulders, as they were all looking toward the buffet tables. At first I thought they were poised for a signal so they could jump up and be among the first in the buffet lines. I was tempted to subliminally steer them toward my spinach salad by softly whistling "I'm Popeye the Sailor Man." Then I leaned far enough to the side to see around the back next to me and got a clear view down the middle of the table to the floor show my tablemates were watching—Shirley and Mercy wrestling with a stand-up microphone.

It was hard to tell what the twins were trying to do to, for, or with the microphone—adjust the height was my best guess. It was also hard to tell if they had any competency for the task or any business touching the equipment, although it appeared to be dawning on the irritated woman waiting to use it that they had neither. When things looked darkest, Angela appeared. It would take longer to describe what she wore than it did for her to separate the twins from the microphone, twist and adjust unseen parts of the microphone's pole, move it over in front of the waiting woman, and slide from view. She did all that without appearing to make eye contact or saying a word. Because of my tunnel vision down the table of transfixed guests, I couldn't tell where she'd appeared from or returned to.

For the record, Angie wore black jeans and a tight, low-cut pink tank top. It was the shade of pink that was my new least favorite color.

The twins made one more effort to be helpful. Shirley stepped up to the microphone, turning it away from the waiting, now fuming woman. Shirley tapped it and spoke into it, presumably saying "Testing, testing." No sound came. Mercy started toward it with a finger extended, no doubt aiming for a switch, but the fuming, no longer patient woman had had enough by then and shouldered Mercy aside. She flipped the switch herself and leaned into the microphone, which promptly deafened the room with wrenching feedback.

My hands instinctively clapped to my ears and I turned, shoulders drawn up, to see how Ardis and the others were coping. Ardis was still on her feet, standing at the head of our table, regarding the scene unperturbed—the picture of a strong woman, sure of her purpose and enjoying herself.

The feedback gained the audience's attention the way no other amplified request would have. When we were all quiet, the impatient, now feedback-shy woman introduced herself from a safer, though not optimal distance.

"Good evening. I'm Evangeline Lavender."

She didn't look violent or excitable. I turned to Ernestine, my eyes asking the question, and pantomimed tipping a pitcher of iced tea.

Ernestine shook her head, as John had before, and mouthed, "Not here."

I turned back and listened to Evangeline Lavender—slender, permed, bespectacled, and good with improvised weapons. Her pastel shirtwaist dress must belie her true nature. Or at least a hot temper. In fact, she looked like a weedy Margaret Thatcher.

"As president of the Blue Plum Historical Trust," she said, "it is my pleasure to welcome you to the thirty-eighth annual annual, er, the annual, the thirty-eighth ann . . . , yes, the Blue Plum Historical Trust Annual Meeting and Potluck. It is our thirty-eighth." She held several index cards in her hand and at that point decided it would be better to read straight from them.

"It is so nice to see so many familiar faces here tonight," she read without looking up at any of the faces, "and also exciting to see faces new to our lovely and historic town. You can be sure I will be calling on you new faces in the very near future to sign you up and get you involved in our wonderful annual Blue Plum Preserves Heritage Festival, which we hold annually in July." She did look up then, and straight down the middle table at me. "Is that Ivy McClellan's granddaughter I see?"

"We told you it was," came a Spivey voice from somewhere off to the side.

"Thank you, yes," Evangeline muttered in their direction. "A friendly warning, then," she called, shaking her finger at me and smiling to show how much fun we were having. "I know where you live and work, so brush off your volunteer hat. I've got something special in mind and I'm going to come looking for you."

There was polite laughter. I laughed too and nodded. Then I moved into the lee of the back to my right and wondered what Evangeline was planning to talk me into and how easily I could keep myself out of it. Maybe her threat was good news, though. Maybe she was the one the Spiveys said was looking for me. Judging from her puny proportions and dependence on note cards for simple opening remarks, I felt confident I was a match for her, with or without a pitcher of iced tea.

After that, Evangeline reminded us that the business portion of the meeting would follow quickly on the heels of dinner, including an update on plans for Blue Plum Preserves from the festival chairman.

"We will keep the business meeting and any accompanying discussion brief," Evangeline read from her note cards and to an undercurrent of skeptical snorts, "so that we may move on to welcome this evening's very special guest, Grace Jenkins, who is going to tell us about her fascinating research into the local china-painting trends of the 1920s and thirties." That was met with several delighted "ohs" and one soft groan. "And back by popular demand," Evangeline plowed on, "is our 'Stroll Down Memory Lane' slide show, just beyond the dessert table there, so don't forget to stroll over and spend some time in yesteryear." This was met with more than several groans, punctuated by an "oh" that sounded more like an "oof," as though a groaner had been corrected.

"Will you all please join me now," Evangeline said, "in a prayer of thanks for the wonderful town in which we live and for the wonderful food and fellowship of which we are about to partake? After our blessing, please remember to form two lines at the buffet table and be mindful of those in line behind you. You may go back for seconds, but please don't take your seconds along with your firsts. Let us pray."

Some heads bowed, some eyes closed, and when Evangeline said, "Amen," the audience surged forward.

Our group, under Ardis' superlative leadership, ended up very near the front of the two buffet lines. I wasn't sure how we did that, considering the location of our seats—back end of the middle row of tables—but no one else in our group or anyone around us showed any surprise at all.

Chapter 24

"I've been looking for you." A hand with long fingers appeared before my face. "By the way, you'll want to take some of that in the yellow bowl next to the hummus." The fingers indicated the dish in question before helping itself to a deviled egg from an adjacent platter. It was Joe Dunbar suddenly in the line across from me. He'd somehow ambled out of the crowd and made it to the front of the line behind Mel and John without my noticing. No complaints of line jumping rose from the line behind him, though, so I shrugged and took a dollop of the brownish, greenish mashed . . .

"What is this?"

"Here." He reached over and redolloped my plate with a larger helping.

"Hey."

Before I pulled my plate out of range, he added a helping of the hummus to it and pointed to a basket of small flatbreads. I started to ignore him, and them, to prove myself capable of making my own choices. Luckily I recognized the feeling of self-defeating perversity bubbling up within and ignored *it* instead. Those flatbreads—slightly puffed, beautifully mottled with darker brown, lightly brushed with oil—called to me and to the hummus on my plate. And to that other stuff Joe had talked me into, whatever it was. Despite fried chicken being the first and most prevalent aroma to cross paths with my nose that evening, I had the beginnings of a decent-looking Middle Eastern meal in my hands.

"I forgot," I said, feeling more kindly toward his bossy dining instructions.

"Forgot what?" He moved forward, casting a critical eye on the acres of green salads ahead of us.

"That you told me you were an expert hunter-gatherer at these dos."

"Honed through years of experience. You'll want to avoid most of the salads," he said, "except for the spinach there in the green lettuce-leaf bowl. It's probably decent."

"I'm glad you think so. I brought that."

"I know. I recognized Ivy's bowl." He smiled and took a helping. "Why the skirt?"

"Why not?" That was probably too quick, too snippy. I glanced along the table. Thea was too far ahead and I couldn't be sure I'd hit her if I winged a roll at her. Joe had on a pair of jeans less faded than usual and a dark blue sweater. Probably his evening wear.

"No reason," he said. "You look nice."

"Thanks."

I passed my salad by, figuring I'd be taking most of it home as leftovers and eating it for lunch for the next five days. I passed the others by, too, opting for a few pieces of julienned red bell pepper, a baby carrot, and a broccoli floret from a vegetable tray. Joe looked at the veggies and shrugged, but when we came to a dish of lasagna in a pretty red baking dish and I reached for the serving spoon, he shook his head.

"Why not?" That came out louder and more irritated than I'd meant, considering I *was* feeling more kindly toward him, but I was feeling even more kindly toward the looks of that lasagna.

"Shh," he said. "Keep moving. Here." He put a scoop of another pasta dish with tomato sauce and cheese on my plate.

"This stuff looks like—"

"But the flavor is amazing and Shirley's lasagna always has too much sugar in it."

"Sugar?"

"Try not to think about it. Do you like green beans? The blue bowl in the middle there. Superb. And the baked beans in the brown bean pot. Made with molasses. Wonderful dark brown flavor. Not the ones in the slow cooker, though."

"Why not?"

"Canned."

"What did you bring?"

"The stuff in the yellow bowl," he said. "I'm a little worried no one will try it." He caught my look. "It is good, though. And it has a name. I'm just not sure of my pronunciation."

I browsed surely and quickly to the accompaniment of Joe's low-volume commentary, taking dibs and dabs and staying mindful of the lines stretching behind us. When we reached the dessert table, we'd ended up with no fried chicken (no matter what the source, all of it always too greasy—according to Joe) and none of the scalloped potatoes (canned milk, fake cheese), but we'd each scored a small wedge of roasted asparagus quiche made by John (asparagus roasted just to the point of crispy tips, extra sharp cheddar—five stars from Potluck Juror Joe).

"What do you recommend for dessert?" I asked, noting the presence of not one, but two of Mel's coconut cream pies.

"I'm not really a dessert guy." He surveyed the selection anyway. "Mercy's brownies always disappear fast." He pointed to a plate of light brown squares.

"Gah. Oh, sorry." I looked around guiltily.

"Gesundheit," he said.

"But what about that?" I pointed to the few slices that were left of a single round dark chocolate layer.

"No idea. I've never seen that one before." He sounded . . . what? Annoyed? Offended?

Judging from the cross section, it was dense, moist, and covered with a dark, dark chocolate ganache . . . mmm.

"Never mind," I said, server already in hand. "I'll be your guinea pig and give you a review later."

We took our plates over to the table. He seemed to assume he was part of Ardis' seating scheme. I assumed he was right, and, sure enough, he greeted the others who were already back and eating, and Ardis, who'd just taken a bite from a chicken leg that looked crispy and not especially greasy, pointed with it toward the place opposite mine. Before I'd moved from beside Ardis, he'd threaded between the tables, put his plate down, and threaded back out.

"Why were you looking for—" I started to ask.

He interrupted. "Tea?"

"Sure, thanks."

I squeezed past Ardis, who, besides the chicken, had a nice portion of my spinach salad on her plate. I stopped beside Thea—beside Thea who had a large slice of coconut cream pie on her dessert plate. The low growl I heard might have come from my own throat. Thea didn't notice the growl, though. She was communing with a helping of cheese grits. Joe had had reservations about those cheese grits, but Thea made them look worth trying another time. I was about to subtly catch her attention by kicking her chair, when Debbie waved her fork and caught mine.

"I was looking for you," she said.

That phrase again. "You, too?"

"Um." Debbie looked at Ardis, then Mel, then Thea.

Thea looked at me over her shoulder. "Why so jumpy?"

"Hang on a sec." I finished my squeeze past her and Ernestine, put my plate down at my place, and squeezed back up to the head of the table so I could see all of them. "Okay, sorry, but I've heard something like that from three different people tonight and so far not one of them has told me *why* they were looking for me."

"She's paranoid in pink," Mel said.

"It's a lovely shade," said Ardis. "And she looks very pretty in it."

But I suddenly felt very exposed standing there. More people were sitting and most of them were tucking into their suppers, but I was inviting a few curious looks. That was only natural, I knew, because I still had plenty of the "she's not from around here" sticking to me. But that didn't mean I had to like it. At least I didn't see the Spiveys watching me—although now that I'd thought of that, not knowing where they were made me nervous, too.

"Mel's right," I said and started back around toward my seat.

"Wait, Kath," Debbie said. "I only wanted to tell you that we decided to reschedule the dye workshop. Ardis suggested we do it at the Cat, though, to save travel time. I've still got dyes mixed and ready and I can bring them in, no problem."

If I knew Ardis, she also hoped the change in venue would separate the pleasant activity from its association with that tragic morning.

"We can each dye an extra skein and give it to Bonny," Ernestine said. "Sort of in memory of Shannon. We thought she'd like that."

"Isn't that a nice idea?" asked Ardis.

"It is," I said, moving back toward my seat again.

There went my theory of separating the dyeing from the dying, though. And after that homophonic thought, maybe I should steer us back toward using the original term of "hand painting" instead of dyeing. "Hand painting," I said, giving the substitution a boost. "Great idea. Looking forward to it. Let me know when you choose a date."

"Tomorrow morning," Debbie said.

As much as I wanted the safety of sinking out of sight into my seat, that stopped me in my tracks again, *so soon?* evidently clear on my face.

"Plus," Mel said.

"Plus?"

"It's a perfect cover story," Ardis whispered, "for all of us getting together so we can report to you and compare notes."

I looked at them sitting together there, right then, and felt I must be missing something. My open and readable face was open for misinterpretation, too, though, because Ardis and Mel both scanned it, appeared satisfied, and nodded.

"I told you she'd get it," Ardis said. "She's quick and crafty as Ivy ever was. Kath, we're calling it the Double Blind."

"Sounds good," I said, completely lost. I crouched over the table, going for conspiratorial while at the same time lowering my profile and hoping to be less conspicuous among the now mostly seated diners. "Tell you what, though. Run through the gist of it so we're sure everyone is on the same, um, is using the same dye lot."

"Good use of jargon, hon," Ardis, murmured, patting my arm appreciatively. "It adds real luster to our cover story." She looked around to see who else might be listening. The diners beyond my place and Joe's were laughing at something from their end of the table. "*Pssst*, can all of you hear me if I keep my voice this low?" Debbie, Mel, and John nodded on one side of the table, Ernestine and Thea on the other.

"Wait for Joe," Mel said.

"If we always waited for Joe, we might as well be waiting for . . ."

"Godot?" It was Joe's voice behind me. "He probably isn't such a bad guy, Ardis."

"Good. Now, sit down," Ardis said. "I'm laying out a plan."

"Hmm. Well, first I have a message for Kath from some woman who saw us talking in the chow line. She seemed kind of grumpy. She wanted to know where you're sitting."

I resisted the urge to straighten up and look around for a grumpy woman. Instead, I groaned.

"I didn't tell her anything," he said. "But she said that if I saw you again I should tell you she's looking for you."

I resisted the urge to groan again. Instead, staying in my semicrouch, I squeezed back to my seat. He squeezed in along the other side of the table.

"Who was she?" Mel asked over her shoulder as he passed behind her.

He shrugged. "No idea. She didn't say please, though, so I didn't feel obliged to ask her name." An interesting set of scruples Joe Dunbar the sometime burglar had.

"What did she look like?" I asked.

"Here's your tea." He handed me a sweaty glass. "Late twenties, brown hair." He put his own glass of tea down and indicated the length of hair with a hand at his chin. "Didn't strike me as the outdoorsy type. Especially the hair."

It sounded like Carolyn Proffitt. That didn't bode well.

Joe sat down and fussily arranged his tea glass, utensils, dinner plate, and a dessert plate he'd also come back with. When he finished, our place settings, except for the raw veggies on my plate and the deviled egg on his, were mirror images, right down to the slice of dark, dark, delicious-looking chocolate torte.

"I thought you weren't a dessert guy."

"This is primary research," he said.

"Pfft."

"If I'd asked, would you have given me a bite of yours?"

"No."

He shrugged.

"Psst," came from Ardis at the head of the table. "Let me finish so we can put this in motion. Joe, Kath had a brilliant idea. We're calling it the Triple Blind."

"I thought it was the Double Blind," I whispered back.

"I've added something else. It'll produce better results and faster."

Why was this beginning to sound ill-advised?

"It'll be more exciting, too," she said.

That could be why. Still, none of the others looked apprehensive at the idea of adding excitement to the evening, so maybe I was listening too closely to the paranoid-in-pink side of myself.

"We'll think of it in terms of dyeing," Ardis said.

I had a nanosecond of homophone trouble again but shook if off.

"Say we have two skeins of wool, both a subtle, hush-hush gray. One skein represents tonight, when we gather information. The other represents tomorrow, when we analyze it. But—this is the clever part—we overdye the hush-hush gray skeins with more intense colors. We disguise our purpose. Tonight we're convivial community members, chatting and laughing; tomorrow we're artisans being inspired and creative. Are you with me so far?"

"Yes, and your food is getting cold," said Mel. "Mine is almost gone because I've been eating. Nutshell the rest or you won't get seconds and I know you want some of the pie Thea and Ernestine carried in for me."

I was glad I hadn't kicked Thea's chair.

"Right, then. Here's the new twist," Ardis said. "Just like you can't count on always getting the exact color you want when you use natural dyes, we can't count on hearing the information we want this evening if we just depend on the natural flow of conversations. I, for one, don't want to hear about Evangeline Lavender's hammertoe. So we don't depend on the natural flow. We do something better. We start the conversations we want to hear. We talk and laugh and reminisce—about the river and Will and Shannon. We are old friends remembering better times. Other people will overhear *us* and they'll start remembering and talking and the talk will flow to the next table and the next and, with any luck, information will be ripe for the overhearing. We will be the mordant in the dye bath, ensuring better results." She had trouble keeping her voice down with that last rallying statement.

"Ardis?"

"Yes, Kath?"

"If we're all sitting here, talking amongst ourselves, what conversations will we be overhearing?"

"And that, friends, is why Kath is our able leader," Ardis said. "Here's the important part I left out. When people start going for seconds, we spread out. We sit at other tables, with other people, looking entirely innocent and keeping our eyes and ears open."

"This is all your idea?" Joe whispered across to me.

"Apparently."

"And then . . ." Ardis went on.

"I thought you were finished," Joe whispered again.

"Apparently not."

". . . we meet at the Cat tomorrow at ten . . ."

"Nine would be better," Debbie said. "It'll give us more time."

Sunday was Ardis' morning for sleeping in. A look of pain came and went from her face. "We meet at the Cat at nine, reports in hand. Any questions?"

"You're including me in this?" John asked.

"Yes. Ivy trusted you."

"Thank you. Although I'm not entirely sure what we should be listening for when we spread out among the tables."

"Kath will bring you up to speed," Ardis said.

John nodded and looked at me. Joe was looking at me, too.

"Why don't we get the talk and reminiscence going first," I said.

"Absolutely right." Ardis turned to Thea and turned up her volume. "Do you remember the time that Will . . ."

John took his cue and told Ernestine about running into Shannon at the post office not two weeks earlier and how pleased he was when she remembered him. Debbie and Mel turned so the people at the next table could hear them laughing over some shared memory. Joe continued looking at me. I'd finished my dinner while Ardis talked. Now I took a bite of the chocolate torte. It was superb.

"Why do you call this plan the Triple Blind?" Joe asked.

"You'll have to ask Ardis. She knows more about the wily machinations of my brain than I do. You could call that stuff you brought in the yellow bowl the Triple Blind, though. It's just about as mysterious. What's in it?"

"Did you like it?"

"Maybe not as much as this cake, but yeah. It was great with the humus and the flatbread."

"It's in a different category than the cake," he said, sounding put out by my comparison.

"Right. You're right, and it was really good. In fact, if you're willing to share, I'd like the recipe, whatever it's called."

"Basically, mashed squash," he said. "Or maybe squashed squash. Anyway, it's zucchini and a lot of garlic, some mint, lemon. Simple." He relaxed and started eating his own piece of the torte, looking it over bite by bite, no doubt storing his assessment in a mental file labeled Potluck-slash-Dessert-slash-Chocolate.

He and I weren't contributing to Ardis' mordant, though, so I cast around for something I could say that might spark interest in surrounding ears. The trouble was I hadn't known Will or Shannon and hadn't ever spent much time on the river. So no memories to dredge up. What to do, what to . . . ah. I could ask questions.

"So, Joe, did you ever find out who Otterbank is?"

Joe choked on the last bite of his torte.

Chapter 25

John Berry gave Joe a few pounds on the back. That did the trick for Joe, but it was the beginning of the downward slide of the evening. While we'd been laying our plans and starting them in motion, someone else had arrived at the potluck, causing a stir and the kind of rolling wave Ardis had pictured our happy chat and reminiscences creating. No one had expected Bonny, so recently and tragically bereaved, to appear at this, the social and entertainment highlight of the year. Surprise and excitement didn't begin to cover it.

She looked amazingly normal—makeup, hair, stylish pantsuit. The makeup didn't hide her red eyes, though. She reached our table just as John finished pounding Joe, as Joe was avoiding my eye, and just as one of those spontaneous, communal silences occurred—into which Debbie tripped.

"Yeah, I could've fallen for Will," Debbie's sweet, clear voice said for the whole room to hear, "but he was so in love with Shannon."

Mel saw Bonny before Debbie did. Mel is a good friend. She tried to get up and out of her chair and around Debbie's chair fast enough to deflect Bonny. But the woman sitting behind Debbie scooted her chair back at the wrong moment, blocking Mel. The communal silence continued, only now it was also an uncomfortable silence. And whereas Debbie had tripped into it, Bonny barged headlong.

"Don't you dare talk about my daughter in the same breath as that murdering son of a—"

"My dear—" John started to get up.

"And don't you start, John Berry." Bonny rounded on him. "You and your brother didn't have any more use for Will Embree than I did, and don't pretend you ever did. This one, though"—she jabbed a finger at Debbie—"is spreading despicable lies. My girl was a good girl and she was going to marry a good man."

She faltered then, seeming to realize, suddenly, that she didn't have just an audience; she had the *whole* audience. She looked unsure, vulnerable, and I hoped she would stop or just slip away. Debbie had made herself small and sat staring at the table, biting her lip. Someone near the doors coughed. One chair scraped back—Ardis. She watched Bonny closely but didn't move to interfere.

Then Bonny sucked in a breath. She'd made up her mind and she set her jaw and she plowed forward.

"Shannon was engaged to Eric," she said, her voice choked. "Did you know that? Did any of you know that?"

There was a murmur down the table to my right and movement, and Evangeline appeared. Ernestine uttered a small "Oh my" and I wondered whether she was worried or hoping that Evangeline carried a pitcher of iced tea. Evangeline went to the microphone, though. It was a good move on her part. If she could draw the audience's attention, maybe someone—Ardis—could ease Bonny away.

There was a screech of feedback; then Evangeline's voice came through loud and clear. "Bonny, our thoughts and prayers are with you at this sad time, but this is neither the time nor the place for confrontations. Please sit down and wait for the business meeting to begin."

A smaller "Oh my" came from Ernestine. She put her fingertips to the bridge of her nose and shook her head.

"He's a good man," Bonny said loudly, regaining the audience. "She was engaged to a good man and my baby was going to have a baby."

"That good man shot her with his gun," Debbie said, finally reacting and looking up into Bonny's face. Her voice was steady but raw with pain. "Bonny, Eric killed her. Will couldn't have."

"Why, because you can give him an alibi? Because he was in bed with you?"

"No, Bonny."

"Then you're lying because you *can't* know he didn't kill her!" Bonny howled. "Will Embree was a bastard and a coward and he killed my baby!"

"Bonny," Evangeline said into the microphone, "please sit down." Several people shushed Evangeline, but Bonny had the final word.

"Shut up, you stupid cow!" she bellowed.

At that, Ardis rose and folded Bonny in her honeysuckle arms, and Bonny let herself be led away. Thea went ahead of them and opened a side door so they didn't have to go past the entire roomful of people.

"I've got a line for a song if anyone wants to write it," Mel said. "There were potshots at the old potluck tonight." She sighed and looked at Debbie. "Are you going to be all right?"

Debbie brushed the question aside. A minute later she got up and walked quickly, head down, to the main doors. Mel gave her a short lead, then indicated to us that she'd go after her, and she left, too.

"Poor thing," Ernestine said when I asked why she thought Bonny had come. "I imagine she's still on autopilot and not really thinking. She came because that's what she knows to do. She's the treasurer of the trust.

She takes her responsibilities seriously and she probably had it in mind that she would come to the meeting and give her report."

"Wow. Really?"

"That's how some people get through stressful times," Ernestine said. "Marching to their internal orders. I'm more of a wailer and neck hugger, but it takes all kinds."

Evangeline tried one more time to gain the audience's attention, but no one was listening. When I glanced toward the microphone, the Spivey twins were there patting Evangeline on the back and shaking their heads. People around us were talking and getting up. Some of them went to browse what was left of the potluck; others drifted toward the doors. Ernestine, John, Joe, and I just sat.

"You historical types sure know how to throw a party," a voice I didn't appreciate hearing said. Clod Dunbar dumped himself into the vacated chair to my right. "Evening, Ms. O'Dell." He nodded to Ernestine. "John. Ms. Rutledge." He was in jeans and a gray flannel shirt instead of his uniform, and I wondered if he'd been at the meeting all along, but then he said something that told me he hadn't. It was also something I really didn't appreciate hearing. "I've been looking for you."

I almost snapped something in return that *he* wouldn't appreciate. Then I realized he wasn't talking to me.

"You don't answer your phone, Joe. You don't call back when I leave a message. I'm beginning to think you don't love me anymore."

Joe half smiled, and they both made small noises that came close to being quiet laughs. They didn't come close enough to convince me that either of them thought it was a joke, but Joe's lanky frame didn't tense and Clod stretched his long legs out under the table. They went in for the understated in their brotherly interactions, these two.

"I can use your help," Clod said.

Joe raised his eyebrows.

Clod covered a yawn, then picked up Joe's tea glass and rolled it in his hands. "Been a long day. Long and frustrating." He put the glass down and looked at Joe. "Looking for things I couldn't find."

"What kind of help?" Joe asked.

Clod glanced at John, Ernestine, and me, then back at Joe. "Looking for Eric Lyle."

"Why on earth do you think Joe can find him if you can't?" Ernestine asked.

Clod didn't answer her. "Joe? Tomorrow morning?"

Joe's smile was slight and possibly rueful, then gone. "There's something going on at the Cat in the morning."

Clod shot me a look. "Tomorrow afternoon, then."

"Sorry, fishing."

Clod said something that made Ernestine say "Oh my" again. And then I heard those words I'd grown to despise, and they were definitely directed at me.

"I've been looking for you, Kath Rutledge." It was Carolyn Proffitt sounding in full snit. She wore heels again, but this time with skinny jeans and a faux peasant blouse. Joe was right. Not the outdoorsy type. But the heels and her tone of voice and the perfectly sprayed hair were all at odds with her hesitant step and the way her shoulders drew in as she approached the table. Then, when she saw Joe sitting across from me, she stopped and she actually pouted. "I thought you said you didn't know where she was sitting."

"Then I didn't. Now I do. Time passed."

That Zen-ish statement didn't put her any more at ease. Neither did realizing the man sitting next to me, the one who'd had his back to her as she'd approached, was Deputy Cole Dunbar. She acknowledged his greeting by backing up a step.

"Why were you looking for me?" I asked.

Her eyes flicked to me, then back to Clod. As I watched, his relaxed-brother persona disappeared and his chest-puffing, "well, little missy" cop took over. He sat up and plunked his feet flat on the floor and all but stuck his hands on his hips.

"Ms. Proffitt?" he said. "Is there something you want to share with Ms. Rutledge that you can't share with all of us?"

And that brought the snit she'd arrived in back in full force. "No," she said. She looked over at me. "Only that I stand by what I said Tuesday morning. I had you figured wrong."

"What?" That couldn't be it. That was a ridiculous reason to come looking for me.

Clod snorted and looked away.

"Wait."

But she'd turned her eyes to the side door that Ardis had taken Bonny through and she was already squeezing behind me and Ernestine to get to it. I reached to stop her. I barely caught her sleeve before she pulled away. My fingers didn't feel anything more than skin-crawling polyester slipping through them, and then she was gone.

"Do you think I should I go after her?" I asked.

"Why?" Clod snorted again. "She just insulted you."

I wasn't sure she had. There was something in her eyes when she said it. And if Clod hadn't been there, or if he hadn't played his cloddish-cop card . . . but she was long gone. Besides, if she was really so all-fired keen on talking to me, she *did* know where to find me.

By then the others were on their feet, making leave-taking noises, and I got up, too. John said something about this potluck ranking right up there with the year of the Cola War. Ernestine shushed him. Joe, hands in his pockets, was ready to amble. Clod, into nonverbal vocalizing that evening, blew noisily through his lips, not directing the commentary at anything in particular. It sounded more like a general summary of his day.

I looked toward the side door one more time and was thinking I might collect my salad bowl and leave that way when I felt a chill at the back of my neck and Geneva trickled into view.

"Have you been looking for me?" she asked.

Chapter 26

"You see? I did understand you perfectly," Geneva said.

I didn't know what she was talking about. I was trying to ignore her and act normal while saying good-bye to the others. It wasn't easy. She was keyed up and going on about her "latest genius invention." She made it hard to think, much less keep my eyes focused. John and Ernestine waved and headed across the gym for the main doors, but they kept turning and looking back, as though they sensed something more than my distraction. And Joe didn't help, because he didn't amble off after all. He hung back. Waiting? To talk? I didn't know, but Clod noticed, too.

"You two have plans?" Clod asked.

I missed Joe's answer. Geneva had finally said something that caught my whole attention.

"So, on your instructions, I infiltrated the potluck. Get it? While you and the rest of the posse took care of the gossip and the research, the G and R, I did the I at the P. I got a grip! Just like you! Only my grip was much more useful to the investigation than the way you do it with your eyes squeezed so tightly shut. I overheard quite a few conversations and picked up a piece of information we should label Key Information. Isn't that wonderful news? And none of this would have happened if you hadn't told me *not to come with you.*" She might as well have added *wink, wink, nudge, nudge.*

I couldn't help it. I closed my eyes.

"Do you see what I mean?" She sighed. "That doesn't look productive. It just looks painful."

Chapter 27

Our dye workshop once again didn't materialize. Debbie called me early Sunday morning and said only that she couldn't. I didn't press for an explanation beyond "couldn't" and told her not to worry about it. As if telling her that would ease her mind. But I said I'd call the others and she should take care of herself. I forgot to ask her about the notes she'd made for me the day before on her impressions of Will and Shannon and the other people she knew who were involved in the case, but I didn't call her back. Maybe she'd left the notes at the Cat. Maybe Ardis knew where they were.

When I called Ardis, she said she didn't care about canceling the workshop. "The potluck ended before we completed the Triple Blind," she said. "We gathered no gossip. We reaped no tidbits for further research."

"You didn't get anything else out of Bonny when you walked her out of the gym?"

"Nothing but tears, hon. She's a shattered woman. And I am a woman wakened too early on a Sunday morning. My mind will think more clearly in an hour or three. In the meantime, I am rolling over and going back to sleep."

Ardis really must have needed a few more hours' sleep if she didn't realize that we'd gleaned at least a few tidbits from our efforts at the potluck. We'd learned that

Shannon was engaged to Eric Lyle. According to Bonny, anyway, and that the baby was his. Again, according to Bonny. Those tidbits added something to our swirl of data. I didn't know how, or if, they changed anything, or if they just added a different color, but that was why we were investigating—to find out how things sorted out and added up. Of course, Ardis had missed Carolyn Proffitt's appearance and cryptic insult. And she'd missed Clod's admission that the authorities needed help looking for Eric Lyle. But none of those tidbits needed to keep Ardis from rolling over and going back to sleep. Before she did roll, I asked her about Debbie's notes. She said I'd find them on the desk in the little office behind the counter at the Cat.

"Debbie looked like she was pouring her heart into writing them, hon, so I let them take the place of that heart-to-heart. Good night."

Thea apologized for not giving me the dossiers that she'd compiled on all the players at the potluck, but with one thing and another . . . She said she wasn't sure they amounted to much but hoped they'd fill in some gaps or spark more questions. "I'll put them in an envelope and slip it through the mail slot at the Cat on my way past."

Everyone else was fine with canceling the workshop, too. Everyone was feeling subdued. No one asked if we planned to re-reschedule. I decided we probably should, though. We needed something creative and colorful and fun to look forward to. I hoped the others would agree.

Without the workshop, I had the morning to stew over Geneva's Key Information and time to wonder if Joe's casual, not quite an invitation to go fishing with him that afternoon constituted going on a date. That was why he'd hung around the night before, eventually outwaiting Clod, who'd snorted one more time, then taken off in a huff.

"Two o'clock sound good to you?" he'd asked. "We can take my canoe."

Geneva thought the invitation *was* a date. "I will act as chaperone if it will make you feel more comfortable," she'd said as I drove her back to the Cat, "because he might be planning more on canoodling in that canoe than fishing. Although you should be aware that the effect of my presence on the worms and fish might put a damper on fishing, should that really be what's on his mind."

"That's a kind offer," I said, "but you make a good point about scaring the fish, and I'm sure Joe will appreciate it if you stay home."

"Just so I'm clear, are you saying you want me to come with you or you want me to stay home?"

"I tell you what—let's make a deal. Let's not use backward or reverse instructions anymore."

"I do miss that television show, and I wish you hadn't brought it up. Missing Monty makes me melancholy. But do you mean that you will use backward or reverse instructions or you won't?"

We got that straightened out, I hoped, and I even extended one of my every-so-often invitations to come home with me rather than go back to the Cat for the night. She never accepted and didn't this time, either, saying she liked the comforts of her own room.

"Besides," she said, "Kojak would miss me."

There really wasn't much to stew over in Geneva's Key Information. She'd heard the Spivey twins tell Angela they were close to cracking the case, thanks to information received, and that they intended to come find me after cooking Sunday dinner for their aged mother and rub it in my face. That excited Geneva until I told her it was the cracked case they meant to rub, not chicken, mashed potatoes, and gravy. I thanked her for telling me, though. Knowing they were going to come looking for me was definitely Key Information. Knowing that gave me time and extra incentive to disappear up a creek with Joe the Unfindable Fisherman.

I did wonder from where or from whom they'd received case-cracking information, and I still wanted to hear what they knew about the wannabe journalists, but on my own terms and not in a Spivey ambush. And, I assured Geneva, not for one minute did I believe Shirley and Mercy had really done anything to even come close to cracking the case.

My memories from that afternoon were stored as a series of impressions—the creaking of Joe's car as we lurched slowly along a nearly invisible, almost impassable Forest Service road down to the river, me laughing as I stretched up trying to help Joe lift the canoe off the car, the touch of gray at his temple that I hadn't noticed before, birdsong, pines, leaf mold, moss, and the liquid soundtrack the river gave to our lazy fishing as we drifted downstream.

Woven through the impressions were the colors of east Tennessee: cathedral wood green, leaf-filtered sky blue, river-polished speckled gray gravel, and water—water rippling, smooth, and clear—dappled yellow, olive, and brown by the sun and darkening from emerald to black in the shade of overhanging trees.

The impressions were only dashed-off sketches, though. Incomplete. They were scraps of watercolors, a snippet of embroidered cutwork, as slippery to describe or bring wholly to mind as the wash of blues and greens in the beautiful silk scarf Sylvia wore the day she and Pen came into the Cat. The impressions were all those fragmented things with the addition of a single splash of red for accent.

Everything else beyond those impressions I would as soon have forgotten. It would have been fine to forget the red, too.

We didn't catch many fish and released the ones we did. We hadn't started too far upriver, not as far as Cloud Hollow, and Joe took us along slowly, mindful that we'd have to paddle harder to get back upstream. There were any number of questions we could have asked each other, but we didn't say much, either, letting the river and the birds do the talking. But at one point I made a joke when I caught sight of something under the trailing willows in the still water lapping an undercut bank.

"I didn't know there were alligators around here."

And of course there weren't and it wasn't.

"That's a nasty head wound," Clod said when he arrived on the riverbank. "I kind of hoped, though, if you went looking for the poor sap, that you'd find him still on his feet and breathing."

"It is Lyle, then?" Joe asked.

"Oh yeah," Clod said. "A shame, too. I had a few questions he could've answered for me. Now I've got a couple more. Did he fall and hit his own head or did someone hit it for him? And what's that trailing from his back pocket? See there? How it moves in the bit of current and catches the light a little farther out from the bank? Kind of pretty. Looks too pretty for a guy like that. Why's he got that jammed in his pocket? Whose is it?"

"Sylvia's," Joe said. "Sylvia Furches."

He was right. And again, it was the quick impression and the colors that stayed with me—the beautiful watery blues and greens of the silk-and-something scarf her sister wove for her. But I hadn't told Joe the scarf was hers. I hadn't done anything since he called his brother. I'd only sat in the canoe with my hand over my mouth and refused to get out.

"How do you know her?" I asked, moving my hand from my mouth to the side of my face so it blocked my view of Clod and whatever his colleagues were doing with Eric Lyle.

"And what's she doing here?" Clod asked. "I thought you two didn't have plans."

Joe shrugged one shoulder. The only way from the canoe to the bank was to carefully step over the side and wade to the mossy bank. He'd done that and then been able to pull the canoe closer in, but I'd stayed put. Joe sat crouched on the bank now, holding the canoe steady. He was looking toward Clod, so I assumed his shrug answered Clod's question and not mine.

"Well, did you see anything on your way downriver?" Clod asked. "Anything obvious? Any idea where she might have gone in? Or were you too busy fishing?"

The emphasis he put on "fishing" was more than I could bear. "I'd like to go home now," I said loudly, possibly close to hysterically, and I started to stand up in the canoe.

"Whoa, there," Joe said calmly, and he held a hand out to me.

"Yeah, watch yourself," Clod said. "I don't need you falling in and muddying up the waters."

They hadn't taken Lyle out of the river yet, and the thought of tipping and falling in anywhere near him had me sitting back down. With my hand clamped over my mouth again. I shook my head at Joe, and he dropped his hand.

"I didn't see anything," he said to Clod. "It'd be hard to know what to look for, though."

"Of course, there's the bridge on Arnold Road," Clod said.

"And a few others farther up. Any idea how long or how far he . . ."

Clod shook his head. "Not even a day, but that's only a guess. How far, hard to say. So how's this Furches woman tied up with Lyle? What do you know about her?"

"*I* told you about her, night before last," I said taking my hand from my mouth again. I wished he wouldn't look at me that way. It always made me say things I should regret. *Should. Didn't. Who gives a flip?* My own contribution to Zen philosophy. "She's one of the journalism students who's been nosing around. Maybe you don't remember because it was so very long ago, but the other one broke into Debbie's workshop night before last. Holy cow, what if in all their nosing they found something incriminating against Eric Lyle and he found out? What if they confronted him? What if Sylvia or Pen is in the water, too . . ."

At that not-necessarily-logical thought I was on my feet and pretty much leapt right over Joe to the bank. It might have been more of a scramble from the looks of Joe when I turned around and stared, horrified, back at the water. But Granny was right when she told me not turn my back on that river for a minute. I might never go near it again. Clod, as ever, was unimpressed by my deductive reasoning.

"Okay, here's what you two are going to do. You, Cupcake"—he jabbed a finger at me—"are pulling your nose out of this case. You're leaving it alone. You're letting the professionals handle it. You're sitting on your butt with your knitting needles clacking and you are minding your own business. Am I clear? And you, Tonto"—he jabbed two fingers at Joe, and the fingers looked like a Moe Howard poke in the eye—"are taking her outta here and taking her home. Shorty will give you a lift back to your car. You can leave the canoe. I'll make sure you get it back. And thanks for all your help."

Ooh, I could hear the drip, drip, dripping of sarcasm. I wanted to kick him.

Joe started to take my arm. I yanked it away. Forget the sitting and the knitting. What I was going to do was go to the Cat, locate Debbie's notes and Thea's dossiers, and climb the stairs to the study, and somewhere in all that information, I was going to find the threads and shreds of evidence and clues we needed to solve three murders. And then that was exactly what TGIF and I were going to go out and do. And I just hoped we didn't find any more bodies along the way.

Joe and I didn't talk much on the way back to town, either, until I asked him how he knew Sylvia. He thought about it far longer than seemed necessary, maybe wondering whether to answer. He did, though, and at first I didn't see why he'd been reluctant.

"We met in class."

"What class—wait, the *journalism* class?"

He nodded, shrugged. "I thought it might be interesting."

"You aren't the one who told those two to stop by the Cat, are you? Or how to get to Cloud Hollow?"

"I never gave them the opportunity."

I could believe that. Quiet Joe, Journalist Burglar. "Huh. So, we know what their big project was. What's yours?"

"Already finished and turned in."

"Okay. Good. And what was it?"

Only a slight hesitation. And a slight blush? "You read it," he said.

"I did?" I thought for a second. What . . . "Oh my gosh. You're Otterbank."

Joe wouldn't say any more about the interview or Aaron Carlin, except to say he was protecting his source. I didn't point out that he'd *named* his source, because naming Aaron Carlin and telling how to find him were two different things.

I asked him to say hi to Aaron for me next time he saw him, though, and then we were back in town and I said he could just drop me at the courthouse. I waited until he drove away before walking to the Cat. I wasn't sure why I waited. He could have figured out where I went easily enough. But I was feeling secretive and decided not to worry about why.

I spent the evening in the study, cell phone off, avoiding Spiveys and the rest of the world, and reading through Debbie's notes and Thea's dossiers. It was better than thinking about Eric Lyle and wondering about Sylvia and Pen. It took less and more time than I thought. More because there were inconsequential details that had to be read and considered before setting them aside and moving on. Less because Geneva insisted on doing her share. If I flipped the pages for her. And if she could read the dossiers, because she found Debbie's handwriting too flowery for her taste.

When she finally settled down to read, we made progress. Although she did insist on saying "ping" every time she wanted me to turn a page, and the cat insisted on sprawling in the middle of the desk so I had to reach around him to turn her pages.

Debbie's notes were more personal than I'd expected. That made me glad Geneva insisted on reading the dossiers. It wouldn't have felt right turning the notes over to someone else, even if that someone else couldn't spread gossip. The notes went on for pages, stream-of-consciousness memories flowing in a cathartic cascade. I hoped it was cathartic, anyway. Parts of them were confessional, too. Will and Debbie's late husband had been good friends. She believed he was innocent of the death in the river. He *had* occasionally slunk by the farm for a meal or a night out of the coldest winter weather, which he would spend in the roughly finished attic space above her dye kitchen. The notes showed her conflicted honesty, too. She was telling *me*, she wrote, but she'd lied to Cole Dunbar about Will's visits. That made me stop reading and try to stop thinking.

"Ping."

It was getting late. I was hungry and wanted to go home—not just home, but home-home to Illinois and my organized life that didn't exist anymore.

"Ping-ping-ping."

I turned Geneva's page and mine and continued reading.

The rest of the notes only confirmed that Debbie was as confused as I thought. She really didn't get it, didn't see that it mattered whether she'd loved Will Embree, because she'd made sure he never knew. And with this glimpse into her honest, steady mind I could maybe understand why she didn't think it mattered. She used the analogy of dyeing—something that made sense to her. She knew that Will loved Shannon—they were a true, clear color. She knew that if she allowed her own feelings for Will to show, they would introduce another element into the dye bath that would taint and muddy everything that followed. I raked my fingers through my hair. I needed to do something. But what? What was I supposed to do with all this?

Geneva provided the answer.

"Well, I'll be a monkey's uncle," she said. "Is that something people say in real life?"

"Not much. Why are you saying it?"

"Or only on *I Love Lucy*?"

"Geneva, did you find something?"

"Not much. There's just something here that I forgot the adorable twins mentioned when they said they were about to crack the case."

"What?"

"Don't snap at me. I'm being extremely helpful."

"I wasn't snapping. I was being focused. So will you please focus and tell me what the Spiveys mentioned?"

"The little hideaway cabin."

"Oh," I said, working hard not to focus to the point of snapping. "What cabin is that and what did they say about it?"

"It sounds darling, doesn't it?"

"Sure. Darling."

"I thought so, too. The twins said it belonged to Shannon's granny's family, and according to this note it's on several acres the family kept after selling the rest for oodles of money to a paper company. And the Spiveys said it belongs to Shannon's mama now, but Shannon and her friends go there more often than her mama because her mama is such a hoity-toity, tooty-fruity, highfalutin city girl. That sounds like a song, doesn't it?"

I rubbed the cat between his ears, using his head as a furry worry stone. It helped. He purred and that helped, too. "You heard the Spiveys say all that?"

"Are you doubting my excellent memory?"

I rubbed the cat harder. He purred harder. Such a good animal. "I'm not doubting you. This sounds like important information, though."

"I think so, too," she said. "That's why I told you as soon as I remembered."

"And I'm glad you did. Did the Spiveys mention how they know about the cabin?"

"The snooty one, Carolyn Proffitt, told them. She was

looking for you and they told her they assist you in all your cases."

"Mm-hmm." And that shed light on Carolyn's "I had you figured wrong" remark. If she knew anything about the Spiveys and if she now believed the Spiveys and I were sleuthing pals, then she couldn't help but think I was wrong top to bottom and inside and out to boot.

Word came the next morning that Eric Lyle had died by drowning in the Little Buck River. Ardis and I heard it from the first customer to jingle the camel bells on the Cat's door and almost every customer that came after. Lyle had sustained two head injuries, either of which might have occurred from falling or jumping in the river and landing on a rock. There were plenty of rocks in the Little Buck, and as Joe and Clod had discussed, there were numerous places from which to fall or jump. Secondary to news of Lyle's death came a report that Sylvia Furches was missing.

"It's a sorry way to go, however it happened," Ardis said, shaking her head over Lyle's death. "And I am so sorry you had to be the one to find him. I'm glad Joe was there."

I nodded.

"And Lyle is somehow connected to this woman's disappearance?"

"He has to be. Her scarf . . ."

"Do you think he went in the river on purpose, then? Took the coward's way out?"

I was about to say that although I didn't know what to think, I intended to find out, when Debbie called. Ardis answered, and her end of the conversation started out sounding positive enough.

"Hon," she said to Debbie, "it looks like things are about to be over, maybe not in a way that's to everybody's liking, but you've held on and handled yourself real well."

I couldn't hear Debbie's end, but it played out on Ardis' face in a way that was obviously not so positive. She filled me in after she disconnected.

"The police are working their way up the river from where the body was found," she said, "looking for the point of entry. That's what they're calling it, 'the point of entry.' But Debbie said she overheard one of them also say they're looking for a crime scene."

"In case he was pushed, so of course they're looking at Cloud Hollow."

"Bite your tongue," she snapped.

"*I* don't believe Debbie . . ."

"Oh, hon, I'm sorry. I know you don't." She picked up a copy of the pattern for the argyle vest the mannequin still wore and started fanning herself with it. She fanned with such frenzy that, if she could have, she would have blown Debbie's troubles out the door and out of sight.

"But you see how it doesn't look good, don't you?" I asked. "When you look at it from their point of view—starting with Will and Shannon? And Debbie was the one who wanted to have the dye workshop yesterday and then she suddenly canceled."

"But now they've found Eric Lyle," Ardis said, almost pleading, "and you *know* he had more to do with all this than Debbie, and she would have no reason to kill him. Oh my Lord, I can't believe we're even saying these things."

"But you see how the police have to look at it. It doesn't mean they're only looking at Debbie, but that's where Will and Shannon were found and they found Eric in the river below Cloud Hollow. And Debbie did catch Pen Ledford out there. And now they need to find Sylvia."

Ardis moaned almost as well as Geneva.

"What else did Debbie say?" I asked. "Anything hopeful?"

"She has an appointment with a good lawyer."

"That sounds like a punch line."

"To an appalling joke. Kath, hon, you need to call the posse together. Things are happening too fast and you can't wait until Friday for a meeting."

"No. You're right."

"So tell me what you're thinking. I can read the concentration in your eyes only so far and your mind not at all."

Thank goodness for small favors. "Okay." I bounced a pencil on the counter. Ardis reached over and took it away. I put my hands flat on the counter. "Okay. Suspects. I'm thinking about suspects."

"The plural is good there, hon. My heart needs the emphasis somewhere other than Debbie."

"And that's what we'll do. Look somewhere else. The police will be putting enough effort into sifting over Cloud Hollow—and Debbie. We'll look at Sylvia. The police will be looking at her, too, but—"

"Doesn't matter," Ardis said.

"No." Because we had to do something. "So here are my questions. Is Sylvia dead? Did Eric Lyle kill her? Is that why he had her beautiful scarf in his pocket when he died? Or did she kill him? Do you think that's a stretch?"

"Doesn't matter," she repeated. "That's why we're investigating. And the Ledford woman—she was capable of breaking into Debbie's dye kitchen."

"Murder is kind of a stretch from that, though."

"Doesn't matter."

"Okay. Then I think we start with the information Thea dug up on Sylvia and Pen. And we find Pen Ledford and talk to her."

"We make her talk."

A vision of Mel and Thea holding Pen while Ardis made her talk swam through my head. Ernestine and John would stand at the ready, brandishing knitting needles. Another vision jumped in with Pen holding all of them at gunpoint. "Being very careful."

"Of course, hon." She patted me on the shoulder. "Whyever wouldn't we be?"

Whyever indeed, considering what I was planning to do. "I'd likc to leave that in your hands, then. I've got—"

"Another lead?"

"Maybe, but—"

"Ah, it's sensitive." She nodded.

"Can you handle the shop alone later this afternoon?"

"With my hands tied behind my back."

"Thanks. But please don't say things like that."

That left convincing Geneva to go for a drive with me. She was in the study listening to the "episode" of *Still Life* I'd started for her. I paused the recording, which annoyed her, but she didn't need much persuasion when she heard the plan.

"How would you like to come with me to find the darling hideaway cabin?" I asked.

"Can we leave immediately?"

"We'll wait until three or four."

"Ohhhhh . . ."

"Please don't whine or moan."

"Well, then I call shotgun."

Her choice of words almost made me reconsider.

As we drove out of town and up the winding river road, I ignored the tiny voice of wisdom in my head telling me I should let Ardis know where I was going. I also ignored the "why" behind that decision. I told myself I was simply treating my friend the ghost to an outing. And while we were out, and because I felt the need to be doing something, I would take the opportunity to clear up a possibility—that Will Embree had been staying in that hideaway cabin as Shannon's guest. What that would prove, I didn't know, except maybe that Shannon did return Will's love. And that Debbie was right, that the color of their love ran clear and unmuddied.

Geneva floated in the passenger seat and hummed. Her tune was familiar, but I couldn't name it. I was just happy she was droning something other than her usual dirge-like lullaby about murk gathering in a glen. And although she managed to turn most tunes into mournful ditties, this one was cheerful, almost jaunty. Then she sang a few bars.

"'Help me, help me, help,' he said,

"'Or the hunter will shoot me dead.

"'Little rabbit come inside, safely to abide.'"

It was "Little Cabin in the Woods," an old campfire song. It was the worst kind of old campfire song, too, because it wouldn't make any difference if I asked her to stop and hum something else. The damage was done. "Help me, help me, help" was stuck in my head.

Chapter 28

The little cabin *was* in the woods, farther up the river than I'd ever been. We'd slowed at each of the few-and-far-between mailboxes, Geneva singing out the names and me trying not to sing about the hunter shooting me dead. We found the right name on a mailbox marking a gravel drive winding into the woods on the river side of the road.

"What do we do now?" Geneva whispered as I hesitated before making the turn. "Ditch the car and creep in on foot?"

"No. We drive in. If no one's here, we get out. If someone *is* here, we act like we got lost, we turn around, and we drive out."

I made the turn and we crept in on wheels.

"Or," Geneva said, "if anyone's here, we can say we're plainclothes police and we can grill them."

"That's probably not a good idea."

"But then I can be the bad cop and I'm so good at that."

"Sorry."

"You're no fun . . . *Oh*, will you just *look* at that darling hideaway cabin!"

It was very cute—a modern log cabin, probably built from a prefab kit, with a deep front porch and a green tin roof. It was a life-size Lincoln Logs house sitting on a rise in a clearing. What I liked best about the place was the absence of cars.

"No smoke from the chimney," Geneva said. That was good, too.

I lowered the windows and turned off the engine, and we sat in the car for a few minutes—watching and listening. Nothing moved. Birds and a sighing breeze in the trees were all we heard.

"I'm getting bored," Geneva whispered.

We got out of the car and listened again. Nothing happened. We left the car, circled the cabin. Heard the same birds. Didn't see anything interesting except a burn barrel out back. The barrel was cold but there were ashes in the bottom. It was hard to tell what they'd been, but they hadn't been beaten down by rain.

"Get a stick," Geneva said. "Stir them up and see if there's any human bones."

"No!" I jumped back from the barrel.

"There's nothing nasty about bones," she said mildly. "We've all had them at one time or another. But never mind. You stay there. There probably isn't much to see in here anyway. No, I was right. Mostly burned paper." She looked odd, almost upended, with her head in the barrel. "There are a few words still showing."

"Can you read any of them?"

"This is funny. I think one of them actually says 'ash.' They are very pale, though. Like word ghosts. You should come look."

I did. The word she saw was on something that had been sturdier than paper. Cardboard, maybe. And the word began with a capital *A* and had an *E* after the *H* followed by the beginning slant of another letter. The rest of it was burned away to nothing. Ashe. Asheville? And what I hadn't noticed before—there was a coil of blackened wire in the ashes. A spiral from a notebook. Sylvia, Pen, and Joe were taking their journalism class at a community college in Asheville.

"Is it evidence?" Geneva asked. "Should we take it with us?"

"I think we'd better leave everything we find here. Let's look at the cabin."

Unfortunately, the cabin's side and back windows were covered by blinds and we couldn't see in.

"Bored again," Geneva said.

"We'll go up on the porch."

I'd saved the stairs and the porch and peeking in the front windows for last, and climbing those half dozen steps made me more nervous than the skulking around back. There weren't any inviting rockers on the porch. Leaves had blown into a drift against the cabin logs. Heavy curtains in the front windows were drawn, and the door was solid, rough pine. All of that made me even more nervous because I knew then that I was going to ask Geneva to do something that strictly speaking . . . pretty much almost certainly . . . wasn't *really* . . . quite . . . legal.

"Geneva, would you, um, would you consider floating through a window or something and looking around inside? You know, check the fridge, the bathroom, see if it looks like anyone was living here recently?"

"You mean *break in*?"

"Well, technically you wouldn't be *breaking* in, and you shouldn't stay more than a few minutes, five or ten tops, so . . ." Who knew I could channel my inner Joe Dunbar so easily?

"But it's against the law?" Geneva asked.

"Well . . ."

"Well, nothing. Stand back and watch how a bad cop does it right." She added an extra flourish by loosening her shoulders and shaking out her arms; then she flew through the wall of the cabin and was gone.

And I sat on the steps and wondered. I didn't go so far as to wonder if I was crazy, but I did wonder if I knew what I was doing.

Five minutes later, Geneva was still gone and I was beginning to wonder in earnest when I heard a car. At first I didn't think the car was coming down the drive. When I saw the sun glinting off the windshield as it approached, I decided to brazen it out—pretend I belonged or was waiting for the homeowner or . . . crud. The car belonged to Deputy Clod Dunbar.

My big mistake, I realized, was in not giving careful enough consideration to Geneva's iffy connection with time. One, ten, twenty minutes, two days—I should have known they'd all be the same to her. My other mistake was in not arranging an "abandon cabin" signal in case of trouble. Of course, those mistakes were in addition to the other rather big ones I'd made in being there in the first place and asking her to go inside and snoop. But in for a penny—I went ahead and tried to brazen it out by smiling and waving and saying hi to Clod and the deputy who got out of the car with him.

"You must be Debbie's cousin Darla the Deputy," I called. It was more of a shout in hopes Geneva would hear and take the hint. She didn't.

Even in her uniform, Darla looked pleasant. Her hair was a shade darker than Debbie's and she wore it pulled back in a tight bun, but she had the same smile and general shape. She started to wave back until Clod turned his mirrored sunglasses on her in what must have been an official "look."

"Ms. Rutledge," he said, "I am going to ask you what you're doing here and then I'm going to ask you to leave."

"Okay." It wasn't nice of me, but I sat there and waited for him to go ahead and ask me. In the twenty or thirty nanoseconds it took him to become furious, I madly wondered what would happen if he made me leave before Geneva reappeared. What would she do if she floated back out of the cabin and I was gone? As he began to stew, he trained his starched face and sunglasses on me with increasing intensity, and suddenly I knew what to do. I slipped my own sunglasses from my purse onto the porch where he couldn't see them.

"Oh, were you waiting for me to answer?" I said, sounding as clueless as I could. "I thought you said you were *going* to ask, but I guess that's kind of what you already did, isn't it? Okay, well, I was just basically taking a drive, you know? And then I saw the name on the mailbox and I thought, oh, hey, why not stop by? No one's home, though, but it's such a nice evening I thought I'd enjoy the peace and quiet for a while sitting here on the porch. It's really pleasant. So what are you doing here?"

"Slemmons," he said.

"Pardon?"

"I *thought* so." He might as well have said, "Aha, gotcha," but the joke turned out to be on him. "You don't know the owners and you didn't just happen to stop by," he said. "You're sticking your nose in again, aren't you? Slemmons is the name on the mailbox. What are you doing here?"

"You don't know?"

He started to snarl.

"No, I mean, you really don't know, do you? Slemmons is Bonny's mother's maiden name. Bonny inherited. This is her land. This is her cabin. I guess she's never cared about changing the name on the mailbox."

That was when Deputy Darla contributed her only

speaking lines that afternoon. I liked them a lot. "You didn't know that, Cole? Sorry, I thought you knew that."

"And now I will ask you to leave," Clod said. From the grouse in his voice and the look he gave me and then Darla, he might have been speaking to both of us. She knew better and didn't seem to take offense. She was going to make a fine, even-tempered deputy. "Leave now," Clod said, now looking only at me, "or I will arrest you for trespassing."

"I don't think you can do that just because you want me to leave, can you?"

"Now."

I got up, wanting so badly to go pound on the door for Geneva. Instead I gave Deputy Darla another wave and walked to the car without looking back. I got in. Started it up. Beeped the horn accidentally on purpose. Looked toward Clod standing at the bottom of the stairs, arms crossed, waiting for me to leave. Gave him a sheepish shrug. Didn't see Geneva anywhere. Sighed and drove away.

I went about a quarter mile down the road to the next gravel drive, turned around, and drove back for my sunglasses. When I pulled back into the clearing, neither of the deputies was in sight, but there was a patch of damp fog at the bottom of the stairs. It must be Geneva, I realized, but I'd never seen her from such a distance. She was happy to see me get out of the car. Clod, who appeared from behind the cabin, was not.

"I thought you would never come back," Geneva said.

"Why are you back?" Clod demanded.

The two of them in stereo, both prissy and pissy, came close to making me laugh.

"Deputy, you made me leave so fast, I accidentally left something behind," I said.

"You mean you didn't leave me on purpose?" Geneva asked.

"Left on purpose, you mean," Clod said. He held up my sunglasses.

"No," I said, answering both of them. "Not on purpose. Deputy, if I you'll give me my sunglasses, I'll make sure I don't leave anything else behind and I'll be on my way."

"Good," Geneva said. She made a rude noise at Clod and floated to the car, nose in the air.

"Good," Clod said. "All except the part about giving you the sunglasses." He stuck his other hand in a pocket and pulled out a clear plastic bag. He slipped my sunglasses inside. "These are evidence."

Chapter 29

I missed my sunglasses all the way back to town, but not as much as I missed my sanity. Breaking into a house? Leaving behind incriminating evidence? Where was my common sense? Neither of those charges, if they really were charges, would stand up to any kind of legal scrutiny—especially the breaking-in part because, technically speaking, no living person I knew *had* broken in. But it was the principle of the thing. I was a law abider and I should not be contributing to the delinquency of my ghost. Geneva moaned in the seat next to me.

"I am so sorry I had to leave you behind like that," I told her.

"And I am sorry," she moaned, "for myself, because who will turn on my audiobooks when they throw you in the hoosegow?"

"I'm glad to know you'll miss me."

"I am thoughtful that way. I am also observant. For instance, I saw a flat-screen television in the cabin and I thought that, as long as we were already breaking one law, you might like to take it home for me. It looked like a very good one, so I thought about that for quite a while. I would say there's always next time, but for you, locked up with the key thrown away, there isn't." She moaned again.

"What else did you see in the cabin?"

"It wasn't to my taste, really."

"But did it look like anyone was staying there? Was there toothpaste in the bathroom? Milk in the fridge? Dishes in the drainer? Had someone been sleeping in a bed?"

"Of course I don't know what their housekeeping standards are, but I would say there are signs of recent occupancy."

"What signs? How recent?"

"Your voice is getting shrill."

"Sorry."

"There were mustard and ketchup in the refrigerator."

"They could've been there for months. You didn't happen to check their sell-by dates, did you?"

"Their what?"

"Never mind. What else did you see?"

"A stack of newspapers next to the woodbox. Kindling *in* the woodbox."

"Did you check the date of the newspaper on top of the stack?"

"If you were so keen on details, you should have better prepared me or done it yourself."

She was right, if annoying, and we rode in silence as I tried to figure out if I'd learned anything useful. I'd learned several useful things, I decided. That I'd been one up on Deputy Clod. That Geneva, much as I'd wished to the contrary, was not a reliable partner in crime and was possibly a dangerous one. And that, much as I didn't want to intrude on a grieving mother, I needed to go see Bonny. And now was as good a time as any.

"Geneva, do you mind if we make one more stop?"

"You mean on your way to the slammer?"

Such a way she had with words.

But when we got to Bonny's there was an ugly beige

Buick parked out front—the Spiveymobile. Maybe I did need to talk to Bonny and to the twins, but there was no way I was going to make myself talk to all three of them together. I dropped Geneva back at the Weaver's Cat and then called Ardis for an update on her end. She was in the middle of getting her aged father to bed.

"Wheels are in motion, hon, and by that I mean Ernestine and John are in motion. Full report in the morning."

Hoping "wheels in motion" didn't in any way involve Ernestine behind a wheel, I treated myself to a frozen pizza for supper followed by a half pint of cookie dough ice cream—with the curtains drawn and the porch light off so no one knew I was home.

The combination of pizza, ice cream, and peace and quiet produced a full night's sleep—in both senses of "full." I woke in the morning to a message on my phone from Joe. He said he felt bad about the way the fishing trip ended and wondered if I'd care to meet him in the park along the creek behind the courthouse for a picnic supper to make up for it. Maybe Geneva had been right and the fishing *was* supposed to be a date. Funny that I still couldn't tell for sure, but I decided I didn't mind spending a little more time trying to find out, so I called and left a message on his phone saying sure and I'd meet him in the park at six.

Feeling brave and strong after that, and willing to give everyone another chance, including myself and my ghostly sidekick, I straightened my spine and went to see Bonny. There was time to do that before opening the shop, although I stopped by on the way and invited Geneva to come along.

Bonny's house up on Fox Street was a showcase Gothic Victorian with upper and lower porches and the most elaborate display of fretwork, brackets, spindles, and spandrels I'd ever seen in architectural gingerbread. It was like embroidery rendered in woodwork and as beautiful inside as out. Bonny herself looked worn-down.

She met me at the door and her salon-fixed hair and neat pantsuit of Saturday night had given way to an inefficient run-through with a comb and baggy sweats. It wasn't cold outside or in, but she'd also pulled on the sage green sweater she'd worn that day out at Cloud Hollow. The sweater had been the only thing soft about her then. Now it might be the only thing holding her together. So much had happened that it was hard for me to believe it was barely more than a week since the deaths in the meadow. For Bonny it must have been more like one never-ending hell of a day. She wasn't overjoyed to see me, but she wasn't angry, either. She asked me in and took me through to the kitchen. Geneva followed.

"I don't know why I spend most of my time in here," she said as she moved some library books off a chair for me. "But this is where I live."

I could tell her why. It was because the kitchen was as unlike the other magazine-photo-spread-perfect rooms we'd walked through as the Weaver's Cat or my whole house was. The kitchen was alive with a flower garden of colors and textures—in the curtains, in the crockery displayed in the antique corner cupboard, in the rag rugs scattered on the brick floor, in the shelves of cookbooks, and in the baskets of yarn sitting handy to her chair.

"The rest of the house needs an intervention," Geneva said. "It reminds me of her not-so-darling cabin. As my very darling mama used to say about houses that put on such airs, there's no place to put your feet up and no place to spit. But this room is more like it."

I coughed. It was a signal I'd come up with on the way

over. I'd told Geneva it meant "pay close attention; this might be important." What it really meant was "shut up." Her very darling mother didn't sound especially so to me, but Geneva rarely mentioned her family, so at least it was an interesting insight.

"How are you holding up?" I asked Bonny.

"I'm dead. That about sums it up," Geneva said.

I coughed. Bonny brought me a glass of water. Geneva slouched over to droop on the corner cupboard and sulk. I drank the water to be polite and to cover the fact that I didn't know how to start after my initial lame question. Straightforward was probably best.

"Bonny, I . . ."

"Your grandmother saved my life," Bonny said, looking me in the eye. "Did you know that? After my snake of a husband left—after he slithered out in the middle of the night—and I couldn't see which way to turn or where any hope lay, Ivy saved my life."

"How?" I asked, afraid of what I was about to hear. I'd heard a few stories start out like that, lovely tributes to Granny, tributes that ended with a fey warning bell . . .

"She threw me a lifeline made of the loveliest soft green wool you've ever seen. I don't know how she did it. How she knew exactly what I needed when I didn't know myself—but as soon as she put that yarn in my hands, I knew she was right and I sat down and I knit this sweater." Her hand stroked her sleeve. "I suppose it was that knack that made her such a good businesswoman."

Or a good businesswitch. I gulped and asked my next question. "Do you know, did Granny dye the wool?"

"Of course. And isn't it a beautiful color? I call it sage. She called it the color of old growing things. It's what got me interested in dyeing. It rekindled my whole interest in needlework and fiber art. There, now, I didn't mean to choke you up. I might've told you that last week, but we didn't really have a chance to talk, did we. But I wanted you to know all that because we've each just lost a piece of our hearts and it's good to know the good stories and remember them."

"Thank you." Choked on tears or choked on fears, I was glad they sounded the same to her. Granny and those dratted secret dye journals—could her hocus-pocus be real? How could it be? And why hadn't I been able to find the journals? Oh, right. Because I kept putting off really looking for them by doing other things like learning to run a business or playing girl gumshoe. With a ghost. Hoo boy.

"There's a book here you should see," she was saying. She reached for the stack from the library she'd taken off my chair and checked through it, putting aside a brochure with a photograph of her house on it and a caption that read "Steamboat B&B."

I nodded at it. "Ardis told me you'd had plans to turn your house into a bed-and-breakfast."

"I've been clearing out garbage," was all she said. She didn't find what she was looking for and she stroked her sleeve again. I could see her mind working through to where she'd last seen the book, but she was coming up blank there, too. Not surprising under the circumstances of her week. "Well," she said vaguely, "it must be upstairs. It's a beautiful book." She looked toward the kitchen door but didn't seem to have the energy to go up and find it. "When I heard about Ivy's passing, I sent money to the library and I asked Thea to buy the best book on natural dyes she could find."

"That was very kind of you, Bonny."

"As soon as she told me she had it, I went down and checked it out. It's a beautiful book."

"Thea told me about it. She put it on hold for me."

"Well. That's all right, then." She'd run out of steam and sat back, the fingertips of her right hand still making tiny circles on her left sleeve, her eyes focused on the tabletop or nothing at all.

I'd touched that sweater when I held her in the field and been shocked by the violent hate that had overpowered her raw, deep sorrow. What would happen if I touched the sweater now? I was still feeling strong, feeling brave . . . I reached my hand toward her arm and . . . couldn't bring myself to do it. I put my hands in my lap and started to tell her what I'd come to say.

"Bonny, you know how you asked me to look into what happened?"

"Mm."

"I drove out to your cabin yesterday."

"I'm selling it," she said abruptly, still staring at the table.

"You are?"

"I can't stand the thought of it anymore." She looked up. "I can't stand that it's on that damned river. Can't bear the idea of driving anywhere near where my baby died. Where her baby died. Where her fiancé died. I cannot bear it. Can you understand that?"

I nodded.

"Do you know what the sheriff's people came and asked me yesterday evening? If Eric could've been hiding in the cabin. If maybe Shannon told him about it, gave him a key, and that's where he was hiding. But I'll tell you what I told them. If he was, then it was because he was scared out of his wits that he'd be blamed for killing her, and now he's going to be blamed anyway because it's convenient and he's dead and he can't answer anyone back. But I'm not making it easy for them. I told them they'd better get a search warrant."

I didn't know what to say. "Wow" fit, but it wasn't appropriate. Telling her what we'd seen in the burn barrel didn't seem appropriate, either, so I just nodded again.

"I'm selling it," she repeated. "I never did like it. I'm sick to death of all of it."

I thought back on waiting there for Geneva the day before, sitting on the steps, enjoying the woods. I'd told Clod it was pleasant and it was. What a shame. What a sad, bitter woman and what a shame she'd never liked it.

"When was the last time you were out there, Bonny? I bet it's pretty along the edge of that clearing when the redbuds bloom."

"I haven't been." She jerked her chair back and stood up, taking my water glass to the sink. "Not since before I left for Florida in January. And I don't plan on going out there ever again. You couldn't drag me out there. I'll get someone to handle the sale for me and be shut of it all."

Ardis was waiting behind the sales counter when we got back to the Cat. She looked solid, sane, and sensible. Out of place, too. It was Tuesday, one of Debbie's mornings, and Ardis wasn't due until noon. Did that mean the police had arrested . . .

"Ardis? What's happened?"

"Debbie's appointment with the good lawyer is this morning. I told her to take the day or several days if she needs them to get things sorted out. Oh, now, I didn't mean to frighten you like that. Come on over here. A rough night, hon?"

"The night? No, the night was fine. It's this morning." I didn't add what I wanted to—*It's this ghost*. The ghost in question floated to the end of the counter, her nose in the air. We'd had words before leaving Bonny's. Now Geneva was feeling miffed and I was feeling far from sane or sensible for having taken her with me on a delicate visit like that. I turned my back to her. "So Debbie's going to be in good hands. We hope. That's good and one less worry. Any news from Ernestine and John? Did they find Pen?"

Ardis held up a hand. "I promised you a full report and you will have it. But first, I want to hear about the lead you were following yesterday. I was so tied up with Daddy last night, I didn't think to ask."

I told her about the trip to the cabin, the ashes in the burn barrel, Cole Dunbar and Deputy Darla arriving.

"What on earth were you thinking going out there by yourself?"

"Don't be angry. Except for losing my sunglasses, nothing really happened."

"Angry? Jealous, more like. And angry, too. Don't you go off being foolish like that and almost getting arrested again. Alone, anyway. And none of *that* gave you a rough night? So what's happened this morning to leave you this way?"

"I went to see Bonny."

"And missed a golden opportunity," Geneva said with a sniff. She was sulking because I hadn't gone along with the "brilliant plan" she'd suddenly dreamed up as we were about to leave Bonny's. The "brilliant plan" consisted of me distracting Bonny while Geneva investigated every nook and cranny in the house to see if Pen Ledford was tied to a chair in a secret room or dungeon. I'd had to pull my phone out and say, "Please don't" and "It makes no sense" and "Do not even think you're going to do that." I'd finally held the phone directly in front of my mouth, squeezing three years' life out of it, looked straight into Geneva's eyes, and shouted, "No!" Amazingly, she'd listened.

Of course Bonny had heard all that, too, and although I apologized for taking the disagreeable phone call in the first place, for overeager and insistent friends in the second place, and for shouting in the third, there was a new wariness in her eyes when she showed me to the door. Just before I went out, her wariness flashed to comprehension and she pointed at the phone still clutched in my hand.

"Spiveys?" she'd asked.

"Mm." I felt bad letting the twins take the blame. But not that bad.

"For my money, Angie's the only Spivey worth spit," she said, mixing metaphors and surnames willy-nilly, Angie being a Spivey only by virtue of her mother's maiden name. "Angie used to babysit Shannon. Had a real gentle way about her and Shannon thought the world of her."

After we'd both shook our heads and clucked our tongues, Bonny shut the door behind me.

"Bless her heart," Ardis said.

Geneva hmphed.

"But Pen Ledford, Ardis. What about Pen?"

Ardis suddenly looked proud enough to burst. "Found her. You'll love this. Thea invented, named, and initiated a new search protocol. The Online Photographer's Organizations, Societies, and Social Media Undercover Search. OPOSSUMS, she calls it, except the *U* is in the wrong place."

"Ridiculous," Geneva sniffed.

I had to agree with Geneva. "Sorry, Ardis, that's um . . ."

Geneva was doing her sulking in a heap on the end of the counter. She acknowledged my comment with another sniff, but she sat up straighter.

"That's all right, hon," Ardis said. "I told Thea she should probably leave acronyms to you from now on. But the search worked. That's what's important. Thea identified half a dozen likely free online photography communities. She and I each joined three, and in between customers here and patrons at the library yesterday afternoon, we chatted online and asked around for Pen. Of course, first we tried her phone."

"Don't tell me it was that simple and all you had to do was call her."

"Wouldn't that have been a kick in the pants? No. She wasn't answering. But we tracked her down online, found out where she is, and Ernestine and John hopped in the car and drove on down there to talk to her in person. And before you ask, I believe John drove."

"Thank you." I was surprised how relieved I was to hear Pen was alive. And that Ernestine hadn't been driving.

"She's lying low in Pulaski," Ardis said.

"Really? Huh. It's as good a place as any, I guess. But why? And how long has she been there? Is Sylvia there, too? Does she know Eric Lyle is dead?"

Someone near the door clapped in slow, sarcastic applause. I didn't bother to look over to see whom or wonder how he came through the door without jingling the bell. Dunbars had a way with doors.

"Good questions, Sherlock," Clod said, "for which we might have better answers if meddlesome-minded citizens would butt out and leave the investigating to the professionals."

Ardis made a furtive gesture suggesting she kick his butt out the door. I did want to see that, but I shook my head. She got a couple of verbal jabs in anyway.

"Hat, Coleridge."

He removed his Smokey Bear hat.

"Now, tell me," she said, "who found Pen Ledford first? You? Or did we do that?"

"Oh, yes, ma'am," Clod drawled. "Y'all are supersonic. In fact, Shorty called me just now to say he'd pulled over a couple of your speed demons. You'll be happy to know that John Berry and Ms. O'Dell will be attending traffic safety school sometime in the near future. Shorty stopped them on their way back from Pulaski. Apparently, they were perfectly happy to share with him what they learned there. Ms. Buchanan, I take it you have been in communication with Ms. O'Dell, although perhaps not in the last half hour? Would you like to fill in the details for Ms. Rutledge?"

"That's all right, Coleridge. You go right ahead. I will be perfectly happy to correct you if you go wrong."

"Thank you. Ms. Ledford has been in Pulaski at her brother's since the early hours of Saturday morning, having driven straight there after her run-in with Hotshot One and Hotshot Two in that outbuilding at Ms. Keith's."

"Excuse me, Coleridge," Ardis said. "Which of those hotshots are you identifying as Kath? One or two? Just so we're clear."

I didn't wait for Clod's opinion on that before jumping in. "Pen couldn't have killed Eric, then, could she?"

"No." Clod shook his head.

"Does she know where Sylvia is?"

"No." Ardis and Clod looked at each other, having both answered that time. Clod scowled. Ardis smiled and waved for him to continue.

"This will all have to be verified by someone in authority, of course—"

"Oh, of course," Ardis agreed.

"—but according to your supersleuth speedsters, Pen Ledford has not been in contact with Sylvia Furches. They are acquainted through the class project, not friends. Ms. Ledford did, however, hand Ms. O'Dell a file containing two-year-old newspaper clippings concerning the incident at Victory Paper. Ms. O'Dell turned that file over to Shorty, saying the Ledford woman claims she and Sylvia Furches were caught up in the thrill of investigative journalism, got carried away, and took the file from the library. Shorty will return it. And that," Clod said, sounding particularly smug, "is all there is to say about that." Then, in a brave show, he looked Ardis in the eye and clapped his hat back on his head.

"What? No!" I slapped my palms on the counter and leaned toward him. "That isn't all. It can't be. What about Sylvia? Where is she? We need to find her."

"No, ma'am," Clod snapped. "You don't. Ms. Rutledge—Kath—I want you to think about something. About a couple of things. Shorty just stopped two senior citizens who had no business careening down the highway, endangering themselves and everyone else, and no business whatsoever involving themselves in a police investigation. And did you even stop to think about what could have happened if you'd blundered around that cabin yesterday and someone had been there? Someone dangerous? Eric Lyle?"

It wasn't smart, but I had to say it. "In case you don't remember, Eric Lyle is dead, so I was probably safe on that count. We found *him* before you did, too. Also Bonny's cabin. Are you getting a search warrant for it?"

Clod's starched face handled it well. He looked at me and only blinked once. "Believe it or not, Ms. Rutledge, I care about the people I come in contact with in the course of my duties. I do my job. I'm good at it. I will not be discussing the ongoing details of this case with you any further. You need to go back to what you're good at. Go back to your"—he waved a hand at the shop—"hobby business."

I was about to spit when Ardis put her hand on my shoulder and squeezed. "Thank you for your concern, Coleridge."

He touched the brim of his hat and opened the door

to leave. I should have taken that squeezed hint from Ardis and let it go, let him go, but I couldn't help myself.

"Why?" I called after him.

He turned. "Why what?"

"Why did you interrupt your busy, professional-criminal-investigation-type day to drop by our hobby business?"

He stopped with his hand on the door and a smirk on his face. "Because I love a good cautionary tale. But let me be completely clear about its moral. You"—he aimed a finger at me for emphasis—"are no longer involved in this investigation." He turned the finger to Ardis. "And neither are you."

"Oh, goody," Geneva said. "That leaves me."

Chapter 30

After Clod's warning, Ardis was unhappy all over again that I'd gone out to the cabin without her and without telling her. Geneva was unhappy I didn't have an immediate assignment for her, our only operative not reprimanded or grounded by the authorities. I was unhappy I'd forgotten to get my sunglasses back from Clod. I was willing to bet he couldn't keep them for evidence, anyway, having found them on private property without a search warrant.

Ardis accepted my apology for scaring her after the fact and we rebonded over insults to Clod and his disparaging description of the shop as a "hobby business."

"He's a flat-footed Philistine," Ardis said.

"A career klutz," I agreed.

"And most of us in TGIF are hampered by the fact we have these day jobs," she said, "which Mr. High-and-Mighty Deputy Dunbar doesn't. He can spend all his time investigating. I call that unfair advantage."

Clod would probably argue that point, but I didn't see any particular need to defend him.

"So what's our next move?" Ardis asked.

"I'm not hampered by anything but your lack of imagination," Geneva said. "Why don't you assign me to tail someone? That would be a good move."

"Speaking of tailing, I never found out from the Spiveys if they learned anything useful when they tailed Sylvia and Pen that first day," I said. Apropos of nothing as far as Ardis was concerned.

She looked at me, sucked a tooth, and said, "Uh-huh."

"Just thinking out loud," I said. "You know, kind of jumping in midstream."

"Uh-huh."

"It keeps my brain nimble. Here's another example. Speaking of things that come in twos—"

"Which we weren't," Ardis said.

"Exactly. See how well it works?"

"Kath be nimble," said Geneva.

"Yeah, that's good." I paused, realizing I was getting confused about who was part of the conversation. "Um. Anyway, things that come in twos. Have you noticed we're missing two cars? Eric's and Sylvia's. We've known Eric's car was missing, but now he's been found and the place he was probably hiding has been found, but his car is still missing. And where is Sylvia's car? Maybe she's with it somewhere far from here, the way Pen is."

"The shame of it is we haven't really got the wherewithal to trace cars," Ardis said. "I wonder if we can work on that."

"Here's another set of two to consider. We have two competing stories of Shannon's love life. Bonny claims Shannon was engaged to Eric and having his baby. Debbie said in her notes that Will told her *he* was engaged to Shannon and he was the baby's father. Two versions, both secondhand."

"Hearsay," Geneva said. "Inadmissible in a court in *Law and Order*."

"And which version do we believe?" Ardis asked. "And why? And how do we prove it's true?"

"Or how do we prove the other one isn't?" I said.

Proving anything that day proved difficult, hampered as we were by our hobby business day job. In between customers we toyed with the idea of contacting Debbie's cousin, the still-green Deputy Darla, and offering her a free knitting class, plus materials, if she would give us access to certain official files. Ardis might have toyed more seriously than I did. Geneva, of course, was all for it.

"I would enjoy corrupting a policeman," she said. "I would also enjoy being a corrupt policeman."

Ernestine stopped by and John Berry called. Neither of them had anything to add to the tale of their adventure in Pulaski. I asked John to let me pay his speeding ticket, but he just hooted.

"It was good for me," he said. "Got my old heart pumping the way it used to when I'd try to outsail a squall. It was good for the car, too. It belongs to my brother and it probably hasn't gone over twenty in the last twenty years."

And speaking of things that came in twos, I did finally make myself call Mercy Spivey, after tossing a coin to decide between calling her and calling Shirley. A purely imaginary waft of her scent came through the phone when she said hello, followed by an annoying conversation. The gist of it was that they stood by their confidential source, who had told them that although Shannon was being stalked, she was not being stalked by Will; they would not give up that confidential source; they had followed Sylvia and Pen to the library, to a bed-and-breakfast on Depot Street, and then they'd remembered a sale at the Western Auto and broken off the tail; they'd written down the make, model, color, and tag number of the car Sylvia and Pen were driving, but Shirley had used the other side for a grocery list and then thrown it out;

they were ready to give further assistance anytime they were needed.

I took a chance at that point and asked a question. "Will you ask if your confidential source knew Eric Lyle or knew who Eric Lyle hung out with?"

"With whom," Mercy said. "I'll ask her and get back to you."

Geneva was unhappy, again, when I told her I wasn't going to spend the evening playing audiobooks for her.

"Oh, fine, you run along," she moaned when I went up to the study to say good-bye to her and the cat. "And don't even worry about me and Nero."

"He hasn't gained nearly enough weight to be called Nero Wolfe," I said.

"Yes, that's it. Find fault and then leave. I'll just disappear into my room and maybe you'll see me again and maybe you won't but you won't care and you'll just leave Nero to pine away to nothing so that he never suits his name."

"You don't have to be like that, you know."

"Then what are you doing that's so much more important than spending time with us?"

"Do you remember the fishing trip I took with Joe that might or might not have been a date? I think we're trying another one. We're meeting for a picnic in the park behind the courthouse at six."

"Considering how well the first one turned out, maybe I *should* come with you as chaperone this time," she said.

"Mm, no, probably not."

She came anyway.

Joe brought wedges of a new sandwich Mel was experimenting with.

"She told me how she made it," he said. "It's roasted

vegetables layered in a hollowed-out round bread loaf. Then she pressed it overnight under a gallon jar of pickled jalapeños and this afternoon flash-baked it for ten minutes at five hundred degrees. We're part of her test group. What do you think?"

The single bite I had was fabulous. Eggplant, zucchini, red bell pepper, sweet potato, with a caramelized balsamic red onion sauce . . .

Before I could take a second heavenly bite, before I had a chance to try the handmade cracked-black-pepper potato chips he brought, or the whole-wheat chocolate chip cookies, Geneva appeared on the picnic bench next to Joe. He looked around, shivered, and moved over.

"How's it going?" she asked.

"The sandwich is fantastic," I said to Joe.

"If I can't taste it, I'm not interested," Geneva said. She looked at Joe's profile. "He has a kiss of gray at his temple, just like you. I always think a touch of gray is attractive. On a man."

"Oh darn, there's my phone vibrating," I said, sounding completely wooden due to being completely torqued. "I should have *left it at home*."

"You could ignore it," Joe pointed out.

"You're right. Whoever it is will call back or leave a message if it's important, *which I seriously doubt*." I sounded ridiculous.

"Oh," Geneva said. "That reminds me. I nearly forgot why I came. It *is* important and you have my very excellent memory to thank for remembering it."

I didn't know whether to believe her or not.

"You look worried," Joe said. "Go ahead and answer it or call back if you want. No big deal."

"That's okay. I'm sure I'll hear all about it soon enough."

"It might not be soon enough," Geneva said, "if

Bonny realizes where she left that book she wanted to show you this morning. I saw it next to a newspaper article about that man Ardis was so rude about. You know, the Smoky Carlin. I saw them both—the book and the article, not Mr. Carlin—in the not-so-darling cabin in the wood."

I put my sandwich down and stared at her. That would mean Bonny had gone to the cabin recently. She couldn't have forgotten, but why lie? Did it mean she knew Eric Lylc was there . . .

"Are you sure?" I asked Geneva. Oops.

Joe shrugged. "Go ahead."

I gave him a quick "thanks" and a "sorry" and yanked my phone out to make the pretend call. I needed a way to "know" what Geneva had just told me. She enjoyed the charade and, wonder of wonders, she repeated the details exactly.

"Aren't you glad I have such an excellent memory?" she asked.

"Yes. Will you do me a favor?"

"Rouse the villagers and bring the pitchforks?"

"No. Please don't get carried away. Please keep quiet for now and I'll talk to you back at the shop, okay?"

She gave me a hideous wink. I disconnected and told Joe about the book.

"If your brother or another deputy got a search warrant and even noticed the book there, he wouldn't have known what it meant."

Joe chewed a bite of sandwich and nodded at the phone still in my hand. "Who's your friend with 'inside' information?"

"Um, I don't think you've met."

He looked at me, head cocked. "You should call Cole."

"He isn't real keen on what he calls Nancy Drew–ish

clues, and the Mystery of the Mislaid Library Book is about as Drew-ish as they come." Although it was better than the Disclosure of the Dispirited Spirit, which he'd really hate.

"So what are you going to do?" he asked.

"Call the posse."

"You should call Cole." This from Blue Plum's premier part-time burglar.

If we were having a second date, then it didn't end well, either.

Ardis agreed we shouldn't call Debbie for a couple of reasons. We didn't want to wait for her to drive into town, and given Bonny's attitude toward her, we didn't want her to become a focal point for Bonny's reaction.

"'Focal point' and 'reaction' sound less scary than 'target' and 'ballistic,'" I said. "But that's really what we're saying. You don't think Bonny's going to get violent, do you?" I remembered the jolt from touching her sweater and I scrubbed my hands together to make them forget.

"No, hon. She's tactless and humorless at the best of times and she's out of her mind with grief right now at this worst of times, but . . . I'm making a good case for leaving Debbie out of it and safety in numbers, aren't I?"

"Maybe I *should* call Cole."

"Now, there is the ultimate in tactless and humorless for you," Ardis said. "No, we won't bother him. We don't know for certain that Bonny has anything to tell."

"And we wouldn't hear the end of it if we wasted his evening."

"We would not. So we'll call Ernestine and Thea and go on over there ourselves—you don't think Joe will change his mind?"

I shook my head. He'd eaten his cookie, said one

more time I should call his brother, then ambled off to I knew not where.

"All right, then. We have two things going for us—the element of surprise and the fact we're all friends. Make that three—because Bonny is a woman who knows how to do the right thing, and she will."

"Make that four," Geneva said, "because how can those other three things go wrong when you've got me?"

Chapter 31

It was too bad the rest of the posse couldn't see Geneva. Or so she obviously thought. She swaggered around Bonny's living room doing a bad imitation of John Wayne while everyone else made settling-in small talk. It was one of those times when I *really* wished I didn't see her. But sitting down on Bonny's brocade love seat next to Ardis and immediately closing my eyes so that I couldn't see her wasn't an option. At least we'd reached an agreement on interruptions—she would keep her comments to a minimum and her voice down if I promised not to cough at her. She said the coughing disturbed her sensitive nature. I told her I reserved the right to clear my throat if her sensitive nature got out of hand.

"Isn't this nice," Bonny said, making no attempt to sound as though she meant it. She sat in a chintz wingback, still in the sweat pants she'd worn earlier, still in her sage green sweater. The only thing about her that had changed was the look in her eyes. It had gone from lost to confused.

Our group had gone from four plus a ghost to five plus a ghost and we'd had a change of cast. Thea was babysitting her niece for the evening, so Ardis called Mel. Mel came straight from the café and smelled vaguely of roasting vegetables. John Berry, looking his part as an old sailor in a Greek fisherman's hat and Aran sweater he'd probably knit himself, came with Ernestine. They'd been playing Scrabble.

"Too many," Geneva whispered to me. "We'll spook her. Why don't you send the old coot out to guard the horses?"

I cleared my throat. Everyone turned to me.

"Oh, um," I said, always the smooth ad-libber, "so it's nice to see you, Bonny."

"You were just here this morning."

"Well, yes, and then there we all were"—I waved a hand at the others—"down at the Cat, having an impromptu dye workshop . . ."

"Really? Down at the Cat?"

We exchanged nods and murmurs.

"And we got to talking while we worked," I said.

"I don't believe it," Bonny said.

"I beg your pardon?"

"You aren't dressed for it. You and Ardis are still dressed for work. Ernestine's wearing a white blouse. None of you is dressed for dyeing."

Geneva raised a hand. "I am."

"This isn't some kind of intervention, is it?" Bonny asked. She looked down at herself and pulled her sweater straight, flicked something off her knee. "I'll admit I wasn't at my best Saturday night and I shouldn't have yelled the way I did. John, I apologize if I offended you or insulted your brother. I was right, though, about your opinion of Will Embree, wasn't I?"

"No, not really. I hardly knew him," John said.

"My daughter said you knew them both, Will and Terry, and she also said Will tried to convince the police that you could clear him. I told her to forget Will Embree. That if the police believed Will for even one minute they would have tracked you and your sailboat down. I also told her that if you knew they needed your account to nail Will's hide to a tree, then you'd be back here so fast it would make Will's head spin."

"No. I didn't know him well enough to feel that way," John said. "But when I left they were saying Terry's death was an accident. And then I was out of the country and out of touch for so many months and I never heard about Will's troubles."

"Boats are convenient that way," Bonny said. She studied John's face. "But it's true you were there the day Terry died? So you do know the truth of Will's guilt."

"John?" Ernestine asked when he didn't answer.

"I know that Will is dead," John said quietly. "And that piece of truth about Terry's death doesn't matter anymore."

"Unless," I said, puzzling something through, "unless Will heard you were back." They all looked at me again. "And he could have. You said it the other night at the potluck, John. You said you talked to Shannon at the post office. If she was in contact with Will, then she would have told him you were back. What if Will was coming back to turn himself in because he was sure you could clear him? And that could be why Shannon was afraid. Not *of* Will, but *for* him, because maybe you couldn't or wouldn't. It fits. But was Will right? *Can* you clear him?"

"That's the saddest part," John said. "I don't think I know anything that would prove it one way or the other. Not a thing."

Bonny made a dismissive noise and I turned back to her.

"How do you know Shannon and Eric were engaged? Did she tell you?

"What?"

"Did she tell you about the baby?"

"No. It's disgraceful. I had to hear it in the autopsy report."

"She kept it from you. She didn't tell you about being

engaged to Eric, either, did she. Because she wasn't engaged to Eric. But did he tell you that? Did Eric tell you?" By then I'd stopped looking at Bonny, stopped waiting for her to answer. I was in the middle of a one-woman brainstorming session, staring at the pattern in the Aubusson carpet on her floor as though I could follow its colorful lines far enough to find answers to the questions racing ahead of them.

Geneva nudged me with an icy elbow. "Take a gander, pardner. The little lady looks volcanic."

I glanced up. Bonny's face was as unreadable as the rug. And about as ugly.

"Bonny . . ."

Mel's good sense leapt between us. "Kath, you're tripping over your tongue, there, and I need to be home and in my bed sooner rather than later because, try as I might, I cannot get the breakfast biscuits to bake themselves. Why don't you ask Bonny what you came to ask her so I can be on my way?"

"Shucks," Geneva said, making a spitting noise. "I was looking forward to the eruption."

I cleared my throat. Everyone looked at me. I needed to come up with a different "shut up" signal.

I'd ruined our hastily thrown together plan to chat casually and meander into asking Bonny to show us the library book. Acting natural and sounding curious weren't going to cut it with Bonny anymore. Her face still looked dangerous, so I went with my own element of surprise—Kath being clear and concise. But not brutal. Bonny was still a mother mourning her only child, and I tried to give her room to explain.

"Bonny, where's the book you donated to the library in Granny's memory? We'd like to see it."

Bonny stared. "That's why you're here? I told you this morning, it's upstair—"

I watched the progression of thoughts from *huh* to *you're kidding* to *oh* . . . pass through her eyes. The only change in her face was the set of her jaw.

"The book is in the cabin," I said. "When did you leave it there?"

She said nothing.

"Did you know Eric was there?"

Nothing.

Mel shifted her feet. Ernestine leaned forward, peering intently at Bonny's face. Geneva unfurled from behind me and floated closer. Bonny blinked as Geneva floated around behind her.

"Ask her where she was the night of the twenty-third," Geneva said. "Ask her who she's working with and where she's hidden Sylvia."

"You did know Eric was there," I said.

"She isn't going to talk, sweetheart," Geneva said, sounding like a bad Bogart or Cagney.

I looked at Ardis. She was so sure Bonny would do the right thing, but I was afraid Geneva was right.

Geneva was moving back and forth behind Bonny, shoulders hunched and slapping one hand into the other. "Give me ten minutes alone with her," she said. "That's all I'm asking." She was starting to billow. Not a good sign.

Ardis hitched forward on the love seat and leaned toward Bonny, her elbows on her knees, hands clasped in front of her. "Bonny, honey," she said, all earnest honeysuckle, "we know you're a good woman—"

"No!" Geneva said. "Don't let her take over. Two minutes alone with her is all we need. She'll tell me what I want to know."

I cleared my throat. Loudly. Everyone looked at me.

"Sorry. I had a ghost in my throat." They still looked at me. "Frog. In my throat. Sorry."

Ardis looked at me longer than the others, with slightly more narrowed eyes. Then she patted my knee and turned back to Bonny. "Bonny, you need to tell us about Eric—"

"No!" Geneva shrieked, swirling at me. "This is *our* collar. *You* ask the questions. Ask her if she killed them."

I tried to bat her away.

"Ask her if she shot Samuel and Martha on their way home from the schoolhouse and left them in that field!"

She was frantic, howling, out of control. I put my hands over my ears. It did no good. She was all around me with horrifying, heart-wrenching shrieks.

"Ask her if she shot Sam and Matty!"

"She *didn't* shoot Sam and Matty," I shouted. "It was *Shannon and Will*!"

"No," Bonny said into the silence that followed my outburst. "Only Eric. And I only wanted him to do what was right, to turn himself in. But he didn't. He wouldn't listen, so I hit him upside the head to make him see sense. Hit him too hard, I guess. Stunned him . . . he'd been drinking . . . he stumbled off toward the river and I let him go."

"What did you hit him with?" Ernestine asked. She seemed more interested than appalled.

Bonny closed her eyes and shook her head. "The book. The book on natural dyeing."

"Who're Sam and Matty?" Mel asked.

"Shh," Ardis said. "Shh, let's all just have a moment of silence for all the dead." She had her arm around me and I cuddled against her, feeling vacant, wishing I could cry like a big baby.

Geneva watched me from the mantelpiece, howled out and looking desolate and depleted. But then she turned her head toward the door, listening. I couldn't hear anything. She looked back at me and opened her mouth, then covered it, maybe afraid of the look on my face. But then she couldn't help herself.

"I'm sorry," she said in a voice as small as I'd ever heard her use, "but I know you like things in twos, so there are two more things, and then I won't bother you anymore. First, you should have let me look for Pen this morning. Second is a riddle. What is the sound of one twin snooping?"

Her first sounded like a riddle, too. I didn't have time to puzzle it out, though, because I knew the answer to the second. "Spiveys," I spat.

Then they were all looking at me again, but I didn't care. I jumped up, crossed to the hallway door, and pulled it open. Mercy Spivey, caught with her ear pressed against the door, fell into the room, her horrible scent wafting in behind.

Chapter 32

The exclamations surrounding Mercy's stumble into the room were followed by more exclamations at the appearance of Shirley. Shirley tried to enter more gracefully, though her success was questionable due to the unattractive combination of gloating and looking flustered with which she did it. She was flustered because Clod Dunbar and Deputy Darla followed directly behind her; she gloated because she was thrilled to point at Bonny and say, "Arrest that woman."

Clod, to his credit, put his hand to his forehead, and along with the rest of us, looked at the floor, shaking his head. I might have heard him mutter something rude, but if he did I didn't blame him. Bonny's Aubusson carpet had more people using it as a convenient focal point that night than any other in its life.

"Ms. Goforth," Clod eventually said, "may I have a word with you?"

"It's about the two cars," Shirley said.

"Which don't belong in your garage," said Mercy.

I stared at the twins. Two cars? *Two* cars. Eric's and . . . "Sylvia!"

"Oh, my word," Ardis said. "Is she really dead, too?"

"No—"

"No," Bonny cut in on top of me. "She's in the basement. She's fine, but you should probably let her out."

Sylvia wasn't exactly fine, but she didn't appear much worse for her confinement in what turned out to be a windowless storage room. Deputy Darla brought her up from the basement. For some reason she wasn't happy to see us, which I thought was a little harsh considering we were instrumental in her release.

"How on earth did you end up down there?" Mercy asked.

"Tricked." Sylvia said. Her voice was slightly husky and her beautiful silver hair hadn't been washed or brushed for several days, but her eyes still had snap to them. "And my own stupidity. I dug up a lead for the story Pen and I were working on. I followed it up myself, though, because Pen left me high and dry without a word. I heard about a cabin and drove out there. She was there." She nodded at Bonny sitting quietly next to Clod. "And the missing security guard, Eric Lyle. They were talking, arguing. I was stupid. He grabbed me, grabbed my scarf, started choking me." She put her fingers to her throat and I saw the bruises. "Then I was retching and coughing and he was gone. When I could breathe, I told her why I was there. She told me to follow her back to her place, that she had a B and B, that she'd feel better if she could give me a free night there and keep an eye on me. I thought she meant so she could make sure I'd recovered. She was showing me over the house and saying she'd give me something more for the story. I was so stupid. I followed her to that room in the basement and she locked me in. When I first came to Blue Plum, met you at the Weaver's Cat"—she nodded to me—"I thought I could see myself living here. Now I think I hate the place."

Leave it to a Spivey to ask what all of us were wondering. "For God's sake, Bonny," Shirley called over to her, "what were you thinking, locking this poor woman in the basement?"

"I didn't know what else to do with her."

Deputy Darla offered to accompany Sylvia to the emergency room. Sylvia held her hands up, warding off any further contact with us. "Home. My own bed. My own doctor tomorrow. My car keys?"

"Seat of the car," Bonny said.

Deputy Darla shrugged and took our names and contact information. Ardis and Ernestine each gave Bonny a hug. Bonny didn't seem to care, but the ugly, obstinate look was gone from her face.

"Can't we stay with her?" Ardis asked Clod.

No, he said. We couldn't. When we left, Bonny was nodding to whatever Clod was quietly telling her.

We said our good nights on the porch, Mel yawning, John taking Ernestine's arm in the dark. Ardis whispered, "Debriefing, tomorrow," in my ear, then made a face and rolled her eyes toward the Spiveys. The Spiveys waited while I dithered after the others were gone. I wanted to sprint down the sidewalk, leaving them in the dust, but I was looking for Geneva. I didn't see her.

"We'll walk you home," Mercy said. "See that you get there safely, what with all the crime these days."

"Or we could just follow you at distance," said Shirley. "It's what we did when you came up here tonight. We're getting good at tailing."

"Thanks," I told them. "But I'm going to the Cat, not home. Things to do." Ghosts to deliver, if she was there somewhere and would come with me. "Oh, but hey. Can I ask, is Angie your confidential source?"

"If we told you who the source is, the source would no longer be confidential," Mercy said.

"True." I nodded, pretended to start down the stairs,

then turned and asked, "But did you remember to ask Angie if she knew Eric or any of his buddies?"

"She said she didn't." Shirley's answer ended on a yip when Mercy's elbow found her ribs.

"How did you know?" Mercy asked.

"You referred to your source as 'her,' and Bonny told me that Shannon thought the world of Angie. It was kind of a guess, but Shannon confided in someone, who then confided in you." What I didn't add was, *And how many people in this world would do that?*

I said good night then, and trotted down Bonny's front steps and on down the sidewalk. I didn't know what else to do. Maybe Geneva knew her way. Maybe she was already back at the Cat. But maybe she was making good on her words *then I won't bother you anymore.* With that thought, I ran the rest of the way.

Chapter 33

The posse-plus-one met for an early breakfast the next morning at Mel's before she was open to the public. Ardis complained about the hour, but she was the one who'd set it up and called all of us. Mel, today in a ketchup red apron, ducked in and out of the kitchen, keeping an ear on us and an eye on the biscuits and her new apprentice baker. If things worked out, she said, she looked forward to sleeping in every once in a while—maybe even until the decadent hour of seven.

We sat in the back half of the café, behind the folding screen Mel used to break up the space in the long, narrow room. She wanted us out of the public eye so other early birds or Spiveys didn't get ideas. We ate family-style, from bowls and platters she brought from the kitchen. The eggs, grits, sausage, potatoes, toast, and coffee were excellent. The family, with Ardis playing mother and John Berry playing father at the ends of the table, was beginning to feel just like that to me—a family.

"I didn't have to come, you know," Clod said, helping himself to seconds of Mel's roasted rosemary garlic potatoes.

"We know that," Ardis said. "Pass the sausage, will you? But please, help yourself first."

Thea, Debbie, and Clod sat on one side of the table. Ernestine and I sat on the other. The empty seat next to me was for Joe. Ardis said he'd thought he might have other plans.

"At six?" Thea asked.

"A man has to fish when a man has to fish," John said.

Clod snorted and helped himself to more eggs. "I'm not obliged to tell you anything, either."

"Of course not, hon," Ardis said. "But we would have heard the rest of it last night if you hadn't made us leave. Plus I'm buying your breakfast and the *Bugle* comes out day after tomorrow, so you might as well."

"We know most of it, anyway, and we beat you to quite a bit of it," Thea said.

"And we'll be happy to fill in anything you haven't figured out." Ernestine beamed an angelic smile at him.

"And let you know where you're wrong." Mel's smile was different.

"John, Ms. Rutledge, Ms. Keith," Clod asked, "any digs? Any quips?"

I shook my head. I hadn't said much and didn't plan to. Part of my "family" was missing. I'd stopped by the shop before going to Mel's. The cat met me at the door. Geneva was nowhere to be seen or heard. I couldn't help remembering her asking me not to remind her of the other dead souls in that other field, wherever or whenever it was. She'd remembered them anyway, remembered their names, the horror. What if it had been too much for her?

Debbie was talking, staring at the food on her plate. "They were always opposites, always. It didn't matter what it was about. He listened to rock and she loved country. She liked anchovies on a pizza; he wanted veggies. But no olives. She liked olives. So they'd go half and half. Always meeting halfway. It worked for them, even when she got the job at Victory. Somehow they always made it work."

"Cloud Hollow," Clod said.

She nodded. "Halfway between Blue Plum and Victory Paper. I talked to him a few days before . . ." She took a deep breath, stared at her plate. "He knew she was pregnant. He said things had changed. I thought he meant he'd gotten tired of running. It made sense to me."

"I honestly had no idea Will thought I could do anything for him," John said. He looked sadder and a little less shipshape that morning. "I hate to think I precipitated this tragedy."

"You didn't." Clod banged his mug on the table, sloshing coffee.

"Do you think life is easier if you see it so clearly in black and white?" Debbie asked, sounding as though she really wanted to know.

"Piece of cake," Clod said.

Ardis blotted the spilled coffee with a handful of paper napkins. She smiled and handed the damp wad to Clod. "Mopping up, Coleridge. It's why we're here. What did Bonny tell you last night?"

He looked around the table and then toward the back door, as though gauging whether he could make an escape before we could tackle him. The odds must have appeared too great. He sighed and dropped the napkins on his plate.

"Bonny said Eric showed up at her house that Monday night—the day of the deaths. She said he told her it was his gun, that he gave it to Shannon for protection. He told her they were engaged and having a baby. He said he'd be blamed for Shannon's death because of the gun. Ms. Goforth believed him, put his car in her garage, drove him out to the cabin. She told him not to worry, that she had someone who would uncover the truth." He looked at me. I stared back.

"He played on her good nature," John said.

"And her grief," said Ernestine.

Clod nodded. "And Shannon's assistant, the Proffitt woman, gave credence to that whole fairy tale by misinterpreting phone calls she overheard. Another case of muddying facts by meddling."

He was probably looking at me again with that dig, but I studied my nails until he continued.

"Bonny says his story changed after he broke open the liquor cabinet and got to feeling 'confessional,'" Clod said. "She said in Lyle's new story he was obsessed with Shannon but she rejected him. Shannon told him she was meeting Embree but didn't tell him where. He tried to talk her out of going. She left early so he couldn't follow. That's why she was in the field hours before Embree. But Lyle did see her leave because he'd gone by her place at the end of his shift and waited. When he showed up in the field, they argued, and the kind of stupid thing happened that does when stupid people carry guns. Bonny says he claimed it was an accident. He panicked. Dropped the gun. Thought about going back for it because his prints would be all over it. But then he realized Embree would find it and figured Embree, the known killer, would get the blame. It worked out better than he hoped because Embree, in his romantic despair, shot himself. Both Lyle's and Embree's prints were on the gun. Shannon's were not."

"So Eric hadn't really given her the gun," Debbie said.

"Unlikely," said Clod.

"And when Bonny heard this version of his story, she told him to turn himself in," Ardis said. "And that's the day Sylvia Furches showed up out there. Bless her heart and bless Bonny's, too."

"Before or after the potluck?" Debbie asked.

"Before," Clod said. "Bonny came to that potluck

with a lot on her mind and a strong desire to believe Lyle's original story."

"Is that why she didn't turn him in?"

"She said she was working up to it." He scraped his chair back and stood. "Thank you for the fine breakfast, Ms. Buchanan, Mel. Ms. O'Dell, Mr. Berry, Ms. Keith, I hope you're able to put all this behind you. Ms. Rutledge, as always, it is a pleasure to leave you." He put on his hat, touched the brim, stifled a belch, and left. Stupid Clod.

The cat turned and meowed hello when I dragged up to the study after that awful breakfast. He blinked and sneezed and turned back to the wall. He sat with his nose inches from it, his ears cocked forward, listening.

"Mice," I said. "Great."

I hadn't been able to eat the wonderful food Mel fixed for us, thanks in part to that large rodent, Deputy Clod Rat Dunbar. And now I had mice. Perfect. I dropped my purse on the floor, dumped myself in the desk chair, and sank my head in my hands.

"Mrrph," said the cat.

I peeked through my fingers, afraid I might see him pounce, and instead saw Geneva float through the wall. The cat stretched and followed her to the window seat.

"I don't allow mice in my room." She sniffed. "You're rude to say I do."

"I worried about you last night," I said. I didn't ask her about Sam and Mattie. I might never ask her about them, or I might work up my nerve, or . . . "How did you get home? Did you come with me when I walked here?"

"You ran. And you might let mice swagger around out here, but my room is too genteel."

"Well, it's nice to see you, too . . . What do you mean when you say 'your room'?" I looked at the wall she'd floated through. Her room? Her room. How incredibly dense I was. She could move through walls. She could move through floors. "Where do you go when you float in and out of the wall like that?"

"To my room," she said. "Haven't I told you? It's the most darling space. You wouldn't like it because it hasn't got mice and you'd probably think it's a cupboard and not a room, but it's just my size, when I curl up, and it's warm and dry. And it's mine."

"When you say cupboard, do you mean it was built to be a cupboard?"

"That's usually the way with cupboards. And this one is mine."

"Does it have a door?"

"Yes. And a secret latch and hidden hinges. And it's quite cunning and beautifully made," she said, sounding livelier as she got caught up in describing her "room." "It's painted deep blue and there are words painted along the edge of the shelf that divides it in two. They're lovely words."

"What do they say, Geneva?" I closed my eyes, picturing those words, and I whispered them along with her, knowing what they would be. What Granddaddy always called Granny: *"My dearest, darling Ivy."*

"Would you like to see them?" she asked.

It took some fumbling on my part and a lot of fussing and inaccurate directions on Geneva's part before I was able to spring the latch my grandfather had made and swing the cupboard door open and see the deep blue he'd painted inside and the lovely words. And to find the dye journals my grandmother kept there. I could hardly breathe. I wasn't sure I wanted to touch them.

"I haven't contaminated them, you know," Geneva said. "I'm dead but I try not to spread it around."

There were three of them. I took them out. They were warm and dry and ordinary, like any of the other binders

Granny used for her records. She had always been a meticulous documenter. She'd kept detailed notes of her dye recipes, their variations, and her experiments with different materials, mordants, and means. Her journals were filled with samples of dried dyestuff and fibers. Were these journals really any different?

I took them over to the desk, sat down, and flipped one open at random to a recipe with the heading *Calming Chamomile for Colic: soft yellow, sleeping babe.* Hmm. Okay. I flipped to another page and read, *Goldenseal to Heal: antibacterial material.* I glanced through the recipe itself but didn't see anything outlandish. No magic words. No woo-woo for the wool. But.

But what? Did Granny use these recipes and believe they worked? Did that make her *a bit of a witch*?

Geneva watched me struggle with that. A ghost was watching me try to think through the confusion of finding my grandmother's secret dye journals—the dye journals that, in the words of the letter my dear, daft grandmother left for me to read upon her death, would *reveal all.*

This really wasn't the life I'd expected to be living at this point in my career as a textile preservation specialist.

Geneva clucked and sighed and told the cat I was suffering untold sorrows. I decided I probably was and wondered if Granny had a dye recipe to deal with that small problem. Maybe something that took care of disbelief, indecision, the collywobbles, and the jimjams all in one blow. Preferably in a color that complemented my stark raving red hair. I flipped to another page and read, *Dandelion: for the person who suffers from everything.*

"What are you laughing at?" Geneva asked. "You sound like a lunatic and you're upsetting Argyle."

"Who?" I laughed.

"Argyle," she said. "Our cat."

I quit laughing. "Oh my gosh."

The cat stretched and yawned and stood up in the window seat. He shivered his tail and let me scoop him up in my arms.

"Is your name Argyle?" I asked.

And then we finally had our dye workshop. It was Debbie's idea and a bright, beautiful one at that. We gathered the next Sunday morning in the kitchen at the Weaver's Cat, where Granny had for so many years set pots to steam and steep and she'd hung her skeins of yarn and lengths of wool roving to drip and dry. Debbie arrived early with gallon jars of vibrant colors. She wore one of her swirling denim skirts and looked brighter, more herself, than she had in recent weeks.

She set skeins of undyed wool to soak in the double sink and then directed Joe and Thea in setting up a long folding table beside the kitchen table and covering both with heavy plastic. When they'd finished, Ardis laid three parallel strips of plastic wrap down each table's length. Ernestine stayed out of the bustle, perched on a tall stool, looking less mole-like than usual and more like a fluffed and inquisitive owl.

"No fishing today?" I asked Joe.

"A day is full of hours," he said and went to open the back door for Mel, who came burdened with an insulated carafe in one hand and a bakery bag and another carafe in the other.

John followed Mel in. He carried a tray of sandwiches from the café for lunch. I was glad to see more spring in his old step than he'd had when he left our debriefing breakfast at Mel's.

The kitchen was large enough to hold the two tables and the eight of us. Plus a ghost and a cat. Geneva and Argyle sat next to each other on top of the refrigerator, happy in each other's company and happy to watch. We hadn't advertised the workshop, thinking of it as a day of fellowship for the members of TGIF who had been involved in the investigation, a day for renewal and celebration.

It turned out to be a day with surprises, too. While we pulled on rubber gloves before dipping into cups and pots of color, a knock came at the back door and Debbie's cousin, Darla the Deputy, stepped in. She wasn't in uniform, but even so, a little chill of unease came into the room with her. Until she smiled.

"I hope you don't mind," she said with a question in her voice. "Debbie told me she was doing this here today, and, well, I don't know if you all know what my last name is. Debbie does. But it's Dye. I'm Darla Dye and I'd like to try my hand at it."

Ardis and Joe moved down, making room for Darla. Debbie brought out another pair of gloves.

"It's not a full house yet," Geneva said from the top of the fridge. She raised her arm and pointed out the window over the sink. For a brief moment of panic, I was afraid the Spivey twins had tailed Darla and discovered what we were doing. I controlled the panic, though, and ever so nonchalantly sidled over to surreptitiously peek out the window in the back door . . . And there on the stoop was Sylvia, silver hair swinging at her chin, another pretty scarf at her neck, and with a plate of brownies.

"I came to the back door because that's what friends do," she said.

It became another day best remembered in snippets and impressions—and appropriately so because the hand-painted dye method Debbie showed us produced lengths of yarn as fluid with color as impressionist paintings.

Sylvia had decided she needed closure. She'd made gooey, fudgy brownies and driven over the mountains from Asheville. Ardis doled out one of her honeysuckle hugs to her and found yet another pair of rubber gloves. Ernestine got as much dye on herself and the sleeves of Thea's sweatshirt as on her yarn. Neither of them seemed to care. John worked mostly in blues and greens, maybe dreaming of deep water and green hills and hollows. Joe said he'd give the yarn he meticulously painted in even stripes of olive and tan to Cole for his birthday. Mel brought out a white apron and had everyone add splashes of color to it.

And I stood at the stove, occasionally giving the wool in my dye kettle a stir, as happy watching the others as Geneva and Argyle from their refrigerator aerie. I'd actually told a convincing lie about the kettle, saying I was trying one of the dye recipes in the book Bonny donated to the library in Granny's memory.

"How's it going over there?" Debbie called.

"Fine." I hoped. I hadn't been sure I would be brave enough for this—trying one of Granny's secret recipes. I wasn't even sure it was bravery that I needed. But as soon as I'd seen the subtitle Granny added to her aloe dye, I knew that I was going to do it.

Geneva floated down from the refrigerator and hovered over the kettle. Argyle thumped to the floor after her and came to twine around my ankles.

"It's pretty," Geneva said. "I like pink. I hope Bonny likes it."

I hoped so, too. *Aloe Vera: for healing, protection, and affection,* Granny had written in her clear hand. It sounded like three magic wishes—healing, protection, and affection—three wishes for Bonny in the days, weeks, and months to come.

"How's Argyle doing over there, hon?" Ardis called. "That's a good name for a good cat."

Argyle purred.

Catnip Mouse

Designed by Kate Winkler, Designs from Dove Cottage, for Molly MacRae's Dyeing Wishes

MATERIALS

Worsted weight yarn, about 6 yards
Size 6 double-pointed needles
Wool roving or yarn scraps for stuffing
Tapestry needle

OPTIONAL MATERIALS

Catnip
Jingle bell
Crochet hook, size G (but see note below)
6"–8" of dark yarn for eyes

Abbreviations

K = knit; st(s) = stitch(es); dpn(s) = double-pointed needle(s); kfb = knit in front and back of same stitch (increase); k2tog = knit two stitches together (decrease); R = round; ch = chain; sl st = slip stitch; sc = single crochet

I-CORD MOUSE TAIL

Cast on 4 stitches. Do not turn work. Slide stitches to the other end of needle; bring yarn across back of work, and k4, beginning with the first st you cast on.

*Slide sts to other end of needle, bring yarn across back of work, and k4.

Repeat from * for 3 inches, or desired tail length.

Note that the same side of the work will face you throughout. As you work more rounds of I-cord, you will see that you are knitting a narrow tube.

Alternative: You may work the tail using a knitting spool (aka "knitting Nancy" or "French knitter"), and transfer the stitches to dpns when it is time to increase for the body of the mouse. That way a young child who doesn't knit yet can help make the toy by spool-knitting the tail, with the body of the mouse knitted by an older child or adult.

Increase for Body

R1: Slide stitches to other end of needle and kfb in first 2 sts. With third needle, kfb in remaining 2 sts–8 sts on 2 needles.

Turn work. You will now be working in the round, as you would for a sock.

R2: Kfb in first 2 sts. With fourth needle, kfb in next 2 sts. Kfb in next 2 sts. With fifth needle, kfb in last 2 sts–16 sts on 4 needles.

R3: *Kfb, k1, rep from * around—24 sts.

R4: *Kfb, k2, rep from * around—32 sts.

R5–14: K around.

Decrease for head

R15: *K2, k2tog, rep from * around—24 sts.

R16: K around.

R17: *K1, k2tog, rep from * around—16 sts.

R18: K around.

R19: K2tog around—8 sts.

R20: K around.

Stuff mouse with wool roving or bits of wool yarn. Add catnip or jingle bell in center of stuffing, if wanted.

R21: K2tog around—4 sts

Break yarn, leaving a 4" tail. Thread tail in tapestry needle and sew through 4 remaining sts, removing them from needles. Run tail through sts a second time and bury tail in center of stuffing. Run cast-on tail through center of I-cord.

Note: From a cat's perspective, you now have a fully functional cat toy. If you wish to add ears and/or eyes, you may; in my experience, however, cats are wholly indifferent to such details.

OPTIONAL EARS (MAKE 2)

With crochet hook and same yarn used for mouse, make a slipknot and ch 4. Join with a sl st in first ch. Ch 1, 4sc in center of ring. Sl st in center of ring and fasten off.

Sew ears to mouse's head, even with first decrease round. Bury tails in stuffing.

OPTIONAL EYES

Using tapestry needle and contrasting yarn, make French knots or Xs for eyes. Bury tails in stuffing.

Chocolate Cake with Ganache

CAKE

Nonstick vegetable oil spray
Parchment paper
½ cup unsalted butter (cut into ½-inch cubes, room temperature)
¼ cup unsweetened cocoa powder
½ cup boiling water
1 cup all-purpose flour
1 cup sugar
½ teaspoon baking soda
¼ teaspoon salt
¼ cup buttermilk
1 large egg
½ teaspoon vanilla

GANACHE

1 cup semisweet chocolate chips
3 tablespoons heavy whipping cream
2 tablespoons unsalted butter (cut into ½-inch cubes)

CAKE

Preheat oven to 350° F. Spray 9-inch cake pan with nonstick spray. Line with parchment. Spray parchment. Dust with flour, tapping out excess.

Put butter and cocoa in medium bowl. Pour ½ cup boiling water over mixture; stir. Let stand 2 minutes; whisk until blended. Whisk flour, sugar, baking soda, and salt in another medium bowl. Whisk buttermilk, egg, and vanilla in large bowl. Gradually whisk cocoa mixture into buttermilk mixture; whisk until smooth. Add flour mixture in 3 additions, whisking to blend between additions (batter will be thin). Pour batter into prepared pan.

Bake cake until tester inserted in center comes out clean, about 30 minutes. Cool in pan 10 minutes. Run knife around pan edges to release cake. Invert onto rack; remove pan and parchment. Cool completely.

GANACHE

Put chocolate chips and cream in microwave-safe bowl. Heat in microwave in 15-second intervals, stirring between intervals, until melted and smooth. Stir in butter. Let stand until spreadable, about 30 minutes. While cake is still on rack, spread ganache over top and sides. Transfer to cake plate. Chill at least 2 hours and up to 1 day.

Joe Dunbar's Versatile Squashed Squash

1 pound small zucchini, cut into large pieces
1¾ cups vegetable stock
1 onion, chopped
1 tablespoon olive oil
2 cloves garlic, minced
1 tablespoon chopped fresh mint leaves
1 tablespoon lemon juice
Salt and pepper to taste

Simmer zucchini in stock until soft. Drain and mash in colander to remove extra liquid (save stock for soup another time or just drink it).

In large frying pan, sauté onion in olive oil until golden. Add garlic and stir just until it begins to color. Add mashed zucchini, mint, lemon juice, salt, and pepper, stirring and mixing well for about 5 minutes.

This makes an excellent dip for raw vegetables or pita chips or a wonderful spread for flatbread or crostini, or can be used as a pizza sauce on a grilled vegetable pizza.

Read on for a sneak peek at the next Haunted Yarn Shop Mystery,

Spinning in Her Grave

Coming in early 2014 from Obsidian

"What do you mean, you won't use your gun?" The incredulity in my voice should have scathed the ears off any self-respecting sheriff's deputy. But the particular deputy standing in front of me did nothing more than momentarily stop staring at the heavy wooden door we were trapped behind and give me some kind of look over his shoulder. There wasn't time to decipher Cole Dunbar's look, though. The smoke was getting thicker and I heard an ominous crackling in the far corner. Scratch that. None of the corners in this misbegotten, soon-to-be-flaming outbuilding were far away enough. By then I didn't care that it might be an early-nineteenth-century loom house—National Register–worthy status be hanged. "Take your stupid gun *out* and shoot the stupid door *down*!"

"You're getting hysterical," Deputy Dunbar said.

"I'm trying hard not to. I am also trying not to be critical or sarcastic, but I'd like very much not to become a smoked ham in here so *please use your gun*!"

"Look at me, Kath. Look at me. Am I wearing my holster?" He was using the infuriating tone of voice of someone who doesn't know how to calm a two-year-old, let alone the woman with whom he's about to become seared tuna. "Do you see my gun, Kath? I did not say I *won't* use my gun; I said I *can't*. I *can't* use my gun because my gun is not here. No gun. Besides, you obviously watch too much TV or not enough of the right kind of TV. Shooting a door, especially a thick oak plank door with iron hardware, isn't the best way to get out of a building. Especially a burning building. Especially a burning building that also contains seven cans of gasoline."

He had to mention the gasoline again. I spun around to see how close we were to being blown sky-high and following the seven cans, the roof, and the whole rest of the building to either North Carolina or Kingdom Come, Kentucky. I'd already dragged the cans from the back wall into the middle of the structure, but that wasn't going to help much. The whole place was only fifteen by twenty feet. The middle of it wasn't a safe distance from any other part of it, smoking, smoldering, crackling or otherwise.

"We'd better finish coming up with an alternative exit plan fast, then," I said, turning back. "*Now* what are you doing?"

He had the palms of his hands on the door. He held them there for a few seconds, and then moved them to another spot, and then another area lower down.

"Testing for heat," he said.

"Now the *door's* on fire?"

He didn't answer. Instead he straightened, reared back, and rammed his shoulder into the door. He made a good thump when he hit, and he let out a muffled "oof," but nothing else happened. The whole sweet little loom house–turned–storage shed may be starting to smolder, but you couldn't fault its stout materials and construction. Deputy Dunbar rubbed his shoulder and clamped his lips on anything further.

"Ouch," I said for him. "Okay, now I *am* going to be critical. Why *don't* you have your gun? What were you going to do if you hadn't found *me* snooping around in here? Did you think of that? What if I'd been someone else who *did have* a gun?"

"You know what the difference is between you and me?" he said, turning from the door to scrabble through a motley collection of yard tools I'd already searched. "It's the difference between talk and action. You can't shut up about the gun." He swept aside leaf rakes and a snow shovel. "And I'm trying to get us out of here."

"With that?"

He held a weed trimmer in his white-knuckled fist.

"No." He tossed the trimmer aside and lunged past me. *"This!"* With a look of triumph, he grabbed a three-foot length of black pipe from the shadows against the wall behind me. He weighed it in both hands like a trophy fish. Then he moved his hands apart and I saw, as though he'd performed sleight of hand, that there were actually two pipes, one sliding in and out of the other, with the inner piece ending in a wicked-looking wedged tip, like a giant screwdriver.

"What is it?" I asked.

"Solid steel salvation."

"Hang on a second, though—"

"No time."

We were both coughing from the acrid smoke by then, and flames licked the back wall, but there was something there in the shadows. . . .

"But there's—"

"No buts. Wish me luck, little sweetheart—then stand back." Before I realized what was happening, he swept me into a one-armed embrace, planted a kiss on my lips, and pushed me behind him.

And then Deputy Cole Dunbar, man of action but not so many listening skills, holding the whatever-it-was like a medieval pole-arm or miniature battering ram, charged full tilt at the door. And in the split second before he smashed our way out of that fiery deathtrap, I knew I should be impressed, grateful, and possibly in starry-eyed love with a true hero.

Instead I felt like a complete heel. There I was, surrounded by smoke, threatened by flames and exploding gasoline cans, being rescued by a tall, fit, gung-ho deputy sheriff, and the only thoughts sputtering in my head were *A kiss? Little sweetheart? Well, this is a disturbing turn of events.*

Ten days earlier . . .

"With guns?" I stared at the man standing on the other side of the sales counter in the Weaver's Cat, my fiber and fabric shop in Blue Plum, Tennessee. I'd only just met him—Mr. J. Scott Prescott, as it said on the card he'd slid across the counter. He was slight and had a well-scrubbed, earnest face that at first glance put him anywhere from his early twenties to mid-thirties. He wore an expensive suit and tie, though, and had the beginnings of crow's feet. Taken together, those details put him closer to the mature, successful end of that age range. He also came across as calm and operating on an even keel, despite the mention of guns. Unfortunately, as much as I wanted to appear the competent, calm business owner so early on a Friday morning, I couldn't help sounding more edgy than even. "You're kidding, right?"

"Your town board already gave us—" Mr. Prescott started to say.

I interrupted, holding up my hand. "But you say they're running through the streets with guns?"

"Only some of them will be running." Again, the gravitas of his suit and tie helped.

"Okay, well . . ."

"Half a dozen. A dozen, tops, and we reconsidered the burning torches and decided against them. Most of the rest of the actual participants will be posted at strategic points around town." He gestured right and left, fingers splayed in his excitement. Thank goodness for the suit—otherwise, he was beginning to look and sound like an eager Boy Scout. "We already have permission to use the park," he said, "and the old train depot and the upper porch of Cunningham house. The main concentration of dispersal will be in the two or three blocks surrounding and centering on the courthouse." His hands outlined several concentric circles, then came together with a ghost of a clap and he leaned toward me. "Oh, and we've been given access to the roof of the empty mercantile across from the courthouse. All of those places are for the visible men; the rest will be hiding. As I said, the plans and permissions have been in place for several months, but one of the property owners was recently obliged to back out, and that's where you and the Weaver's Hat come in."

"Cat."

"Pardon?" He straightened.

"Sorry, I didn't mean to interrupt, but we're the Cat, as in 'meow.' Not 'hat.'"

"Really? I'm embarrassed."

"It's okay."

"Anyway, we'd love it if one or two of the men could sneak in here during the action and watch from the windows upstairs."

"Hmm."

"They won't get in your way at all. They'll watch at the windows and when they see the other men out there in the street, they'll stick their heads out and shoot. They might also do the famous yell, but I'll tell them that's optional, sort of as the spirit moves them, if you see what

I mean. A bloodcurdling yell, like, that really whips up the enthusiasm of the spectators, though, and between that and the shots erupting from unexpected places, it'll keep things off-balance in a realistic enough way that the whole reenactment will have an incredible sense of authenticity and it'll be great." He stopped, eyes wide. I took a step back.

"At this point I should ask you not to divulge any of the details we've discussed," he said. "We're keeping the program under wraps. Looking for the big reveal, if you see what I mean. The wow. Also, I forgot to ask, do the windows upstairs open? Because, you know, there wouldn't be much point in anyone hiding up there and then trying to shoot out of them if they don't."

I'd processed his words and understood his gesturing hands, and it would have taken a harder history-loving heart than mine to ignore the excitement of a good-natured reenactment. The tourists flocking to town for our annual heritage celebration—Blue Plum Preserves—would no doubt love it, too. But my mind kept skipping back to my original question. "With *guns*?"

J. Scott blinked.

"Sorry. I didn't mean to shout," I said. I surreptitiously wiped my mouth in case I'd also spit. "But the stories I remember hearing always made that whole episode sound more like a loud fuss between neighbors—with a lot of that yelling—than a feud. With guns."

"But these days a feud is more fun," he said. "Plus, think of the marketing possibilities. If it goes well this year, just wait until next year. And I can assure you it will be perfectly safe. No projectiles. No live rounds. No actual aiming at people. I think your mayor and aldermen were impressed by how thoroughly and carefully I've choreographed the event. It will be playacting at its finest. Verisimilitude and good fun. We're taking Blue

Plum's worn-out skit and giving it the life it should be living. We're giving Blue Plum's history the voice and resonance it was meant to have. Believe me when I say this will take your festival weekend to the next level. Blue Plum Preserves is going to be on the map and on every heritage tourist's itinerary. The result will be more visitors, more fun, and more money in the merchants' pockets. Win-win-win. And here's something else that will interest you. If I'm not mistaken, one of the originators of the festival, a founding mother, if you will, was a knitter just like you."

"Are you talking about Ivy McClellan?"

"Possibly." He nodded. "Yes. Ivy. That could be the name I read. I see you know your local history. That's wonderful. I think she might be the one who dabbled on the original skit, too. The records aren't entirely clear on that."

"Ivy McClellan was my grandmother."

"You're kidding. Is she still . . ."

"She died four months ago. This was her shop. She and a couple of friends wrote the skit based on their research."

"I am so sorry for your loss." He gave his sorrow half a beat. "But then, this will be especially wonderful. It could hardly be more appropriate for the shop to have a role in this year's celebration. You will be honoring your grandmother's memory and her vision by letting part of the action take place here. And that win-win-win I mentioned? It will go for you and the Weaver's Cat, too. You'll see. People eat this stuff up." He smacked his lips and smiled. "Frankly, I'm surprised you aren't already aware of the reenvisioning of what I believe is a cornerstone activity of Blue Plum Preserves."

I opened my mouth—but to say what? That I'd been busy planning the shop's own festival booth and related activities? Maybe. To tell him my life had been upended and my mind otherwise occupied since Granny died? Probably not, but it didn't matter, anyway. He was primed and ready and got in ahead of whatever I might have said.

"Also, if you stop and think, I feel sure you'll realize that your focus is on the wrong component of the event." He shook his head with a sad cluck of his tongue. "It happens, though. You aren't the first by any means. You only have to mention guns and there are people who will misinterpret what you're trying to do. But I think that, like the others, you're missing the educational importance of this kind of event. You're focusing on a small part of our toolset and missing the bigger picture of our message."

"I could be." I nodded, trying to give him the benefit of a snapless judgment. He was right. I was having trouble getting past the guns. Guns in the streets of Blue Plum. Guns fired out my second-floor windows. Guns in a little skit about a minor land squabble and wandering livestock. I gave myself a shake to jar my focus somewhere other than guns. . . .

"And you can trust me on the gun issue," he said. "The reenactors will not be just a bunch of good old boys playing with fantasies and popguns." He grinned, showing me his ivories and also showing me that he could laugh at a stereotype as easily as the next good old boy. "So, Miss Rutledge—Kath—I know this is short notice, but may we have your blessing and permission to stage part of the Blue Plum Piglet War from the upstairs windows of your charming place of business next weekend?"

ALSO AVAILABLE
FROM

Molly MacRae

LAST WOOL AND TESTAMENT

A Haunted Yarn Shop Mystery

When Kath Rutledge comes to the small town of Blue Plum, Tennessee, to settle her grandmother Ivy's will, she learns she's inherited Ivy's fabric and fiber shop, The Weaver's Cat. She also winds up learning the true meaning of T.G.I.F.—Thank Goodness It's Fiber. That's the name of the spunky group of fiber and needlework artists founded by Kath's grandmother, who now are determined to help Ivy run the shop and carry on her grandmother's legacy.

But when Kath learns her grandmother was also the prime suspect in a murder, solving the case becomes the most important thing on her to do list. Luckily, she won't have to do it alone. She's got the members of T.G.I.F. to lean on—and she's about to get some help from a new friend from beyond the grave…

Available wherever books are sold or
at penguin.com

facebook.com/TheCrimeSceneBooks

OM0086

Sally Goldenbaum

ANGORA ALIBI

A Seaside Knitters Mystery

Yarn shop owner Izzy Chambers Perry and her new husband are expecting a baby. Now she's having the best summer of her life—until an abandoned baby car seat and hand-knit blanket spark a terrible premonition.

Unfortunately, Izzy's fear comes true when a young man who did odd jobs at her doctor's clinic is killed during a scuba dive. When Izzy discovers the man was actually murdered and is connected to the abandoned car seat the crime becomes too close for comfort. It'll take the Seaside Knitters' careful attention to patterns—and their fierce commitment to bringing Izzy and Sam's baby into a peaceful town—to unravel this mystery together...